Lara Temple was three years old when she begged her mother to take the dictation of her first adventure story. Since then she has led a double life—by day she is a high-tech investment professional, who has lived and worked on three continents, but when darkness falls she loses herself in history and romance…at least on the page. Luckily her husband and two beautiful and very energetic children help her weave it all together.

Also by Lara Temple

Lord Crayle's Secret World
The Reluctant Viscount
The Duke's Unexpected Bride

Wild Lords and Innocent Ladies miniseries

Lord Hunter's Cinderella Heiress
Lord Ravenscar's Inconvenient Betrothal
Lord Stanton's Last Mistress

The Sinful Sinclairs miniseries

The Earl's Irresistible Challenge

And look out for the next book coming soon.

Discover more at millsandboon.co.uk.

THE EARL'S IRRESISTIBLE CHALLENGE

Lara Temple

MILLS & BOON

First published in Great Britain 2018
by Mills & Boon, an imprint of HarperCollins*Publishers*
1 London Bridge Street, London, SE1 9GF

Large Print edition 2019

© 2018 Ilana Treston

ISBN: 978-0-263-08155-8

MIX
Paper from
responsible sources
FSC™ **C007454**

To the marvellous, generous, creative and all-round wonderful ladies of the Unlaced Historical Romance Group—you are my surrogate family in Romancelandia, and my little world is so much the richer for my having found you…

Chapter One

Blood was thudding in Olivia's ears, loud in the echoing hollowness of St Margaret's. She had purposely chosen an hour when there were likely to be few people in the church, but she hadn't expected it to be empty. Or dark.

She should have realised they wouldn't waste many candles on a near-empty church on a rainy winter afternoon. The few tallow candles smoked sulkily in their sconces and occasionally shivered in the draught that seemed to come from all directions at once.

Surely if she cried out someone would hear, wouldn't they? Hans Town might not be a fashionable part of London, but it was respectable. Or perhaps it was best to just tuck tail and run…

Too late.

The strike of boots on the flagstones matched the rhythm in her ears and a man emerged from the darkness at the far end of the nave, his greatcoat rising about him like sweeping wings. She was not surprised they called him Sinful Sinclair. She presumed it was merely a play on his family name and less than pristine reputation, but, as he moved towards her in a swift, gliding motion and she noted his pitch-black hair and uncompromising features, she understood the name better.

'Lord Sinclair, thank you for coming,' she said as he stopped before her, pulling a piece of paper from his coat pocket.

'Don't thank me, this isn't a social call. You sent this quaint little note?'

'I did. Lord Sinclair—'

'What do you want and why the devil did you have to choose such an inconvenient location?'

'It is convenient for me. Lord Sinclair, I—'

'I didn't see another carriage in the lane outside. How did you arrive?'

She blinked. She had not even begun and already she was losing control of the situation.

'What on earth does it matter? Lord Sinclair, I—'

'It matters because I prefer to know what I am up against when I come to meet a silly little miss in an empty church in the middle of nowhere. If this is some kind of plan to entrap me I should warn you, you have very much mistaken your prey...'

Olivia's confusion disappeared and she couldn't hold back a laugh.

'You believe I brought you here to entrap you? Goodness, you are vain.'

His eyes narrowed and she felt a new flicker of alarm. Perhaps laughing at him was not advisable under the circumstances.

'Lord Sinclair...' she began again and hesitated. The clear list of points she wished to make faded under the oppressive force of his black eyes. She took another deep breath. 'Lord Sinclair—'

'I know my name,' he said impatiently. 'Only too well. Stop wearing it thin and get to the blasted point.'

'I have some information about your father.'

The draught swirled his coat out in a wide arc about him and cut through the thin fabric of her own cloak and she shivered. He didn't reply immediately, but the impatience was gone, replaced by a rather sardonic smile.

'So do I and very little of it is good. What of it?'

'I have evidence that raises some questions about the circumstances of his death. It is possible that he was wronged.'

The only sound was the faint whistling of the wind through cracks in the high windows. She pulled her cloak more tightly about her and waited.

'Raise your veil.'

'Why?'

'Because I prefer to see people's faces when they are lying to me.'

Olivia considered her options. She didn't know if involving this man was one of her more intelligent ideas, but he had come and she would have to see this through. She rolled back the thick lace veil attached to her bonnet and his dark eyes scanned her face without any change in their expression of amused contempt.

'A little miss, but not silly, I think. Now let us begin anew. Why did you summon me here?'

'I told you, I have some information about the circumstances surrounding your father's death.'

'I see. And what do you want in exchange for this so-called information?'

She hesitated.

'That depends.'

'Not a very clever bargaining approach. You should have come with a clearer idea of what you think your lies are worth. Or what you think I am worth.'

'But that is precisely what I am trying to determine.'

He laughed, a low warm sound that did nothing to soothe her skittering nerves.

'You want a list of my assets? You are by far

the most inept blackmailer I have come across, sweetheart, and I have met a few.'

'I wasn't talking about your financial worth,' she replied coldly. She knew he would be difficult, but she had not counted on him being annoying as well. She wasn't at all certain she wanted to deal with this man.

'I can think of only one other level on which I might be of any worth. But it's a bit cold here for that, however tempting the bait. I have a carriage waiting outside, though, if you like.'

'No, I would not like!' she said, unable to keep the annoyance out of her voice. Really, if only he would be quiet for a moment and let her think. She knew he was a care-for-nobody, but she had expected a little more interest in her story. Did he really not care at all? If he did not, there was no point in continuing. Except that she very much needed help. Mercer, her man of business, was a treasure, but he was only good when told precisely what to do and she no longer knew which way to direct him.

'Are you certain? You have a certain charm and I wouldn't mind seeing just how far—'

'Oh, would you please be quiet so I may think! I had no idea you would be so provoking!'

At least that wiped the mocking humour from

his face. She waited for his anger, wishing she had held her tongue, but he merely took her elbow, turning her towards the exit.

'Come with me.'

'No! Let me go!'

Her confusion turned to panic and she tugged her arm out of his grasp. He raised his hands and took a step back.

'Calm down. I won't hurt you, but it's as cold as a witch's… It is freezing in here and I don't feel inclined to stand around in this draughty church discussing my family for any busybody to hear while you make up your mind about extorting me. If you wish to speak with me, you may do so in the carriage. If not, goodnight.'

His words were calm, but his brisk stride as he headed towards the exit was a blatant dismissal. Olivia stared at his retreating figure with such a wave of hatred she could hardly believe it originated from her. The temptation to throw back her head and howl at the eaves was so powerful she could almost hear her own voice echoing back at her.

Instead she filled her lungs with cold air, lowered her veil and stalked after Lord Sinclair.

She reached the road and for one panicked moment thought she was too late, but then she saw the dark-panelled carriage on the narrow lane leading past the church. The buildings hung low, blocking out what remained of the late afternoon gloom and she could hardly see his face under the brim of his hat, but felt him watching her as she approached. Without a word he opened the carriage door.

She must be mad to be contemplating stepping into a carriage with one of the Sinful Sinclairs. Mad, desperate or a fool. Well, she *was* desperate. And though she might be an utter fool, something about the way he mocked her at least relieved concern for her person. But still...

'Lord Sinclair, perhaps we could...'

He sighed and stepped into the carriage himself.

She hadn't meant to grab the door as he closed it. She felt the resistance of his hold on the handle, then it eased but remained taut, counting out his patience. When he let go she stifled her qualms and grabbed her skirts to take the high step into the carriage. Once inside she pressed herself as far back into a corner as she could. He tossed a rug towards her.

'I wish you would stop acting like a hissing cat being forced into a pond. Put that around you before you freeze; that cloak is about as useful in this weather as a handkerchief. Now, you have ten minutes to tell your tale and be gone.'

She clasped her hands together and began her rehearsed speech.

'My godfather, Henry Payton, was found dead. The constable was summoned by a woman by the name of Marcia Pendle, who claimed she was Henry's mistress and that he died...while...well, in bed. However, I know she isn't the genteel widow she claims to be, but a courtesan at an establishment on Catte Street and that she was paid to make that claim to the constable at the inquest and though I don't know why, I am at least certain she was not my godfather's mistress.'

'Are you? That is charmingly loyal of you, though naïve. But how does any of this sordid but mundane tale relate to my father?'

'Well, it doesn't, not directly. At least not that I can see as yet. But amongst the belongings my godfather left at the leased house where he died were letters written to him by a Mr Howard Sinclair from twenty years ago and with them a note in Henry's hand which read, *"If this is true Howard Sinclair was terribly wronged and something must be done,"* and underneath that he wrote the name Jasper Septimus and underscored it several times. I don't know if there is any connection between this note and his death and Marcia Pendle's lies. The letters appear to be mostly business correspondence and I have no idea who Jasper Septimus is. I know this is all garbled, but I had to see if you could shed any light on this story.'

He listened with the same mocking calm with which he'd dismissed her earlier, as if he was watching a mediocre play just titillating enough to overcome the urge to leave the theatre. With his arms crossed and his chin sunk into his cravat, to her exhausted mind, it looked like the inverted white triangle of white fur on her pet wolfhound's throat. Except that Twitch wasn't in the least frightening despite his size and impressive fangs.

Finally he spoke.

'I grant you credit for a very vivid imagination. Let me see if I have managed to follow this Drury Lane plot. Sorry, two interconnected Drury Lane plots. In the first a doxy is paid by someone to lie to the magistrates about being your godfather's mistress, presumably to mask the circumstances of his death which I gather were at the very least humiliating. In the second your godfather ruminates over the past and comes to the startling conclusion based on the words of a Jasper Septimus, whose name is an insult in itself, that my father was wronged. And this revelation is possibly at the root of the first tale. Have I done your fantasies credit?'

It was evident he was a cold man, but she expected to hear something in his voice when he spoke of his father's death. There was nothing, not a quiver or a change of inflection.

'I am not fabricating any of this. It is the truth.'

'Well, so what?'

'So what?' she asked, shocked.

'The facts you proffered don't amount to much, do they? Certainly not to a murderous plot that spans decades. A much more likely explanation is that you or this woman are attempting to extract money from me on the back of what you believe is my sentimental need to know more about my sire's very ignominious departure from this world. Let me assure you I have no such need. In fact, you might have gathered I am not of a sentimental disposition.'

'You are ignoring a further possibility, my lord.'

'Am I? Enlighten me. I admit to being curious what your rather unique mind will conjure next. You are a very peculiar girl, do you know?'

'I am not a girl. I am almost four and twenty years of age!' She immediately regretted her outburst as the amusement in his eyes deepened. He was baiting her and she was rising to his hook each time. *She* should be the one in control of this conversation and yet she had let him take the reins from the moment he entered the church. She removed the rug, placing it on the seat beside her.

'Goodnight, Lord Sinclair. I shall not waste any more of your time. You are clearly not interested in what I have to say.'

Again that soft gliding motion of his was deceptive. Though she was closer to the carriage door, she had not even reached the handle when his hand was there.

'Don't play me,' he said softly. 'I won't be led. And certainly not by a pert almost-twenty-four-year-old who likes mysteries and hiding behind veils. You have five minutes remaining.'

'Then *listen* instead of being so...aggravating! This is important to me and you keep...' Her voice cracked and she stopped before she crumbled completely. She was shaking, from cold and weariness and the aftermath of tension and fear. She pulled the rug towards her and shoved her hands into its warmth, feeling like a pathetic fool.

He didn't speak, just knocked against the carriage wall and it drew forward. Olivia gasped and reached for the door again, but he put his arm out, barring it.

'Calm down. I won't touch you and I will take you wherever you ask once we are done. But though I don't care for much, I care for my horses and I won't keep them standing further in this cold. Fair enough?'

She nodded warily.

'Good. Now, what is your name?' he asked.

'My godfather's name was Henry Payton.'

'I asked for your name, not his.'

'Olivia, Olivia Silverdale.'

'Olivia Silverdale. Sounds as fanciful as your tale. Now begin at the beginning. Who is this Marcia Pendle and how did you trace her?'

He had changed again—more businesslike but no less ruthless.

'I told you. Marcia Pendle works in a…a house of ill repute in Catte Street.'

'Catte Street. Madame Bernieres'?'

She raised her brow contemptuously. Obviously he would know about the brothels of London.

'I think that was the name. She calls herself Genevieve, but she is really Marcia Pendle from Norfolk.'

He shook his head briefly, but there was no negation there, only a kind of focused confusion as he watched her. Stripped of mocking or anger, he looked more human but no less unsettling.

'So. Marcia Pendle is Genevieve. How and why did you trace her and why on earth would she tell you she was involved in your godfather's death?'

'I traced her because I had my man of business hire a Bow Street Runner, a Mr McGuire. He was present at the inquest into my uncle's death. Apparently Marcia gave a masterful performance about a long-standing relationship where they would meet at the leased house where he died. When she left the inquest he followed her and after some discreet investigation discovered her true identity and occupation. He also discovered she is very superstitious and every week she visits a gypsy fortune-teller near Bishopsgate who is no more a gypsy than Marcia is French, but one Sue Davies from Cardiff. So, I went to see Miss Davies…'

'You went to Bishopsgate to visit a fortune-teller.'

'Yes. And after we had a little conversation and understood one another tolerably well, I paid Gypsy Sue, as she is called, to tell Marcia she must consult an occultist.'

'A what?' he asked. The sardonic edge had left his voice completely. All she could detect there was a kind of fascinated shock.

'Have you never heard of them? Apparently

they are quite popular of late. There is very much a demand for communication with dead loved ones on The Other Side. In any case, the gypsy, or rather Sue Davies, told me how Marcia was obsessed with someone named George whom she loved and mourned and that she asked Sue...'

'Wait one moment... Hell, never mind. I will reserve my questions for the end.'

'Thank you. So I had my man of business lease a house in an unassuming part of town where such an occultist might credibly have her lodgings and Sue Davies helped me set the stage, so to speak. Like Marcia Pendle she was once an actress and was very useful in procuring the correct clothes and artefacts. Then she sent Marcia Pendle to me and under the guise of my occultist's persona I questioned her about her relations with Henry.'

'Good lord. A vivid imagination doesn't even begin to cover it. So we are now at a consultation between a masquerading occultist from Yorkshire, a French madame from Norfolk and a fraudulent gypsy from Wales. Charming. Proceed.'

'How did you know I was from Yorkshire?'

'I have an ear for accents. Proceed.'

'Very well. During this session, Marcia Pendle

revealed she never even met my uncle, let alone became his mistress.'

He held up his hand again.

'Revealed. A doxy and practised blackmailer just handed you this information. Just for the asking...'

'Not quite. I told you she is very superstitious. I told her the fellow she wanted to reach could not meet her in the afterworld unless she revealed all and cleansed her soul.'

'You exposed yourself to a woman who you believe might be involved in murder and she believed a young girl is her gate to the afterlife. I don't know which of you is more unbalanced...'

'Of course I didn't allow her to see me. I was heavily veiled and I wore a rather vulgar dress Sue gave me and she even showed me how to paint my face so that should my veil slip I would not be recognisable. Sue did offer to act the occultist instead of me but I had to be the one asking the questions. I could hardly prompt Sue all through the session, could I?'

'I see,' he said carefully. 'I was apparently right about your imagination. I'm impressed the powers that be have no issue with Marcia Pendle being a doxy, only with her lying to the authorities.'

'There are apparently different degrees of depravity.'

'That is very true, there are. So back to your discoveries—I presume you asked her who paid her to engage in this deceit?'

'Of course. That was where I ran aground. She did divulge that his name was Eldritch, but she was so overset by her communications with George she became quite hysterical with weeping and I felt horrid and halted the session and told her George was being summoned back, but we could try again in a few days once her soul was calm.'

'And she accepted that?'

'Apparently George was never fond of crying females so in fact it strengthened her belief in my powers. So you see, I need to find out who this Mr Eldritch is, but Mr Mercer had no luck and I do not know how to proceed.'

'You surprise me. But before we proceed to Mr Eldritch, I'm curious why you are so certain she was not your godfather's mistress in the first place?'

'I just knew. And I was right.'

'An intuition, in fact.'

The sardonic inflection was back and she shrugged. She had told him enough. It was time to see if he would be of any use at all or whether he was merely enjoying treating her like some freakish fair exhibit.

'Will you help or not?'

'Help with what?'

'Help find out who this Eldritch is and why he paid to defame my godfather and whether it is in any way connected with Henry's suspicions about your father's death.'

'Why?'

'Why?' She threw up her hands in disbelief. 'Because I, for one, will not sit by while someone out there is ruining people's lives. My godmother, Mrs Payton, is in shock and in pain not only at the loss of one of the most wonderful men I have ever known, but at the discovery that he had betrayed her and his family. I must find out who is behind this and make them pay for what they have done to the Paytons. And I don't know how to do that on my own! That is why!'

Lucas stifled a sigh at her outburst. He wished he had tossed her note into the fire rather than succumbing to the siren's pull of curiosity. If he had an ounce of sense he would send her on her way—she was probably either mad or a very creative liar and he didn't have time to indulge in such nonsense, he was already running late for his meeting with his uncle at the War Office. But as his brother Chase always told him, curiosity was likely to be his downfall, which was rather ironic because Chase was just as bad.

For a moment he contemplated taking her to his uncle. Oswald would see through all the girlish dramatics and probably reveal her as the clever trickster she was, because although Oswald was as cursed with curiosity as any of their fated Sinclair tribe, he was never swayed by sentiment. Lucas usually wasn't either, but as much as it galled him to admit, even to himself, mentions of his father's demise still had the power to sink their talons into his flesh. He could stride over most matters without much compunction but the moment she spoke those words he stumbled. Just a little, but enough. He couldn't walk away without at least trying to understand what was afoot. Which meant he had to find out the nature of the peculiar beast sitting opposite him.

Not today, though. However offended she appeared to be by his accusation of entrapment, her voice and demeanour were clearly those of a wellborn young woman and every moment spent in her company as night descended was a moment of precisely the kind of danger he did not enjoy.

'Where do you live?'

'Why?'

'Because as tempting as the thought is, I can hardly leave you in the middle of London in the dark. I presume you do live somewhere. This might be a fantastical story, but you appear discouragingly corporeal.'

For the first time her eyes shifted away from his. She was about to lie, which was interesting in itself.

'Spinner Street.'

'Spinner Street? Isn't it around the corner from the church where you summoned me?'

'Yes.'

'Stranger and stranger. Is that sad neighbourhood populated by occultists now? At what number are you perpetrating your masquerade?'

'Fifteen. But… Does this mean you won't help?' she demanded as he tapped the wall of the carriage and it slowed to a halt on the empty street and a postilion jumped down to take his directions.

'It means it is nearing your bedtime, Miss Silverdale. I will consider what you told me. That is all I can offer for now.'

Again her expression changed, or rather it leached away, leaving her face blank just as they slowed and the gaslight filled the carriage. Now at least he could see what she looked like in repose. She reminded him of a painting he had once seen in Venice. It was a depiction of the biblical tale of Ruth, with Naomi seated on a stone cradling a very unattractive babe and Ruth standing, her hand on the older woman's shoulder and, unusually for such a painting, looking straight at the viewer. She, too, had worn no expression, but the message was clear. Beware. I guard my own.

'If this is a polite way of telling me you have no intention of pursuing this puzzle, I prefer you tell me so outright,' she said as she raised the hood of her cloak over her bonnet. 'Heaven forfend I waste any more of your precious time which could be spent so much more profitably in gaming hells and brothels like Madame Bern—'

Her haughty lecture ended on a squeak when he caught her wrist as she opened the carriage door. He should have kept his calm and sped her on her way. If he needed anything to convince him to have nothing more to do with her fantasies, it was a lecture. His temper had borne quite enough that evening.

'I don't need you to put words in my mouth and I sure as hell do not need your lectures. You do either again and that will be the last you see of me, Miss Silverdale. I said I will think about it and I will. That is all for now. Now run along before I decide to demand compensation for your ruining what had promised to be a very pleasant evening by fulfilling your worst suspicions about my character. Unless that is what you are looking for? Is that tortuous little mind of yours curious about that as well?'

He brushed his fingers lightly across her lips, as much to test his question as to warn her. They were soft and warm and as they shifted under the pressure his gaze caught on them as well, making the question rather more complicated than he had intended. But before he could pursue the thought she drew away so abruptly she bumped into the frame of the door and for the first time he saw real fear in her gaze and something beyond it which surprised him. Revulsion was not the usual reaction to his overtures, but then he never made overtures to proper little virgins and they never made appointments to meet him in a darkened church and proceed to tell him the world was made of cheese and rode along on the back of a turtle.

He opened the door.

'Run along, little miss.'

She didn't run. The blank watchdog expression

returned and she drew down her veil and jumped down nimbly from the carriage, ignoring the postilion who stood by to assist her.

Chapter Two

Olivia looked around the respectable interior of St George's, smiling at the gall of the man.

She might not quite have Lord Sinclair's measure, but she knew without doubt his choice of arranging this meeting in a church in midday was an ironic riposte rather than out of any concern for propriety. The man was living up to his reputation as a care-for-nobody.

Well, not quite. She had expected someone more...spoilt. Indulged and self-indulgent. Not...

Well, whatever he was.

For two days she had heard nothing from him, her already meagre hopes foundering and leaving her even more depressed than before. When her old nurse, Nora, appeared that morning in Brook Street, bearing a sealed note she said was delivered to Spinner Street by a proper footman, Olivia's first reaction was almost stifling relief.

The relief faded a little as she read his note. It was succinct, listing nothing more than a time, a place and a bold, scrawled 'S'.

'At least you are prompt.'

She rose on tiptoes in surprise at the deep voice directly behind her, her stretched nerves bursting into an agitated dance. How had he managed to cross the whole church without her hearing? Blast the man for putting her at a disadvantage again. She turned, gathering her dignity. The windows were small, but the sun that broke through the winter clouds was directly overhead and sunlight bathed him like a benediction, making it clear she had missed a great deal in the darkness. Two days ago he had been a figure of the dark—a shady hulk towering over her, menacing but indistinct. Now Gypsy Sue's words came back to her and she could understand fully why the Sixth Earl of Sinclair was referred to as the sinfully seductive Sinclair. It wasn't merely that he was handsome. She couldn't even get enough distance from the impact of his aura to judge his looks. It was something completely different—his presence chased away everything else, like the sun coming out from behind a cloud with sudden brutality—harsh and demanding a reaction.

She searched for her scattering wits and managed to gather enough to speak his name.

'Lord Sinclair.'

'Miss Silverdale.'

The silence stretched and she felt the edges of her mouth rise against her will. It must be nervousness, understandable given what was at stake. There was nothing amusing about this situation.

'Lord Sinclair,' she repeated, and the humour she suspected gleamed in his eyes and tugged at the corners of his mouth as well. He bowed with all the formality of a London ballroom.

'Miss Silverdale.'

Inspired, she brandished the note she held and tossed back his words from their first meeting. 'You sent this quaint little note?'

He plucked it from her fingers. 'You've mangled the poor thing. Have you been poring over it all morning?'

Blast the man. It was close enough to the truth.

'No, it is merely that I had to rescue it from the cat.'

'I am sorry you had to fight over me.'

'Over the address. There are a dozen St Georges in town and I forgot which one you mentioned. It would have been a little embarrassing to send a note to Sinclair House explaining the cat lunched on your note. I felt my pride was worth a few scratches.'

His black brows twitched together. 'Then you are as foolishly stubborn as I suspected. You should be more careful. Did the cat really scratch you?'

She blinked at the transformation, hoping the heat she felt in her chest would not bloom into a blush. She hardly managed to make the transition from annoyance to humour and now he was undercutting her with utterly misplaced concern based on her nonsensical embellishment. She shook her head and hurried forward, trying to cling to what mattered.

'Well?' she asked. 'Do you agree to help me?'

'No.'

'Oh. Then why are you here?'

'Because two days ago I met a delusional young woman making outrageous claims about my father's death. I told you I don't like being coerced, managed, threatened or interfered with and this qualifies as most of the above. So I came here to say that should I find that you are making any enquiries that involve my family name I will stop you. Am I clear?'

'You are many things, Lord Sinclair, not all of which can be spoken aloud in polite company. You don't like being threatened? Well, neither do I. If you plan to stop me I suggest you begin today because aside from your delightful billet this morning I also received a request from Mrs Pendle. She assures me she is eager for another session with her dear departed and I invited her to Spinner Street tomorrow at five. So I give you fair warning I shall discuss whatever I see fit.'

She marched out of the cloistered entrance, angry with him, but far angrier with herself at the depth of her disappointment at his rejection. She had so been looking forward to sharing her thoughts with someone intelligent, and Lord Sinclair, though he might try a saint's patience, was plainly intelligent and probably resourceful. For a moment the concern in his voice and the softening lines of his beautifully carved mouth had lulled her into believing he could be an ally.

Well, he wasn't her ally. He was an arrogant, cloddish, opinionated...

'Miss Silverdale! Olivia!'

Olivia froze halfway to the carriage where Nora was waiting. Of all the bad luck—the last person she expected to see in London was Henry Payton's son, Colin.

'Colin! I thought you were in Harrogate with your mother and Phoebe.'

'I came to consult Mr Ratchett about the will and see about extending our mortgage. At least until probate is granted...' His voice wavered and she reached out, briefly touching his sleeve. She knew Colin as well as her own brothers and she had never seen him so pale and beaten.

'I'm so very, very sorry, Colin. What can I do to help?'

'I did not mean to worry you, Olivia. We are not on our last legs, though Mr Ratchett did tell me in confidence that Sir Ivo is putting pressure on the bank to foreclose. Still, he assures me they see no need to take such drastic measures as we have always honoured our commitments and he did count Father his friend, despite the... unpleasantness. Still, I think it would be best to sell and remove from Gillingham. I cannot see Mama returning there, not with all the gossip.' He rubbed his hand over his forehead. 'I never guessed... I don't understand any of it. Father always seemed so...reliable. I cannot comprehend why...'

'I don't either, Colin. It makes no sense.'

'Nothing makes sense at the moment. I went by Brook Street, but Lady Phelps said you were visiting this church with Nora. I thought she is your chaperon, Olivia. You should not be here on your own.'

'I am not on my own. Nora is awaiting me in the carriage.'

'Nora is hardly an adequate chaperon in London.'

'It is merely a church, Colin. Not Vauxhall Gardens.'

His eyes widened. 'I trust Lady Phelps is not taking you to such places, Olivia. They are not at all the thing, you know.'

'That was a figure of speech, Colin. If you must know, we do not go about much.'

'Then why not come to Mama and Phoebe in Harrogate?'

'There is some important business I must address in London.'

'Surely Mr Mercer can...'

'No, Colin. He cannot. Please let us not argue. How is Phoebe faring?'

'Still in shock. It is doubly hard for her. She has barely begun to recover from Jack—' He stopped. 'I'm so sorry, Olivia. I know Jack's death was painful for you as well.'

Olivia resisted the swiping claw of anger that demanded she strike out at his unknowing cruelty. She was accustomed, a little, to people presuming her friend Phoebe was the greater sufferer from Jack's death. There was no point in trying to explain that the loss of a twin brother might be even more devastating than the loss of a fiancé. What mattered was that Phoebe herself never presumed her loss was greater. She knew how close Olivia and Jack were. Had been.

'Please don't apologise, Colin. I hate that people won't talk about him with me. It makes it worse. He feels even more dead that way.'

He clasped her hand, shaking it a little. 'You always say the strangest things, Olivia; if you're not careful you will end up like one of those blue-stocking quizzes.'

She smiled a little stiffly. 'Then I shall have to school my tongue. When must you return?'

'Tomorrow. I do not like leaving Mama for long. Phoebe tries, but Mama needs me there as well. When will you complete your...your business?'

The barely veiled condemnation in his voice struck home. She hated not being there to support Mary Payton and Phoebe during their mourning, but she hoped once they knew she was acting on their behalf they would forgive her defection.

'Very soon, I hope. Please do come dine with Lady Phelps and me this evening, Colin.'

She clasped his hand briefly, but as she let go he grabbed it and pulled her back towards the church. She wanted to resist, but her guilt made her weak and she followed. The church seemed smaller now, a little stifling.

'What is it, Colin? You know it isn't proper for me to be here alone with you. I told Nora I would only be a moment.'

'I believe that is the first time you preached propriety to me, Olivia; I cannot recall the number of times Mama had palpitations because of you and your brothers. I am glad to see you are finally growing up.'

'That is one way of phrasing it, certainly.'

'Couldn't you convince Lady Phelps to come with you to Harrogate? We... Mother and Phoebe missed you these past two years since you left Gillingham. I never understood what happened between you and Bertram and of course we followed Father's lead and stood by you, but the truth is I admit I am glad you jilted him. He was never right for you and I must say I don't think the heiress he married last year is very happy with him either, if that makes you feel any better. But the point is I...we all miss you since you left.'

'I will come as soon as I am able, Colin.'

'What if I tell you *I* would like you to come?' He moved even closer, taking her other hand as well. 'Everything is so upended and somehow you always made the strangest things seem… commonplace. Coming to visit you with Father over the past two years while you were staying with Lady Phelps I have come to… I hardly had any idea how much I depended upon your presence until… I cannot say anything, under the circumstances, but once we are out of mourning…'

She forced herself not to move, not to pull her hands from his. This wasn't Bertram, this was Colin, there was no reason to feel so stifled. It was not as if she had not contemplated this solution to her conundrum. She had noted Colin's migration from friendship to admiration during his visits with Henry. If she could not redeem Henry Payton's name and reputation by any other means, marriage to Colin would grant him access to her fortune and he could provide for Phoebe and Mary Payton without them suffering any qualms of conscience.

But as he pressed her hands between his, the gap between good intentions and reality widened and she struggled against the need to pull away.

'You will come soon?' he prompted and she breathed deeply and nodded. He bent to touch his mouth to her cheek and she held herself still even as his lips slid and settled on her own. *It is only Colin*, she reminded herself. *This is not Bertram and you are no longer a gullible fool. No one will ever take advantage of you that way again. Ever.*

He drew back, his blue eyes warm and his cheeks pink, and finally she allowed herself to move, pulling her hands from his.

'I must go or Nora will worry. Please tell your mama and Phoebe... Tell them I will see them soon. Be strong, Colin.'

She hurried outside to the awaiting hackney, narrowly missing a pushcart piled high with casks. Inside, she tugged off her gloves and kneaded her palms, trying to chase away the stinging pressure that always came when memories of Bertram returned.

'I'm so sorry I kept you waiting in this horrid weather, Nora. You will not believe who is in town...'

'I saw Master Colin approach you, Miss Olivia. I told you this was foolishness itself. You aren't twelve years old, hiding in trees so you can listen to your brothers' talk unseen. And you needn't tell me to save my breath, I know you won't listen. Just put this shawl over your legs, it is almost as cold as back home. I take it you didn't tell Master Colin the truth?'

'I cannot, you know that. I may uncover nothing and I do not wish to give him false hope.'

Nora sighed, but didn't answer, and Olivia turned to look out the window and caught herself as she rubbed again at her cheek, as if she could wipe away the underlying memories of her disastrous betrothal.

She did not regret jilting Bertram—marriage to that deceitful wretch would be far worse than heartbreak and ostracism—but she deeply regretted telling Henry Payton the truth and then swearing him to secrecy. Poor Henry had taken her side and then faced the fury of Bertram's family without complaint, even when Bertram's father Sir Ivo made it impossible for Henry to work in Gillingham. She did not even try to escape her culpability—it was her fault he had to spend so much time in London away from his wife, therefore her fault he sought solace with other women, therefore her fault he was dead.

None of this was Colin's fault, but when he kissed her the mocking memory of her fateful confrontation with Bertram surfaced, as sharp and vivid as the reality. Bertram had dismissed her rejection, trying to placate her by the same means he achieved everything—seduction. She had once enjoyed his kisses, convinced they were signs of his love. But that evening the embraces she so looked forward to became unbearable. She could still see his face bearing down on her, feel his wet lips seeking her mouth, the weight of his body pressing her against the wall... Everything she looked forward to in their union became a sign of her gullibility. Colin was nothing like Bertram, but perhaps now and for ever any contact with a man would bear Bertram's taint and that of her disgust with her blindness. All her passionate hopes capsized by the weight of his horrible deceit.

She shook herself. What mattered now was Henry. She had come to London and opened herself to the world again because of him and she would see her task through.

If Lord Sinclair wouldn't help, she would do it alone. She would prove the Henry Payton she knew and loved had existed, even if he was dead. She would stand by him as he had stood by her.

Chapter Three

Lucas waited until the young man exited the church before leaving the shadow of the pillars separating the nave from the chancel. He was tempted to go after him and tell him precisely what foolhardiness his little friend was engaged in. Perhaps a few judicious words about her activities would have her family remove her before she caused real damage. To herself or to others.

He walked outside into the gloomy winter morning, juggling what he knew about her. He was accustomed to making quick judgements about people, but this girl was proving a bit of a puzzle. Perhaps it would be a good idea to discuss this with Chase. They rarely discussed the past, but his brother was not only good at puzzles but this concerned him as well. Not that he would show it, or much else for that matter. Chase went through life as lightly as possible. Lucas considered going to Chase's apartments near St James's, but thought better of it. This discussion had best be held at Sinclair House where they would be assured of privacy.

* * *

'This place grows more cavernous every time I enter it. Shouldn't you consider replacing the carpet on the stairs? I sounded like a herd of stampeding camels on the way up,' Chase said as he entered Lucas's study at Sinclair House. Lucas looked up from his papers and smiled at his younger brother. They were of a height and had often been mistaken for twins once out of school, but Chase's eyes were grey rather than black, as if transitioning between their mother's Italian blood and the Sinclairs' northern heritage. He was still brown from his recent trip to the east, adding to the Latin impression.

'I prefer it that way,' Lucas replied as he went to pour his brother a measure of brandy. 'You of all people should appreciate the benefit of being forewarned.'

'You have the Tubbs clan in the nether regions to do that for you, Luke. Some boy I didn't recognise, but scarcely out of breeches, opened the door for me. I thought Mrs Tubbs called a halt to her share in growing the family.'

'That would have been Richard. He is Annie's boy.'

'Annie's? My God, she was an inch high when I last saw her.'

'Another sign you don't come here often enough. Are you settled in London for now?'

'I don't know yet. A few weeks, perhaps, but I will visit Sam at the Hall before I leave again. I don't like the fact that our little sister is still holed up at Sinclair Hall so long after Ricardo's death.'

'Don't press her, Chase. It isn't Ricardo she is mourning and you know Sam makes her own decisions, including how long and how hard to mourn. Besides, she is keeping busy with her work.'

'I won't press. I merely want to see her. And you? How long before you roam again?'

'I am expected in St Petersburg in a month or so. Why not stay here while you are in London?'

Chase looked around the study.

'No, the Mausoleum is your cross to bear, Lucas. Just walking by the closed door to the Great Hall reminded me why I prefer the uncomplicated impersonality of my lodgings on Half Moon Street.'

Lucas grimaced. 'I always enter by way of the mews myself. One day I will have to do something about this place one way or another. It's damnable that it is entailed.'

Chase swirled his brandy and went to sprawl in a wingchair by the fireplace.

'That is sufficient reason to have an heir, just so you can then break the entail and rid us of the Mausoleum and the Hall.'

'No, thank you. I don't think the world needs more Sinclairs; we've done enough damage as it is.'

'So we have. I dare say the world wishes our Sinclair ancestors had stayed in the far north among our Scottish forebears instead of joining the English court and wheedling good English titles and land out of them. Too late to repine now, though. So why don't you tell me what is bothering you?'

'Why do you presume something is bothering me?'

'Years of experience. Out with it.'

Chase had an impressive ability to remain still while listening, offering neither distraction nor encouragement and certainly no indication of his thoughts, but Lucas knew him too well to be fooled. His very stillness was telling.

'What do you think?' Lucas asked as he concluded his story of the peculiar Miss Silverdale and her theories.

'I think that if anyone else had told me this tale I would be checking them for the fever. Gypsies, doxies and occultists... Are you quite certain that young woman isn't touched?'

'I'm afraid not. She might be unconventional, but she is distressingly sane and as stubborn as a Cossack. Short of kidnapping her and bundling her off to her family in Yorkshire, I don't think I can dissuade her from her fantasies of plots and injustice.'

'Do you think there is a chance there is anything to it?' Chase tipped his glass to watch the firelight undulate in its depths, his sharp-cut profile tense, his dark-grey eyes hooded. Chase was only ten when their father died and though their mother tried to keep the details from them, the gossip was too juicy to be contained and the boys at school were only too happy to share the tale of the duel and its causes. They were both sent down for brawling and the following year they had been only too happy to leave England to live with their grandmother's family in Venice.

'No, I don't,' Lucas replied. 'This is clearly a case of acute denial of reality. Little Miss Silverdale evidently feels indebted to her godfather and has concocted this cock-and-bull story to assuage her grief and guilt. I think she is tilting at windmills, but I don't want her making enquiries about our family. If anyone is to continue tarnishing our name, I prefer we remaining Sinclairs do it ourselves.'

'True. So what do you plan to do about her and her occultist ambitions? What a pity I cannot observe her performance. You should.'

'Are you mad? I prefer a full month of Wednesdays at Almack's.'

'No, you don't. You are curious. Besides, imagine what might happen if that Catte Street doxy discovers she is being duped by this young woman during her occultism session? Not a pretty scene. Might sit heavily on what remains of your conscience.'

'Be damned to you, Chase.'

'Undoubtedly.'

'All the more reason to bundle her off home.'

'Perhaps.'

'It is a waste of time.'

'Well, you have time to waste if you aren't needed in St Petersburg until next month. Unless you wish to go early and enjoy the Russian winter to the hilt? Bonaparte tried that, not very successfully.'

'No, I damn well don't. I was hoping you would have some useful thoughts on defusing this loose cannon.'

'I do. Go oversee your budding occultist and keep the Sinclair name off the dunghill where is appears to enjoy residing all too often. Meanwhile I will go to the Hall and see Sam before I must leave London again.' He stood, straightening his waistcoat and looking around with a sigh. 'Do you know, I am of two minds about your having allowed the Mausoleum to descend into such bare silence. It doesn't do your hedonistic reputation credit, you know. You could hire an acting troupe to stage an orgy or two and leave the windows open on to the square.'

'No, thank you. Besides, the lack of information about what occurs here only encourages the creative minds of the *ton*. God forbid I should confuse them with something as mundane as reality.'

'That is true, especially since you provide them more than enough material with your activities in foreign lands. Speaking of providing material, will you join me at the club tonight?'

'I cannot, it is Wednesday. Almack's calls.'

For a moment Chase stared at him in shock before bursting into laughter.

'Good God, for a moment I thought you were serious. Don't scare me like that. If you ever turn respectable, the world might develop expectations of me as well and if there is one thing I find more abhorrent than Almack's, it is expectations.'

Chapter Four

'What the *devil*?'

Olivia dropped the tablecloth she was holding and ran for the study door. It was probably not a smart thing to do. The sound of a man cursing in what should be an empty house would usually be taken as a good sign to run in the opposite direction. But Olivia recognised the voice and, perhaps foolishly, she wasn't in the least afraid. Alert, but not afraid.

She stopped in the doorway. Lord Sinclair was standing, hands on hips, inspecting her Wall of Conjecture.

'What are you doing here?' she asked, tucking a straggling curl behind her ear. It was absurd to wish she was wearing something more present-able than a simple muslin round dress. He was in riding clothes but he possessed the same ca-sual elegance in his buckskins and dark blue rid-ing coat as he had on both previous occasions. Again she was struck by the sheer power of his face and frame. He looked utterly out of place in her parlour. In her world.

'What the…what *are* all these?' he demanded and she moved a little more deeply into the room despite her discomfort.

'Those are lists.'

'I can see that. I've just never seen so many on a wall. How do you manage to make them stay there?'

'I had felt pasted on the wall over a layer of corkwood and I use sewing pins to secure them. When I tried laying them out on the floor they kept scattering. How did you enter?'

'And the strings? It looks like a mad spider is attempting to build its web here.'

'That is how I remember what connects with what. It helps me think.'

'If your mind looks anything like this wall, heaven help you.'

'Did you come here to insult me or was there some other purpose to breaking into my house?'

'I didn't break, I entered through the area door. You really should have a locksmith install something more reliable than those ancient locks, you know. Your guest is arriving at five o'clock, you said?' He proceeded along the wall and she resisted the urge to tear down her lists before he could read them. She would only look ridiculous and, besides, she wanted him to see them. If he had been intrigued enough to come today, perhaps this would snare him further.

'Yes. I was preparing the room for her. Are you here to stop me?'

'No.'

'Why *are* you here, then?'

'Curiosity. I've never attended an occultist's meeting. I am expanding my horizons.'

He reached the part of the wall dedicated to his father and she tensed, waiting. It was emptier than Henry Payton's side, but even the meagre amount of information about his death Mercer uncovered for her was likely to anger him. But he said nothing and after a moment he moved towards the desk.

'More lists? Famous occultists... Who is Madame Bulgari?'

'I am. Gypsy Sue helped me think of the name, she said people are impressed by foreign airs, but the rest I gathered from books.'

He took a book from the desk, his brows rising as he flipped through the pages. '*Communication with the Other Side*. Wasn't Baron Lyttelton a Member of Parliament?'

'I have no idea. Please don't lose my place.'

'Pericles? Christina, Queen of Sweden? A select grouping.' He tossed the book down and took another. 'And what is this tome about? *The For-bidden Secrets of Occultism* by Madame Vol-gatskaya? That sounds a little more entertaining, though Madame Vulgar would be more appropriate by all the gilt on this binding. I am beginning to think Madame Bulgari an excellent choice of moniker.'

She plucked the book from his hands. 'If you came to poke fun at me, you may leave. I have work to do.'

'Work?'

She didn't wait to see if he would follow. He might be as flippant as he liked, but she knew the pitfalls of curiosity too well not to recognise a fellow sufferer of that malady.

Back in the parlour she drew closed the thick velvet curtains, casting the room into a gloom that would be near absolute by late afternoon when Marcia Pendle arrived. The candles and incense were prepared and she lit the fire so it would calm by the time the magic began. She needed just a hint of light and enough heat to spread the scents Gypsy Sue recommended. She marked the item on her list and continued: tin-derboxes, brandy...

'I don't know which room is more disturbing, this parlour or your spider's lair of a study.

The study by a narrow margin, I think,' he commented behind her.

'Why is that?'

'Because this is clearly for show, that room is in earnest.'

She shrugged. Votive candles. Bergamot oil. Present.

'Did the otherworldly Mrs Volgatskaya inspire this decor? What are these scarves for? Do you perform a dance?'

'No, I bind unwary visitors and sacrifice them to the dark lords.'

'No, thank you. I've never had to resort to binding anyone to get what I want, certainly not women.'

She looked up from her list, her mouth curving into a smile despite her attempts to keep it prim.

'You are rather vain, aren't you, Lord Sinclair?'

He slid a scarf through his hands, his fingers skimming the shimmering fabric absently and his smile answering hers.

'Am I? I wouldn't call it vanity, precisely.'

Don't pander to him, Olivia.

'What would you call it, then? And don't say "experience", that would merely confirm my point.'

'I won't call it anything at all, then. So, what happens next?'

'Next you leave.'

He pulled a chair from the table and sat down in clear disregard for conventions of politeness, still tugging the scarf idly between his hands. The hiss of silk as it slipped through his fingers tingled upwards from her feet, travelling like smoke over her skin. She could feel the warmth it picked up in the friction against his flesh, mirroring on the softness between her own fingers, a faint burning, spreading to her palms like the singe of acid. She held herself back from snatching the scarf away from him.

'Do you really want me to leave, Olivia?'

Her name sounded like smoke and silk as well and she had to breathe in before she could speak. She was losing her footing again which was probably precisely what he wanted. The object of that subterranean rumble of heat was no doubt to soften her, make her pliable to his manipulations. That was all.

'Miss Silverdale,' she amended. The scarf paused for a moment before resuming its tormenting progress.

'So. Do you want me to leave, Miss Olivia Silverdale?'

'If you are here to help me, you may stay. But I don't need you here if all you plan to do is poke fun at me,' she said and he tossed the scarf on to the table. The sultry warmth was gone, confirming her suspicions, but she felt no victory at withstanding his charm.

'I don't find obsessions particularly amusing, Miss Silverdale. I am not here to help you, but to ensure you don't do damage to my concerns with your rather colourful methods. My family name has been dragged through enough mud and we don't need any help from outsiders in adding to our infamy.'

'You said you weren't here to prevent my meeting.'

'I'm not. I am here to…oversee. I will be in the next room, listening as you do your occultist's best to extract gold from Marcia Pendle, so keep that in mind as you delve. When you are done I want you to make it clear to her that her spectral friend will be taking an extended trip on the other side and will no longer be available to your summons. So have her make her tearful farewells and send her back to Catte Street. Permanently.'

'I believe I told you I don't enjoy being threatened, Lord Sinclair.'

'I sympathise. I'm not fond of the feeling myself. So now we understand each other.'

'I am not threatening you, I am merely trying to uncover—'

'Yes, I understood you the first time, Miss Silverdale. You should consider it a serious concession that I am allowing even this meeting to take place. You take another step down this path without my knowledge and I move from threats to actions. Am I clear?'

'To be fair, I did inform you of this step.'

'Don't split hairs.'

'Out of curiosity, what actions are you contemplating?'

Some of the severity faded from his eyes.

'You want me to show you my cards, Miss Silverdale? I'm insulted you think me such a soft touch.'

'Not at all. I think you understand me well enough to know I am more likely to respond to a believable threat than to bombastic words.'

'Very well then. My first action will be to send word to your brother, Guy Silverdale, as to your whereabouts and actions. As the head of your family he might object to his only sister leasing a house in a shabby-genteel part of London and arranging rendezvous with notorious rakes. Is that sufficient to start with?'

'How did you know my brother's name is Guy?'

'I consulted my spectral spirit friends and they had a word with their Yorkshire connections by way of the ghost of Catherine the Great and Julius Caesar. Well, Olivia?'

Perhaps it was the way he said her name again, or perhaps it was merely his presence there and the fact he mentioned Guy's name, as if knowing that would reach her above all else. She ought not to be worried; if he was completely serious about his threat he would have acted on it already. Which meant he was willing to make a concession, even if it was only out of curiosity. All she had to do was ensure he remained curious. It would mean coaxing him along, inch by inch.

She sat and extended her hand.

'Very well, Lord Sinclair. After this evening dear departed George will take a long cruise down the River Styx until we agree otherwise.'

The hand might have been a mistake. Her nerve endings hadn't calmed in the least from his scarf-toying and they leapt to attention as the warmth of his hand closed over hers, revelling in the contact. Her other hand twitched, as if envious, and she pulled away and hurried towards the door.

'Marcia will be here soon so I must dress. I will be down directly.'

She didn't wait for him to respond and, as she rushed upstairs, she didn't know if she hoped he would still be there when she returned.

Chapter Five

Marcia Pendle's cloying perfume rose like smoke from under the door and Lucas resisted the urge to move away. He did not want to miss any of the entertainment in the other room. Miss Olivia Silverdale might not know what a Bulgarian madame sounded like, but her version of a spirit-possessed fortune-teller would do well in a Drury Lane farce.

He had begun his vigil of her little masquerade annoyed as hell, but after half an hour of her antics he was having a hard time resisting the urge to laugh out loud. He couldn't believe Marcia Pendle was taking her so seriously.

To give Miss Silverdale her due she paced her theatrical nonsense well. Just when Marcia Pendle was on the verge of extracting a promise of eternal fidelity from the deceased, who sounded like fidelity had not been his strong point during his corporeal state, Miss Silverdale sent him scurrying at the interruption of a host of avenging angels accusing Marcia of assisting in the perpetration of a heinous sin.

'You must reveal all!' Madame Bulgari intoned, her voice quivering with baritone outrage. 'Only then will the Lords of the Gates be appeased and allow you to unite with George! The wife of the man you maligned has powerful spirits working for her. They can bar your way for ever!'

'No! Please, Madame Bulgari, I only did what this man told me. I swear! He said it was to help someone from ruin. He weren't no flash cove, nor sharp—why, he was nervous as a virgin on her bridal night. I reckoned the lady who rode that fellow so hard was his relation and he didn't want questions. He gave me five guineas just to tell the constable I was this Henry Payton's particular friend these past six months and that I visited him veiled and all. I told him don't you worry, it happens, don't I know it? I didn't mean trouble; I thought I was doing a good turn. Tell the spirits!'

'Calm yourself. They know your heart is true. They will seek the malefactor, but you must name him.'

'The mal-e-what?'

'He who did evil. The man who bade you lie.'

'But I don't know him, I tell you. He shows up and asks for me particular—says he heard I used to be on the stage and offers me five guineas. Five! He shows them to me, too, right there in the middle of Catte Street which shows you he has less sense than a day-old kitten. Clear as anything he didn't want to be seen with me, had me walk three steps behind him the whole way from where the hackney left us. I only know his name because a man he passed tipped his hat and said, "Evening, Eldritch, fancy seeing you south of the river." Poor fellow almost wet himself, turned redder than a duke in a new corset. I'm not saying it's right, lying about who this Payton was frolicking with behind his missus's back, but it ain't a shade on the evil I've seen elsewhere. It ain't right to punish me and my George for trying to help. You tell them that, will you?'

'They hear you, but still you must present him to their judgement. Tell them what manner of man is he. Close your eyes and give him the image you see in your mind, give it to them so they may take away his sin from your spirit. Describe him.'

'I don't know. He was…a man. Not tall. He were dressed like a clerk or one of them better shopkeepers, brown eyes, I think, or black. I see a dozen of those a day at Madame's, they look alike in the end. I'd say by his clothes he's got a wife or someone who sees to his housekeeping, but they ain't too well-padded. There's the darning, neat stitches, but enough to say he doesn't have too many Sunday clothes, see? If he'd have come to Madame Bernieres you can be sure he'd have been palmed off on the country girls who don't know the tricks yet. He looked serious, scared, but then he ought to, oughtn't he? Are they still angry, the spirits?'

The silence that followed her agonised question was punctuated by her tearful sniffling and Lucas reined in his impatience. Surely even the irrepressible Miss Silverdale recognised there was nothing more to be extracted from Marcia Pendle, even under the threat of eternal damnation. Finally there was a rustling and a shuddering sigh.

'Ah, there is much water, fog, they are going away.'

'But they won't keep me from George when my time comes?'

'For now they are appeased. But they say I am not to communicate with them again on your behalf unless they send word first. I dare not defy them.'

Lucas pushed away from the door frame. Marcia Pendle's tale was far more sensible than Miss Silverdale's theories. Perhaps now this outrageous young woman would abandon her fantasies of conspiracies. He glanced at the lists decorating the wall behind him and sighed. Not likely. People believed what they wanted to believe and Olivia Silverdale wanted to believe Henry Payton a wronged man.

When the front door closed behind the sniffling Marcia Pendle he entered the parlour. With the reek of perfume, the guttering candles and the garish scarves, it looked like a struggling brothel. Olivia was unwinding the gold-embroidered scarf that secured her curls and they tumbled down, glinting with copper and gold lights as they settled on her shoulders. She twisted them into a knot and secured it with a wooden pin, but tendrils escaped like trailing ivy, framing her face and curling around her neck and ears. Lucas picked up a discarded scarf to keep his hands occupied. It was a bad sign when he began contemplating helping a woman with her coiffure.

'Well? What did you think?' she asked the silence.

'I think that was the worst Balkan accent I have ever had the misfortune to hear.'

Laughter burst in her eyes but her rouged mouth remained serious. It was a peculiar and unsettling combination.

'It was effective, though, wasn't it?' she demanded.

'That depends on what you consider effective.' He went to the mantelpiece, snuffing the candles. 'I think we should remove to your spider's lair. This room reeks.'

She followed him into the study, untangling scarves as she went and balling them into a rainbowed lump. Without the veil she looked even more a parody of a fortune-teller, her cheeks and lips flared with rouge and her eyes dusky with kohl.

'Can't you take off that paint? You look like an actress from one of the lesser theatres.'

The honey-and-moss eyes sparkled with either amusement or annoyance, but her answer was all business.

'I know we did not learn much beyond the fact that this Eldritch told her what to say to the constable, but at least that is something. We must find him.'

'Sit down, Miss Silverdale. Let me explain something to you.'

She folded her arms, the tangle of scarves pressed against her bosom like a strangled pet, drawing his gaze to the low-cut bodice of the purple satin monstrosity she wore and to the tantalising cleft between what he judged were two delightfully shaped globes, neither too large nor too small. He regretfully removed his eyes from this unintended display and fixed them instead on hers.

'Very well, stand if you wish. I will explain in small but explicit words so there can be no chance of a misunderstanding, and you will have to forgive me for not sparing your maidenly blushes because any woman dressed as you are dressed at the moment and pursuing your present course of action can surely survive a little plain speaking. Your godfather had the misfortune to expire mid-coitus—it is rare and highly undesirable, but it happens. It would have been better if the real person involved in this unfortunate situation had hared off and left Payton to be discovered in due course instead of involving a third party, but the fact remains this is nothing more than an unfortunate accident.'

'But...'

'But nothing. Your godfather was not perfect, no man is. If the worst you know of him is that he had an affair, then he is a man like many others, however regrettable that fact is. I suggest you accept this and move on, and by move on I mean back home at the soonest possible opportunity.'

'What of the note I found with your father's correspondence? What if they are connected after all? What if this Mr Eldritch was involved in his death? Perhaps he had been trying to prevent Henry from doing something or saying something or—'

'Miss Silverdale,' he interrupted again, 'You clearly read too many novels. I have indulged your imagination far enough. You have a day to pack and leave Spinner Street and return whence you came or I will send a messenger to your family informing them of your whereabouts and your activities.'

'Don't you even wish to see your father's letters?'

'No, thank you. Twenty-four hours. By this time tomorrow you should be well on your way out of London. If you need help hiring a post chaise, I can offer my butler's services. He is very discreet.'

Her arms spread wide, the crushed scarves fluttering in a parody of an exotic dance. 'How can you be so certain there is no more to this than a weak heart and an officious relation? Can you honestly walk away without a qualm?'

'Not honestly, sweetheart. Too late for that. But without a qualm, yes.'

'Oh, don't be so glib!'

'Too late for that as well. What the devil do you think you will achieve if you keep rummaging in other people's rubbish heaps? Do you think you will discover a dastardly plot to defame your god-father that somehow stretches back twenty years to another plot against my father? That you will redeem them from their own iniquity and win your godmother's gratitude? The world doesn't operate that way. Just accept that your godfather, like my father, was a weak man who made a mistake, or several. That is the end of this story. Anything else is pure indulgence on your part.'

Except for her garish clothes she looked a model of cool defiance, her shoulders back, her lips pressed firmly together and her eyes disdainful. But her hands gave her away, kneading away at the tangle of scarves, and he was sure he heard the rending of silk. He doubted the colourful fabrics would survive the evening.

Still, when she answered her voice was calm.

'I know you are probably correct. About them. About me as well. But I must do this. If I walked away now…' she shook her head '… I cannot do it. At least when I leave I shall know I did my best.'

She looked ridiculous but peculiarly appealing

with her painted face and beseeching hazel eyes made far too vivid by the kohl. He assessed his options and sighed.

'Do me a favour and scrub your face clean and put on something that doesn't look like you stole it off a demi-monde's back. Then we will talk. Calmly. Is there anything to drink here?'

'Drink? There is brandy in the parlour. Gypsy Sue suggested having some on hand to make Marcia more generous. Or would you care for tea?'

'I will find the brandy. Go and change.'

The brandy was surprisingly good and he took it into the study and poured himself a measure and on second thought poured her a glass, too. Perhaps it would make her more generous as well.

He paused with the glass halfway to his mouth at the thought of Olivia Silverdale being generous, the potency of the image surprising him with a rush of heat that flowed upwards from his stomach and then settled back into his groin with an insistent thudding. It was utterly unwelcome, but before he could push it aside it was followed by the realisation that she was somewhere upstairs, undressing. That the vulgar purple-satin dress was even now hissing downwards over her skin, puddling on the floor at her feet with a whisper like an exhaled breath.

He tightened his hold on his glass and grimaced at the unwelcome thoughts. She might be an appealing little thing, but despite her eccentricity she was clearly gently born and as far outside his areas of interest as was possible without being married with ten children. Besides, from what he witnessed in the church she had no positive outlook on physical intimacy.

The image returned of her standing in the church, chin up, eyes closed as that young cub bent to kiss her. It was a submissive stance except for the fact that her hands had been fisted and her mouth anything but inviting. She looked more like a soldier before a firing squad, defiant but resolved to embrace his fate, than a young woman about to be kissed. It struck him as strange then, but doubly so now. Someone so very passionate about life should not look like that when a young man she clearly cares for steals a very chaste kiss.

I must do this...

He swirled his brandy, watching it lick against the edges of the glass.

It was *not* his concern. She might not be able to tame her curiosity, but he had years of experience doing just that. The fact that his discipline was lagging in his dealings with her was no excuse to slacken control further. She was not his concern. The ragged remnants of the Sinclair name were. Sam should not have to weather any more storms and so his only concern was to push this genie back into her bottle and move on.

'Oh, good. You found it. Is that for me?'

He turned, his body clenching in readiness to either administer or receive a blow. She was transformed again—she was wearing a cream-muslin dress with rows of tiny pale-yellow flowers marking the bodice and sleeves. The makeup was gone, but her lips and cheeks were reddened from rubbing and a faint shadow lingered around her eyes. She had not even tried to dress her hair, but merely twisted her curls a little more rigorously into an off-centre knot and secured them with what looked like short knitting needles. She looked like what he imagined a young woman from the country would look like in the privacy of the breakfast room, still warm from bed and with nothing more on her mind than embroidery and morning calls. Not that he had much experience with that breed or wanted to. What he wanted was to pull one of those needles and see if that knot of burnished curls survived. Then take out the other and watch it all unfurl. Then lead her upstairs and watch her remove that proper dress as well.

Hell and damnation. This was the very definition of unwelcome.

She sat, sipped her brandy, frowned and sipped it again.

'This is rather foul. Do men truly enjoy it or do they merely drink it for the pleasure of becoming intoxicated? By the way, I should warn you I have no intention of leaving London tomorrow.'

'Not voluntarily. I'm aware of that.'

'Not even under duress. I must at least discover who this Mr Eldritch is. If he is indeed merely a concerned relation and there is another woman involved, then…well, perhaps you are right. But I must try. Well? You said you wished to talk. What shall we talk about?'

How I am going to bed you.

He smiled at his unaccustomed descent into folly and shook his head.

'Who was that young man you were kissing at St George's?'

Her eyes widened and a flush rushed over her cheekbones, as vivid as Madame Bulgari's rouge.

'You saw us?'

'I saw him accost you by your carriage and, as

you pointed out, I am a curious fellow, so, yes, I followed you back into the church.'

'I didn't see you.'

'You weren't meant to. So, who is he?'

'Colin Payton. Henry Payton's son.'

'Ah, I see. What is there between you?'

'What does it matter?'

'Are you engaged to that young pup?'

Her mouth flattened and her eyes narrowed.

'He is not a young pup; he is but a good man. But, no, we are not engaged.'

'If you go about kissing him in churches you are as near to engaged as possible without the priest reading the banns. Why didn't you tell me this is one of your reasons for wanting Payton cleared? If I am to help you, you must be honest with me, Miss Silverdale.'

'I didn't tell you because it isn't true.'

'So you kiss men in churches for the sheer pleasure of it?'

'He kissed *me*—I didn't instigate it.' Her ferocity confirmed his observation, though he couldn't tell if it was merely a virgin's inexperience or some deeper objection. Probably the former; her obsession with conspiracies was making him see shadows when there were none. His experience with virgins was thankfully minimal; for all he knew they all reacted like that at the prospect of physical intimacy.

Before he could respond she pressed her hands together, calming. 'But I might marry him, if I cannot solve this any other way.'

'How precisely would matrimony solve it?'

'Well, it would at least solve the financial concerns that Henry's death caused. I am very wealthy, you see. If my brother Jack had married his sister Phoebe they would have had his protection, both financial and otherwise, but he died and now it falls to me to help as much as I can.'

'I see. Very noble of you.'

'It has nothing to do with being noble. I am merely trying to do what is right for people for whom I care deeply. To answer your as-yet-unspoken question, no, I will not cease merely because you tell me to, so I think it is in your best interest to help me rather than try to chase me away.'

'And so we circle back to your agenda. Are you always this stubborn or do I bring out the worst in you?'

'Both.'

He laughed, moving forward to raise her chin with the tips of his fingers.

'Do you know, if you want me to comply, you

should try to be a little less demanding and a little more conciliating.'

'I don't know why I should bother. You will no doubt do precisely as you wish without regard for anyone. So far, the only way I have found of persuading you is either by appealing to your curiosity or to your self-interest. I don't see what good begging would do.'

He slid his thumb gently over her chin, just brushing the line of her lip, and watched as her eyes dilated with what could as much be a sign of alarm as physical interest. He wished he knew which. His blood was simmering, expanding, demanding he find out.

'It depends what you are begging for,' he said softly, pulling very slightly on her lower lip. Her breath caught, but she still did not move. Stubborn *and* imprudent. Or did she really trust him not to take advantage of the fact that they were alone in an empty house in a not-very-genteel part of London?

It really was a pity she planned to waste herself on that dull and dependable young man. What on earth did she think her life would be like with him? All that leashed intensity would burn the poor fool to a crisp if he ever set it loose, which was unlikely. A couple of years of being tied to him and she would be chomping at the bit and probably very ripe for a nice flirtation.

He shook his head at his thoughts. Whatever else he was, and whatever his body was unexpectedly demanding, he had never yet crossed the line with an inexperienced young woman; they were too apt to confuse physical pleasure with emotional connection. It wouldn't be smart to indulge this temptation to see if those lips were as soft and delectable as they looked. Not smart, but very tempting...

'You could always offer a trade,' he prompted gently, testing the line of her lip with another soft brush of his thumb. The sensation was addictive.

'A trade?' Her voice was husky and she cleared her throat.

'I will try to find out who Eldritch is...'

'And what must I do?' Her expression was wary, but she did not pull away and if anything the tension in her shoulders relaxed, as if becoming accustomed to the licence he was taking. He wasn't certain that was an encouraging sign either.

'If it is about turning my back on this, then there is no trade,' she added as the silence stretched.

'I wouldn't think of asking for something I

know you are constitutionally incapable of. It is something much simpler.'

'Well, what?' She frowned and he hesitated. However much he wanted to test this strange need that was sinking its claws in him, the thought of asking her for something she had shown such an aversion to when approached by her friend was too uncomfortable. It was a breach of trust where trust should not be an issue at all, and that was problematic. He breathed in and dropped his hand, stepping back.

'Never mind.'

She moved towards him.

'No. Tell me what it is!'

The command should have served further to convince him he should leave this room, this house, this peculiar woman's fantasy. Instead it prodded further at his own fantasy.

'You tell me. What would that information be worth?'

'Do you mean in monetary terms?'

'No. I have no need for your money. This is pointless. Goodbye, Miss Silverdale.'

She caught his arm.

'Oh, please just tell me. I need your help, but I have nothing else to offer but my money. Nothing someone like you might value, at least.'

'Someone like me?'

Her beseeching eyes fell from his.

'Someone with…experience. I can hardly imagine you would wish for anything along such lines from someone like me.'

'Someone like you?'

'Unremarkable.' The word burst from her as if it had been lodged in her throat. It was not her word, and that was surprising in itself. Who in their right mind would call this woman unremarkable?

'That is one epithet I would never associate with you. Believe me, Miss Silverdale, you are one of the most remarkable women of my acquaintance.'

Her cheeks, already pink, heated and so did every cell in his body. He touched his fingers lightly to the hand clutching his arm so desperately.

'I will pledge to find this Mr Eldritch for you if I can.'

Her hand did not relax.

'You will? Just like that? Without recompense?'

'Without. But then you are on your own.'

She let go and as her tension seeped away he saw the return of her curiosity.

'What *were* you about to ask for, Lord Sinclair?'

'You have what you wanted. What difference does it make?'

'I dare say it doesn't, but I am curious.'

He sighed. 'Of course you are. You will be pleased to find you were spared the noxious experience of being asked for a kiss.'

Her eyes widened in disbelief.

'A kiss?'

'You needn't sound so shocked.'

'You cannot be serious,' she said, her voice scolding.

'Rarely, but in this instance I am. It was merely a kiss, I was not about to ask for your first-born child.'

'But why?'

'Now that is a question worthy of being ignored. You have what you want. Now I had best leave before you further crush my vanity underfoot.'

'I am not... It is merely that it seems a little silly. I mean, the gossip columnists hint you have dozens of mistresses, why would you wish for a kiss from me?'

'I'm beginning to wonder that myself. Do you know you are the most aggravating woman...

girl…whatever… I have ever met? Goodbye, Miss Silverdale.'

'Wait.'

Despite his better judgement he paused at the door. 'What now, Miss Silverdale?'

'Did you really wish to kiss me?' She looked so confused his impatience waned. His frustration on the other hand…

'I do, but it was extremely foolish of me to make that suggestion. I am well aware that despite your Spinner Street fantasies you are a respectable young woman and one with a dislike of being…approached. That much was evident by your martyr's stance when Payton's son did no more than tickle your cheek.'

She pressed her hands to her cheeks.

'It isn't that I… I never did until…'

Anger bubbled up in him at this confirmation of his suspicion. He wondered what clumsy fool had left his mark on her. It probably wasn't the boring Payton boy, she seemed quite fond of him and the kiss they exchanged had been as unthreatening as being accosted with a daisy. Still, it was all the more reason to leave now. She wasn't his responsibility.

'Someone hurt you.'

Her mouth thinned.

'Someone lied to me and used me and that hurt most of all, but he never… It hardly matters, it is in the past. But you are wrong about Colin. I didn't wish for him to kiss me because he would then read into that single kiss a hundred things I am not ready for and I would once again find myself in a corner, with no choices that reflect my own wishes. This is different; you don't want anything from me *but* a kiss and I am still not quite certain why you want even that. Do you understand?'

He refrained from correcting her that what he wanted went quite a bit beyond a mere kiss.

'I think I do.'

She smiled, her eyes narrowing, more honey than green. They were speculative now and he remembered how she inspected him that first day in the church—even though she had been tense and afraid, there was that same assessing gaze, measuring his worth.

'May we try, then?'

'Try what?' He was rapidly losing control of the situation. She could not possibly mean…

'Kissing. I cannot bear the thought that every time I think of it I must think of…him. When Henry died I decided that perfidious wretch had affected my life far too much. So perhaps this is a good idea. I wish to take his power away and I may not have such an opportunity again. After all, I know I can trust you not to tattle. I'm a little worried, though. What if I *do* hate it? Do you think you could contrive to be convincing?'

Only a madman would pick up that hand with the cards so absolutely stacked against him. He might on occasion be a little reckless, though certainly less than society imagined, but he never...

'I could try.'

'Good. Thank you.'

She straightened resolutely, shoulders back. Her cheeks were still flushed, but the animation was fading from her features and she looked as she had in the church waiting for that young man to kiss her.

Contrarily it was the anxiety behind the determination that held him there. It made no sense for someone as intensely passionate as she to react with such a mixture of resolution and fear to a mere kiss. He wasn't certain if he agreed with her experimentation analogy, but it struck him that, his own undeniable interest aside, to spurn her request now would be to add insult to injury. He would just have to be very, very careful. He was well served that his foolish impulse to satisfy his curiosity by bartering for a quick kiss had landed him in such hot water. That would teach his impulses not to escape their fetters again in future.

He raised her chin gently and her lips tensed, pressing together hard.

'Relax, I will not kiss you yet.'

Her eyes flickered up to his.

'You won't?'

'I will tell you before I do and, if you wish me not to, you have only to say so. Now close your eyes.'

'Why?'

He sighed. 'Just trust me. I promise I will not kiss you without asking first. Now close your eyes.'

She obeyed, frowning, and he touched her cheek, moving his fingers lightly over her cheekbone to where a downy wave of brown hair curled over the tip of her ear. He brushed his thumb over its warmth, easing it back from her temple with soft stroking motions, his hand moulding to the curve of her jaw as he tucked it behind her ear. Her shoulder rose a fraction and he watched the flickering of her lashes, surprisingly dark and long, the shifting of her brows as they moved in and out of a frown as if trying to hear something far away.

He kept his touch light and soothing as his fingers explored the contours of her face, wondered what she was thinking. Whether despite her determination to master her thoughts and reactions she was cringing inside, linking his touch with memories of pain and humiliation.

'Is it terrible?' he whispered. 'Shall I stop?'

Her brows twitched again, but she didn't open her eyes or speak, just shook her head. It was hardly an accolade to his appeal, but it did quite a bit of damage, relief flowing through him more potently than her brandy, and he couldn't stop his gaze from settling on her mouth or his head sinking towards hers. So he closed his own eyes and concentrated on touch. On the slide of his fingers over the curve of her ear, her neck, on to the hard ridge of her collarbone and the sweep of her shoulder, then back up again.

Without seeing them there were revelations on the journey. The lobe of her ear was softer than any he had ever felt, so much so he had to feel it again, brushing his palm against it and barely controlling the shudder that rushed up his arms to join the building agony in the rest of his body. Then there was her collarbone. He had noticed it before with the eye of a connoisseur who could appreciate architectural highlights, but under his fingers it was combination of hard lines and velvety skin; it drew his fingers along its definite sweep and made his body imagine her hands touching him in a mirror image of his caresses, sending tingling sensations over his chest to join the rising heat below.

His hands itched to go lower so he made them rise again, rewarding them by touching that impossibly soft skin beneath her ear where her pulse was fluttering as swiftly as his, then moving gently along her jaw and cheeks, resisting the urge to touch her mouth with every ounce of his control. He couldn't remember the last time he had either touched a woman so innocently or been swamped by such mind-numbing need. He gathered his disintegrating control. It was time to either go forward or retreat.

'May I kiss you now? I will stop the moment you ask.'

Her lips parted and she nodded slightly, the words sliding out, hardly audible, but they seemed to enter directly into this chest, two spears dipped in molten lead.

'Yes, please...'

He had never felt such tension at the thought of just kissing a woman. The need to be gentle was in absolute opposition to his desire. But it was imperative that he not scare her, and allowing her to feel one iota of the heat tormenting him would probably send her running.

He touched his mouth to hers. The burn was immediate, like making contact with a live flame under a veil of silk. Her body jerked, her breath hitching, and he fought his own instinctive recoil at the contact. He held himself still, just absorbing the feel of her lips, as her breath, short and shallow, feathered over his lips. It was both torture and exquisite—nothing was happening, but every passing second the sensations shifted, sparking little shivers of pleasure along his lips that danced out through his body like ecstatic messengers preparing the ground for a feast. Her heartbeat thundered where his palms were pressed against her neck and cheek.

Finally, he felt something in the balance of her body shift; a slight quiver ran through her and her lips parted just a little, her lower lip sliding between his, until he felt the perfect point where the pillowy softness was damp, warmer. He concentrated on keeping his movements slight, gentle, sliding one hand into her hair, his thumb brushing over her ear as he pulled her lip slowly between his, tasting it.

His other hand moved over her shoulder, to her waist, holding her as he moved in, trying not to drag her against him as he wanted to, just bringing his body to touch hers. Her own hands, which had hung by her sides, rose languidly, resting for a moment on the lapels of his coat, then with another devastating shiver they slid up and around his nape, her fingers skimming into his hair, moving gently against his scalp. He wanted to arch his head back, force her to go further, to sink her hands into his hair, press her body the length of his, he wanted her to sink her teeth into the stinging need spreading in the wake of the sweep of her lips against his. The disconnect between her languid movements and the raging fire they were feeding finally dragged him to a halt.

He drew back, but he didn't let her go or do more than manage even an inch of distance between their mouths.

'That was nice.' Her breath brushed against his lips, soft and warm as a Mediterranean breeze. But her words were as lacklustre as ditch water and dragged him categorically back to reality.

Nice.

'For someone who was not certain she would like kissing, you did very well,' he managed to say.

She moved back, but his hands remained on the soft curve of her waist. She didn't appear to notice and he wasn't going to call her attention to it because he wasn't quite ready to let her go. Her eyes were half-closed and she pulled her lower lip between her teeth. It slid out, moist and full, and the tense knot of heat and desire tightened like a ship's rigging in full gale winds and then her eyes softened in a smile that hit him like a fist to the gut. If he didn't know better, he could well believe she had conceived of the perfect seduction. It was certainly far too effective.

'I am glad I tried. This was quite…different,' she replied.

Different. Almost worse than 'Nice.' Before he could respond she stepped back.

'Do you really believe there is a chance you will find this Mr Eldritch?'

He let her go and moved towards the door.

'I will do my best. Such a sacrifice on your part shouldn't go unrewarded.'

He didn't wait to hear her response. He was damned if he gave her any more opportunities to make a fool out of him.

Olivia went to sit at her desk, staring at the still-open door of the study until the thud of the area door closing brought her a little closer to the surface.

She touched her lower lip. It felt strange, puffy and sensitive like the time Jack accidently bumped his head against hers while struggling for ownership of a croquet mallet, except that it didn't hurt. Everywhere Lord Sinclair had touched and a few places he hadn't felt strange—tingly and restless and pulsing, as if he had scoured away layers of sheltering skin. *She* felt strange.

To think she had worried it would give even more power to those images and memories of Bertram. The moment his fingertips brushed her mouth her mind latched on to the sensation like Twitch on to a stick. By the time he asked if he could kiss her it would have taken a great deal more strength than she possessed to say no.

Now that he was gone she wondered where she had found the temerity to ask him to kiss her. She had told him far too much, revealed much more than she ever revealed to anyone. She had trusted him. She must be quite mad. He certainly must have thought her mad. She winced at the memory of her comments about experimentation. What had she been thinking to prattle on so? It seemed so natural, so right to share with him that fear, that need, her curiosity…

At least if she had utterly humiliated herself, again, there was some comfort in knowing she was not fated to think of Bertram the moment a man approached her. As much as she enjoyed Bertram's embraces before his betrayal, she could not remember ever feeling them so potently. She remembered Bertram's own excitement, his endearments, and especially the feeling of power over him. And all of those had been lies. This was different. She was not even certain the earl enjoyed the kiss or whether for him it was merely curiosity and dominance.

All she knew was that she remembered every second of it, every element of it. The sensation of his hair sliding between her fingers, silkier and warmer than those scarves, the scent of musk and soap and something far away but so familiar. Even with her eyes closed images filled her mind—the way his eyes narrowed and darkened as he bent over her, the strength of the long fingers bringing her skin to life, his mouth a breath away from hers… And then the scalding moment of contact and the kiss…

She had been utterly present and utterly lost in the moment.

Even now that he was gone she still felt… strong. Alive.

Confused.

She shivered and picked up his glass of brandy,

watching the amber liquid pitch and sway. The packet of his father's letters was right there, the handwriting on them still clear despite two decades having passed. He had looked right at them without a sign of recognition. Surely anyone... anyone *normal* would show some curiosity about letters from their deceased parent, no matter how much they disliked that parent? She wasn't very fond of hers but she would definitely be curious if someone presented her with a packet of their lost letters, even if they were most likely about orchids and other rare flora.

Too much about this man didn't make sense.

She sighed and sipped the brandy and stared at her wall. Then she pulled a sheet of paper towards her and dipped her quill into the inkpot. In her scrawled writing she wrote and underlined the title:

Lord Sinclair. Characteristics...

Chapter Six

Lucas paid the hackney driver and continued on foot. He was a half-mile from Spinner Street, but he would do well to expend some of his excess energy along the way. He wasn't accustomed to rebellions either from his libido or his conscience and to have both of them heading in the wrong direction was surely a good indication to retreat.

And yet here he was. He couldn't even completely blame it on his rebellious body. It had never ruled him in the past, whatever society chose to think, and he had no intention of allowing it to do so at his age. But he couldn't shake the conflicting images of Olivia Silverdale that dogged his steps as he went about unearthing the identity of her mysterious Eldritch—the garish Madame Bulgari in her satins and silks, the coolly veiled woman issuing her demands, and especially the girl waiting to experiment with kissing, managing to look both lost and fiercely determined all at once.

Despite appearances she was no helpless waif—very few women…very few people he knew would have embarked on her course of action and most would recognize an unscaleable wall when they crashed into it. Clearly when Miss Silverdale met a wall she manoeuvred some fool to climb over it for her—in this case himself. He remembered a few generals with similar characteristics from the war, not all of them fondly.

He had to keep in mind she was *not* his responsibility—that sphere was occupied only by a very few. But he couldn't deny she reminded him of Sam. Sam would also have walked across the desert barefoot if that was what she felt was necessary to help her brothers and friends. And he and Chase would do anything for her, which made Sam's present apathy about life all the harder to stomach.

He stopped before the unassuming door of Number Fifteen. Perhaps that was why he was here, tilting at this young woman's windmills. Because he couldn't help Sam. It was a poor reason to be tangling with a delusional little field marshal. She was not his sister and his instincts were screaming at him she was pure, unadulterated trouble. He should make good on his promise and then decamp.

He knocked and after a long moment the door swung open and a grey-haired female version of Napoleon Bonaparte stood glaring at him, a flour-covered rolling pin grasped in her hand.

'What will you be wanting?'

He eyed the rolling pin warily. 'Is Miss Silverdale in?'

The grey brows sank lower. 'What's it to you?'

'Who is it, Nora?'

Nora looked over her shoulder. 'You know this varlet, miss?'

'Varlet?' Miss Silverdale entered the hallway from the study. 'Oh, yes, Nora. I forgot to tell you we might have a guest. Though to be fair I expected he would send word before appearing on our doorstep. Do come in, Lord Sinclair.'

Nora snorted. 'I don't like this, not one bit, Miss Olivia.'

'I know, Nora. I am a sore trial to you. Shall I brew my own tea as penance?'

'Not while I'm in the house!'

The servants' door snapped shut behind the woman and Lucas followed Olivia into the study and inspected her, rather sorry that she wasn't arrayed in another Madame Bulgari costume. It was hard to reconcile the young woman in her proper gown of pale-yellow sprigged muslin with the intrepid occultist of yesterday. Or with the young woman who reacted so sensually to his kiss.

Again he experienced the tug between conscience and lust. Had he really asked to kiss her? Besides being wrong it was stupid. For all he knew she might have misconstrued his interest in her and meanwhile concocted some foolishly romantic fantasy on the back of that ill-judged kiss. If he had an ounce of sense he should indeed have sent her a note with what he had learned because no good could come out of spending more time with her.

He watched her warily as she went to stand by the desk, but the image of the proper young woman hovering on the brink of infatuation caved as she turned and grinned at him.

'You should have seen your face. She is terrifying, isn't she?'

He smiled before he could think better of it.

'I dare say you wouldn't have objected if she cracked my skull with that rolling pin.'

'Oh, no, it would have been very inconvenient. Well, have you found anything? I didn't expect you back so soon. Nora will bring tea, but would you prefer brandy? I should ask Nora to procure some more, but I dare say you won't be coming often enough to merit replenishing my stock of spirits.'

'*You* won't be staying here long enough to merit replenishing them,' he corrected, touched despite himself by her obvious nervousness. She shrugged, her chin rising fractionally.

'Well? Have you found Eldritch?' she demanded.

'It is, for better or worse, a very rare name in London. I found three of them and none are particularly likely as the villain in your drama. One is an octogenarian who has been bedridden for several years. He lives with his unwed son who is the vicar at St Stephen's in…'

'In?' she prompted when he trailed off but he didn't answer. After a moment he picked up the top letter from the pile at the corner of the desk. The paper was soft, the edges frayed and a little stained. Strange how one remembered handwriting, even stranger how similar it was to his own.

There was always a spike of excitement when he saw that handwriting on a letter from Boston. His father's gift for description brought that world to life. Lucas used to believe he could smell the sea and spices on the paper. Those letters were more precious than any of the wonders they described; until they'd stopped.

Now would be a good time to leave. He had fulfilled his part of the bargain. It was time to send Miss Silverdale back where she belonged. He forced himself to continue.

'In Bloomsbury. The third, his elder brother, resides, permanently, in the burial ground of that same parish and has done so for the past few years. There are no other known Mr Eldritches in London, and especially none known in or around the brothels or molly houses near Catte Street. That does not mean it is impossible there are others, but it is unlikely. My sources tend to be reliable.'

'What is a molly house? Is it also a brothel?'

'This is hardly a proper topic for discussion, Miss Silverdale.'

'This whole situation is improper, isn't it? Besides, you were the one to mention brothels and… Molly houses? Is that where they call all the courtesans Molly?'

Good lord, how had he dug himself into this pit?

'No. Molly houses are places for men to associate with each other.'

'Oh, like a men's club?'

'I…yes, like a club. But that is hardly the point, the point is that I have fulfilled my obligation to you and there is clearly nothing more for you to do in London. I suggest you unravel your spider's web and return to Yorkshire before your little ruse is uncovered and you are thoroughly compromised.'

'I have not resided in Yorkshire for the past two years and I have no intention of returning any time soon. Besides, why would I be compromised? Surely there is nothing wrong with a young woman living with her perfectly respectable chaperon in Brook Street?'

'I would hesitate to impugn any woman who wields a rolling pin so skilfully, but your Nora could not pass muster as a socially acceptable chaperon and this is quite a way from Brook Street.'

'No, not Nora. She was my wet nurse as a child and came with me when I left Yorkshire. I was referring to Lady Phelps. We have leased a house on Brook Street for the Season.'

He rubbed his forehead.

'Is this another fanciful manifestation of Madame Bulgari's or is this one a real person?'

'Oh, she is very real. She is my mother's cousin and once led a very fashionable life in London when she was married to Lord Phelps. Unfortunately, when he died five years ago he left her without a penny, but unlike Byron she merely left London for Guilford. Still, she is eminently respectable and very fashionable.'

'She might be all that, but she is clearly remiss in her duties. My experience of chaperons would lead me to expect she would have interceded at least a dozen times since I met you.'

'Well, she and I have an understanding. She knows I am safe with Nora while I am here in Spinner Street and while I am in Brook Street I am the model of propriety, so much so as to be practically invisible. Even before we came to London I sometimes travelled with Mr Mercer and as she becomes queasy in carriages she was happy to allow Nora to assume her role when circumstances require it.'

'Who is this Mercer? You have mentioned him before.'

'My man of business. The point is...'

'*Your* man of business?'

'I was always good with figures and oversaw all the household accounts and my brothers' business affairs, you see. So when I turned eighteen and took possession of my own inheritance I decided to administer it myself and Henry helped me find Mercer. He is very reliable.'

'I see.'

'You disapprove.'

'Not of your financial aspirations. I disapprove of your fantastical theories regarding my father and I take strong issue with your assumption that you are invisible. If you encounter acquaintances while staying here, you will discover that to your detriment.'

'I told you, I rarely leave Brook Street and then only to come here and I do so fully veiled. When I complete my business in London we will likely join the Paytons in Harrogate. There is no reason anyone will ever discover I was here at all.'

'I cannot believe you are quite that naïve, Miss Silverdale. If one was a stickler for accuracy I would point out you were compromised the moment you met with me at St Margaret's. Every moment spent alone in my company is compounding that transgression.'

Her mouth quirked up at the corners. 'You don't look overly alarmed by the prospect, Lord Sinclair.'

'I am not the one who should be alarmed by it, Miss Silverdale.'

'Well, rightly or not, I am not. I admit when we met in the church you looked rather forbidding, but you are far less intimidating than your reputation indicates. And, since it is clear you no more wish to be leg-shackled than I, I am not worried you will use this situation to your advantage.'

'How the devil would I use this situation to my advantage?'

'Well, I *am* very wealthy and it is said you are very expensive.'

'Given my reputation I might be interested in something other than marriage.'

'Are you?'

He gritted his teeth and fell back on evasion. 'I am trying, unsuccessfully, to make you aware of the pitfalls of your situation. Or is it common-place for you to spend time alone with men of dubious reputation?'

He could almost see the moment the thought of that man who had betrayed her rose to her mind; her face hardened, but her voice was very calm.

'Hardly. I lived a very retired life in Guilford these past couple years and I see no reason for anyone to suspect me of doing anything other than visiting London with my widowed cousin. Colin certainly believed me the other day out-side the church.'

'That baby-faced sapling would probably be-lieve you if you told him you were an agent of the Crown on a mission to prevent Napoleon's sup-porters from smuggling his body off St Helena.'

'That is hardly fair. I have known Colin all my life, of course he trusts me. *Is* there a plot to steal Napoleon's body? How macabre. What do they plan to do with it?'

'I was talking hypotheticals. The point is neither you nor I, though for very different reasons, want society to get wind of your current endeavours.'

'All I am asking is that you consider the possibility there is more to this than meets the eye. Won't you at least take a look at his note?'

He dragged his hand through his hair. The woman was relentless. 'Show me the blasted note.'

'Here.' She opened the top drawer so swiftly it almost flew out. She held it out and he read it without taking it.

If this is true Howard Sinclair has been terribly wronged and something must be done.

Underneath, in larger, bolder print and underlined several times was the name she had mentioned in the carriage—Jasper Septimus.

'Is this it?'

'Isn't it enough? Mercer did try to discover if there is someone at Buxted Mallory Shipping by that name, but had no luck. He also tells me the company is managed by trustees for the current Lord Buxted, who is only sixteen, and I admit I'm not quite comfortable making enquiries there about people who are now deceased.'

'I am glad to hear you have even that much compunction. I think you are reading far too much into far too little.'

'I might have agreed with you if it were not for Marcia Pendle.'

'This is merely an unfortunate coincidence. If you search the shadows for shapes, I can promise you you will find them, but they rarely amount to more than figments of one's imagination, and yours, Miss Silverdale, is all too fertile. You are likely to do more harm than good by pursuing this.'

'How?'

'People who turn over stones tend to uncover snakes and other unpleasant creatures.'

'Are you worried I might uncover something even worse about your father?'

'Until the news of my father's death reached us my family and I were convinced that my father was no more a typical Sinclair than I am a Quaker. Since the day I learned of the litany of the sins he committed in Boston and succeeded in hiding from us, I know one can always discover something worse. My own reputation may not be of primary interest to me, but I won't have my siblings dragged through the mire again if I can prevent it.'

'Then help me put this to rest. All I am asking is that you help me look at these letters and tell me if there is anything here you think might be of importance.'

She held out the packet of letters he had been doing his best to ignore. Her eyes softened as he did not move, leaving them more green than brown. He didn't like that look. He could do without pity.

'Haven't you read them?' he asked.

'Only the first three. That was how long it took me to develop a conscience about reading other people's correspondence without their permission. I thought in fairness I should apply to you before continuing. Which I hereby do. Not that the ones I read are very revealing; they are mostly about shipping, but there are mentions of you and your siblings and in the second letter he thanks Henry for ensuring the package of books he sent was delivered safely to your mother, which led me to think your father and Henry trusted one another. Here, take them.'

'No, thank you.'

'Perhaps your brothers would care to have them? I meant to send them to you, but then I thought... Well, never mind.'

He walked away, over to her spider's-web wall. He hadn't looked too closely during his last visit, but now he scanned the lists. There was a short one titled Howard Sinclair—Letters—Names. He read the list again. Lord Buxted. George Buxted. John Mallory. Ada Mallory. Jasper Septimus. His own name was there and his mother's. A pin was shoved into the top half of Buxted's 'B' and a thread connected it to a larger pin near Henry Payton's section of the wall.

'Please take them.'

He turned. She was standing right by him, still holding out the letters. This close he could see the pattern of gold flecks in her green irises. She looked harmless. Just a typical country miss.

He was spared a decision by a rattling in the corridor and with a mumbled imprecation Miss Silverdale took his hand and shoved the letters into it before retreating towards the desk.

He remained where he was as the nurse entered and placed a tea tray rather ungently on the table with a less-than-friendly glare at Lucas. An enormous black cat entered with her, weaving about her skirts like a witch's familiar, but when Nora called to it as she went to the door it flicked its tail in the air and walked daintily up to Lucas and waited. Lucas shoved the letters into his pocket, but his hand was tingling uncomfortably and he bent to pet the cat awaiting his attention. An impressive purr erupted from it and it arched its back and closed its eyes, clearly expecting more of the same.

'Hussy!' Nora shook her head and closed the door with a definite snap.

'You are sinking deeper and deeper into infamy, you know,' Olivia said. 'Nora is very possessive of Inky. She saved her from drowning as a kitten and then from being nearly eaten by Twitch.'

'A friend of yours?'

'He used to be until he passed a year ago. He was my wolfhound and usually quite gentle, but he could be a little jealous of our affections. Just like Nora.'

'She is welcome to it. No, don't sit on my boot, you pestilential feline. Off!'

'I don't think scratching her behind the ears is making your distaste quite clear, Lord Sinclair. Do you need help escaping her clutches?'

'I think I can hold my own against a cat, Miss

Silverdale. No, I don't want tea. I'm not here on a social call.'

'Brandy, then.'

He sighed and sat on a chair by the table and surrendered. She poured a generous measure of brandy and he took it, watching as she poured the tea and placed a slice of a cake smelling strongly of cinnamon on a plate in front of him. Inky came and sat by his leg, its large body warm against his calf and its long white-tipped tail switching occasionally as if to some internal tune. The whole scene was unreal, utterly disconnected from his life. He sipped his brandy and though Olivia Silverdale didn't speak, her silence was both calming and peculiarly full. He hardly even noticed when he extracted the packet from his pocket and unfolded the first letter.

It wasn't so much what was written that struck him. The first letter was mostly a dry account of recent transactions and requests for documentation. It was the voice. Or the handwriting. He refolded it and placed it on the table and took the cake.

The cat raised a paw and swatted the air several times, the big grey eyes round and mournful. Lucas hesitated, breaking off a piece, but Olivia intervened.

'You won't like it, Inky. You don't like cinnamon.'

The cat turned those liquid grey eyes on her in a look that would have convinced Genghis Khan to show mercy, but Olivia merely met its stare until Inky slunk off under the sofa with a resentful mewl, only its long tail visible like an accusing finger.

Lucas felt a laugh build inside him, like a bubble rising to the surface. He had strayed into a madhouse. That explained everything. There was a comfort in accepting that.

He ate the cake, which was the best he had eaten in as long as he could remember, which made sense since he couldn't remember the last time he had eaten cake. If Mrs Tubbs prepared cakes in the cavernous kitchens and lower regions of Sinclair House, she didn't inflict them on him.

He was well into the fifth letter when something about the silence broke through his concentration and he looked up abruptly and met her gaze. The heat that bloomed across her cheeks had an immediate echo through his body.

'Aren't you supposed to be reading?' he asked.

'I *am* reading. It is a copy of an old bond prospectus from Buxted Mallory Shipping and it is thoroughly tedious. I was resting my eyes.'

'Well, rest them somewhere else. If you look at me like that, I might decide to do something about it, such as continue where we left off yesterday.'

She frowned and bent her head back over her papers, but looked up almost immediately. 'May I ask you a question?'

'That sounds ominous. About what?'

'Kissing.'

His body tightened at her words, a wolf catching the scent of prey, and he quieted it with an act of will. But there was nothing he could do about the expanding, drumming heat spreading through him at her words.

'You wish to ask me about kissing?'

'Yes, it is only that it wasn't at all like... Oh, never mind. Would you like some more cake?'

'No, thank you. Like what? Like fairy-tale nonsense you read in books or girls whispered in school? I am sorry to have disappointed you.'

'No, I meant that it was not at all like what I remembered. Which is why I am curious. Perhaps it is merely that you have much more experience. Was that really how people who know how to kiss, kiss?'

He put down the letters carefully and discouraged Inky's claw from testing the fortitude of his boots.

'Just so I understand. You wish to discuss the various levels and types of kisses with me?'

'I don't know. Well, yes, I do. I believe one should always exert oneself to understand a phenomenon before one either embraces or dismisses it.'

'Were you contemplating adopting either course of action?'

'Well, I thought I wanted nothing to do with it ever again, but now I believe I was too hasty. It must be like anything else. Sometimes I make bad investment decisions, though luckily not too often. But I certainly do not allow that to dissuade me from continuing to see to my financial well-being. And yet I realise that is precisely what I have allowed to happen in this case. So when one was thoroughly locked into one conviction and one suddenly discovers it is no such thing, it is natural to wonder about the mechanism underlying both the conviction and the alteration, isn't it?'

He flexed his hands and picked up his glass of brandy, but did not drink.

'You make it sound like a naturalist's experiment.'

'Oh, I leave experiments and such things to Carl, but I dare say he would suggest it should be approached precisely like that. He was always adjuring me to put observations before theories.'

'Who on earth is Carl?'

'One of my brothers. He is brilliant and a firm believer in Francis Bacon's admonitions against preconceptions in the sciences. Have you heard of Bacon?'

'Yes, but I had not realised he had an opinion about kissing.'

'Well, he might, though I doubt it; he sounds a trifle dry. I would not have mentioned him, but you were the one who remarked on experimentation. I was merely saying that your demand we kiss has brought me to reconsider my own opinion of the activity.'

'I most certainly did not demand you kiss me.'

'True, rather it was I who pressed the point, but you were the one to introduce the topic and now I am forced to reassess my opinion and that is bothersome because I should really be concentrated on the case at hand. You see, I have allowed Elspeth, my chaperon, to convince me to attend social functions again and one can hardly avoid the topic once one re-enters society.'

'I am afraid to ask what form of society you are frequenting if kissing is a common topic of discussion.'

'Not of discussion, but though people will not speak openly of financial or carnal consider-ations, I cannot help but notice they are ever pres-ent in those gatherings. I spent an hour today with Lady Barnstable while she and her two sons dis-cussed which members of the *ton* were currently in town and the latest poems published and all the while I could see them assessing my assets as compared with those of the rest of the misses on display so they can decide if I am worth the bother of cultivating.'

'While you were considering whether they were worth the bother of kissing?'

'Well, it was a very boring conversation and I had nothing better to think about. But upon con-sideration they did not appear to have the requisite experience. Every time they met my gaze directly they blushed.' She laughed, looking younger and more carefree suddenly, which didn't reassure him in the least. He must be unhinged to be hav-ing this conversation with her and certainly unhinged to care one way or the other if she was considering kissing her way through the *ton*.

'If you looked at them like you were just looking at me, I am not surprised. You will find yourself in trouble if you are not careful. Didn't any of your multiplicity of brothers tell you that?'

'No, because they know better than to lecture me. Even Jack.'

'Another brother?'

'Yes. He was my twin. He died.'

Inky straightened from grooming her paw. It had been a long time since Lucas had heard pain ring so clear without the slightest inflection. It threw him back twenty years to his mother looking up from a letter. *'Your father is dead.'*

My twin.

Compassion should be an effective antidote to desire, but it wasn't. In this case it only made it worse—he wanted to pull her into his arms and absorb that pain into his own skin and, that being done, he wanted to strip her of her clothes as well.

Olivia shook herself and smiled. 'I did not mean to become morose. So, what are we going to do next?'

Lucas looked down at the letters on the table. He knew very well what he wanted to do next. It was scalding him inside. The sheer intensity of the heat finally broke the pull of her siren's call. There was no scenario in which he would allow himself to bed this unconventional young woman. Spending more time with her would only complicate matters. It was therefore time to return to the real world.

'I am going home.' He picked up his gloves from the sofa and stood. 'I fulfilled my part in the bargain. Unless you think Marcia Pendle's scheming procurer is a respected and unmarried vicar who lives with his bedridden father, I suggest you treat her delusional nonsense as such. You cannot resurrect your godfather or his reputation. Let it lie and move on with your life. It is over. *This* is over.'

She rose as well, but didn't speak. He glanced at her as he took his greatcoat from where he had tossed it on the back of a chair. She stood, one hand palm down on her desk, her knuckles white.

'You cannot win all your battles, sweetheart,' he said and she flinched, but remained silent.

'What the hell do you expect me to do?' he asked, as exasperated with himself as with her. She looked away.

'Nothing. There is nothing you can do.'

'What are you going to do?' he asked.

'I do not know yet.'

He had no idea how she managed to invest that simple sentence with so much. There was confusion and pain and mostly that stubborn inability to let go. She would have made a very effective pugilist.

'Sometimes you have no choice but to admit defeat. That is life.'

'Perhaps.'

'Goodbye, Miss Silverdale.'

He turned back halfway to the door. How much more harm could one more kiss do?

She didn't move as he approached and there was no lightening of the stubbornness in her eyes as he touched her cheek, drawing his fingers along her jawline and touching a finger to the tense swell of her lips. He waited three thumping heartbeats for good sense to prevail, gauging the depth of challenge in her eyes.

'Another attempt to lull me into submission, Lord Sinclair?'

'I don't fight lost battles, Miss Silverdale. I leave them for others and withdraw to a safe distance until the dust settles. This is farewell.'

He bent to touch his mouth to hers. It was meant to be brief, light, but the moment his mouth touched hers the memory of their unfortunately intimate first kiss took the lead. She wasn't the only one curious whether it had been an anomaly.

It was different, but not in the way he had hoped. She didn't stand passively under his caress this time. Her lips parted, rubbing against his, her hands smoothing up over the lapels of his coat to rest for a moment on his shoulders. He felt a peculiar fear as her lips shifted against his, so soft, but seeking something he knew would test his control. He held still, debating whether to continue, but she didn't stop, her hands slid upwards, raising herself as she canted her head, tracing his lips with hers, her breath feathery and warm over his skin, her fingers moving gently against the skin above his cravat, as soft as her kisses and just as damaging.

As during the war, when he couldn't retreat he advanced.

'You wanted to experiment? *This* is a kiss, Olivia,' he murmured against her lips before taking possession of them. She was curious? Hell and damnation, so was he.

He was prepared to pull back at the first sign of resistance or fear, but she was ahead of him again. She pressed against him as he gathered her body to him, as he splayed his fingers deep into her hair, coaxed her lips apart with his, drawing them between his, dampening them with his tongue, tasting and suckling them. She tasted of cinnamon and brandy and beyond it a scent that caught at his chest because it was already so familiar he wanted to bury his face in her hair and fill his lungs with it. Her lips moved with his, making it impossible for him to draw away.

'It feels so good…' Her words were just a whisper of warmth against his mouth, but they felt like a blow from Gentleman Jackson in his prime. The transition from light to dark was so sudden his hands shook against the need to crush her to him. It wasn't supposed to be like this. He was supposed to be in control. After all his warnings to her, he was knowingly walking into cannon fire.

Her lips opened, her tongue darting to meet his, the moment of contact sending a shudder through her, or through them both, he could not tell the difference. After the first moment of shock, he sank into her, finally allowing himself to kiss her thoroughly, without caution or calculation, his hands and mouth exploring and discovering with a hunger he didn't try to mask. Part of him still hoped she would recoil, put an end to it before he was stripped of what little control remained. The knowledge that he would have to stop was eating away at his insides; there was something wrong with the world if he had to stop this.

There was a great deal wrong with the world as he knew all too well.

He grasped her arms above her elbows. 'Enough.'

She shook her head, her fingers tightening in his hair, her lips pressing against his, pulling at them gently, her tongue caressing and tasting as he had tasted her, sending vicious bolts of need through him, as sharp and uncompromising as iron stakes.

'Enough,' he said again, stepping away from her. 'Goodbye, Miss Silverdale.'

Olivia stood, staring at the closed door.

There, it was over, as he said. He was gone. But it didn't quite make sense. She hadn't been prepared, not for him leaving like that. It wasn't just the throbbing aftermath of the kiss. It did not seem possible that he could leave so easily. Somehow she had come to believe she would overcome his resistance and make him part of her quest.

But that was folly. She knew what he was and knowing that she should be grateful he had even done as much as he had in tracing the Eldritches. She should be grateful, but all she felt was emptiness and disbelief.

She looked at her wall of lists. He was right to think her delusional. And right to run. She should do the same. It was foolishness incarnate to allow herself to depend on someone like him. She had put all her faith in a rake before and it had caused untold damage to herself and to others.

Like a bee sting, the likes of Lucas Sinclair were best drawn quickly.

Chapter Seven

'Regarding Brook Street, my lord...'

Lucas looked up from his correspondence as Tubbs, his butler-cum-valet-cum-procurer-of-information, stoked the fire.

'Well, Tubbs?'

'Information about the two ladies was a little scarce on the ground seeing as all the servants accompanied them from Guilford, including a groom and two postilions to tend to their carriage and horses in the stables on Morton Mews, my lord.'

'I have faith that such obstacles did not stand in your way, Tubbs.'

'Naturally not, sir. They merely required some additional effort. My Jem knows a man in the stables and I've had a word with the link boys in the area.'

'And?'

'And word of Miss Silverdale's worth and presentability has spread since their invitation to the Barnstables. The carriage is to take them tonight to Countess Lieven's ball and there is some expectation that a voucher to Almack's is in the offing.'

'Countess Lieven. Straight to the top of the social ladder. I am impressed with Lady Phelps's social prowess.'

'I believe the credit is due to Miss Silverdale in this instance, my lord. I had an easier time with Lady Barnstable's servants who have developed an interest in the young lady seeing as she has been added to the top of their lady's list of possible brides for her son. Apparently while at that good lady's soirée Miss Silverdale held a lengthy conversation with the Countess.'

'Did she? Stranger and stranger.'

'The footman said they discussed something about banks in Austria after the peace.'

'Good God.'

'Indeed, sir. Interesting that she should catch the eye of the Russian ambassador's wife.'

'Miss Silverdale is not connected to our concerns on that front, Tubbs.'

'Of course not, sir. Will you be accepting the Countess's invitation, then? You were considering going, were you not?'

Lucas had not been considering it, but then Tubbs would know that. Despite his friendship with and interest in the Lievens and the concerns of the Russian emissaries in London, he found such society events tedious and more often than not a waste of time. His reputation made any attendance on his part a topic of conversation and speculation and hardly left him room to conduct his own business.

He wondered again at her chaperon. He would not have chosen to catapult someone as unconventional as Miss Silverdale directly into the clutches of one of the patronesses of Almack's and particularly not the likes of the shrewd Countess Dorothea Lieven. Not that it was any of his concern. As long as it kept Miss Silverdale occupied and distracted from her fantastical plots, her entry into society was a boon. In fact, he should do what he could to promote that entry. All the most fashionable members of the *ton* would be present at the Lievens' ball—it would be a true baptism of fire for Olivia Silverdale. Perhaps his presence would draw some of that fire. Or fan it. Either way he could make himself useful. He returned his quill to the inkwell.

'I might attend after all, Tubbs.'

'My dear Olivia, this is marvellous. That will be your second dance with Lord Pendleton in as many days. I think our position is assured,' Elspeth murmured behind her fan as the peer withdrew, having secured the quadrille with Olivia.

'Money has that effect on people and London is apparently no exception.' Olivia kept her voice low.

'Nonsense. You look delightful in that dress. I am so glad Madame Fanchot could provide our gowns on such short notice. Those shades of peach and ivory are quite lovely.'

Olivia resisted the urge to point out that the chief reason Madame Fanchot was so generous with her time and skills was because Olivia was of that rare breed of customer who paid her bills immediately. Whatever the case, as Elspeth said it was an exquisite dress. Growing up in a male household she hadn't thought much about her clothes until Bertram returned from London. Even then her horizons were limited by Mary Payton's modest view of feminine fashions. It was only when Elspeth took her to Madame Fanchot that Olivia realised why Bertram mocked their provincial fashions.

So now she was dressed in the finest London had to offer and perched on an uncomfortable sofa in what was, according to Elspeth, one of the most coveted ballrooms in the realm.

She tried to feel impressed with her sudden

elevation from the modest house outside Guilford or the provincial society of Gillingham, but could only feel bemusement. From the moment she came to London she had been operating in a dream, allowing herself to do things she never would have contemplated in the past, not even before Bertram.

She was no longer the smallest of the Silverdales, tagging after her brothers, or the foolish girl so blinded by a rake's charm she lost all self-respect. In fact, she was no longer certain who Olivia Silverdale was beyond her wish to redeem Henry for the Paytons and for herself.

Certainly Olivia Silverdale would never in a hundred years have flung herself at a man as she had at Lucas Sinclair, without an ounce of modesty. Mary Payton might have called her wild, but she had never been that flavour of wild. Just thinking of what a fool she had been…

Again the wave of both cringing shame and scalding heat spread through her at the memory. No wonder he had run. She had scared away her best asset and now she had no idea what to do to convince him to return. Not that there was anything she could do if he did not wish it done. He was one of those people who were singularly un-doable. But even if that bridge was burnt, she could not imagine returning to her safe sanctuary in Guilford. She had picked up the reins of her life and it was impossible to contemplate letting them slip once again.

'Smile,' Elspeth cautioned. 'Lady Westerby is approaching with her eldest son. She has two unmarried sons and four unmarried daughters.'

'Poor woman. Shall I be expected to provide all their dowries?'

'Hush!'

Olivia did hush and smiled at something Lady Westerby said, docilely accepted her son's invitation for a country dance and resigned herself to another bout of polite patter about nothing at all.

On their return towards the sofas after their dance Olivia heard a rising buzz of voices and stiffened. Just thus society in Gillingham hummed every time she appeared during those horrible weeks after jilting Bertram. Her heart kicked and bucked and she called it to order. An unknown like her was unlikely to be the target of malicious mutterings.

'By George, it is Sinclair,' Lord Westerby said in a half-whisper. 'The Countess must have applied the rack and thumbscrews to have him attend an event such as this.'

Her heart, just settling, went from trot back to canter.

'Sinclair?' she asked.

Lord Westerby smiled.

'I forget, you are not from London. The Earl Sinclair. Friend of the Count and Countess, but your paths aren't likely to cross.'

'Why not?'

He blinked at her directness.

'Well, he's not quite…you know. In any case, he isn't interested in proper young women. Wouldn't want him to meet my sisters, though they wouldn't mind meeting him.' He chuckled a little. 'He's one of the Sinful Sinclairs. Strange family. Always some scandal or other. His grandfather and uncle died under a cloud and his father was killed in a duel over…well, not quite the thing to talk about, you know. Point is, he and his brother, the Honourable Charles Sinclair, rarely attend this kind of function. Spend most of their time kicking up dust on the Continent…'

He faltered as they passed by Countess Lieven and that formidable woman raised a gloved hand, beckoning them. Lord Westerby audibly drew breath before turning them in their hostess's direction. She was handsome—slim, dark-haired and sharp-faced, with a tongue and wit to match.

It was lucky Olivia had not known how feared the Russian ambassador's wife was before they engaged in conversation at Lady Barnstable's. But now Olivia's nerves were not concerned with her hostess's social power, they were fully engaged in preparation for her unexpected meeting with the tall, dark-haired man who stood with his back to them.

Her hostess spoke first. 'Good evening, Lord Westerby. Miss Silverdale. How are you enjoying your first London ball?'

'Very much. Everyone has been most kind,' she answered properly, risking a glance at Lucas as the Countess made the introductions, but he met her gaze as blankly as any stranger.

'You are lucky, then, Miss Silverdale,' he said once the introductions were complete. 'Kindness is not a common virtue in London.'

'Perhaps it is not merely luck, Lord Sinclair,' she replied, meeting his eyes rather more directly than was accepted.

Countess Lieven waved her fan leisurely, her finely drawn mouth hovering on the edge of a smile. Lord Sinclair bowed.

'I shall have to make up my own mind. Has Miss Silverdale received your sanction to waltz, Dorothea?'

'She has not, Sinclair. However, I shall be sending Lady Phelps vouchers for Almack's.'

'Close enough. With town so thin of entertainment, can you not satisfy me? I promise to behave.'

Countess Lieven snorted and closed her fan.

'I look forward to the day. Very well, you have my sanction. But you should apply to Lady Phelps. She may prefer to advise her charge against you. Now let us find Christopher, he will be tickled you have come. And with a wish to waltz.'

'You cannot be serious! I most certainly will not approve such a request. The man is...' Lady Phelps pitched her voice low, the words shoved out between her teeth '...a rake. He is head of the Sinful Sinclair clan.'

'Yes, dear Elspeth, I know. However, should he indeed carry through on his threat and ask me to dance, you will smile and approve.'

'Olivia, I stand here in your mother's stead...'

'Not a good example, as you well know, Elspeth. I trust your judgement far more than my progenitors, but in this case you shall have to trust mine.'

'Olivia, I realise that men such as Sinclair can be fascinating, but there is a reason he is not considered a good marital prospect despite his title and property. Certainly someone like you, without any experience in society and, if you will excuse my plain words, no extraordinary physical beauty or arts, has no possibility of securing him.'

'I do not wish to secure him. Or anyone else for that matter. It is merely a dance.'

'No, it is a waltz. Your first in London society, before you have even been introduced at Almack's. It is a signal honour that the Countess has approved such a distinction, but perhaps given your age and the paucity of entertainment ahead of the Season it is comprehensible. If you must waltz, do so with Lord Westerby or Lord Barnstable.'

'They have not asked me. Lord Sinclair has.'

'Do you even know how to waltz?'

'I learned the waltz with Phoebe and all my brothers practised with me as partner before I left Gillingham so I have become an expert at protecting my toes. Hopefully I shan't make a fool of myself.'

'My concerns are a trifle more serious than whether you trip.'

'You are being uncharacteristically dramatic, Elspeth. What on earth could he do to me in the middle of a ballroom?'

'I hope you do not find out. Oh, dear, here he comes. I was hoping you had misunderstood.'

By the momentary dimming of talk around them, followed almost immediately by a rising buzz, it was clear those around them had noted his approach to that part of the ballroom where the matrons and debutantes held sway. Olivia tensed at the unwanted attention and focused on Lord Sinclair. She could read nothing in his expression but slight amusement as he made his request of Elspeth, though it deepened at Elspeth's barely veiled disapproval.

She waited until they were positioned on the dance floor to speak.

'I am surprised, Lord Sinclair. You were quite clear in your intent to wash your hands of me. This is a most peculiar way to do so.'

He took her hand and placed his other lightly at her waist as the orchestra began the first flourish of the waltz.

'I was clear in my intent not to further your investigations. Those are two different matters.'

'That reinforces my conviction you have a hidden reason to asking me to dance. May I know your agenda? So I can decide whether to align myself with whatever it is you are plotting?'

'I leave the plots to you, Miss Silverdale. As

you pointed out, my besetting sin is curiosity. I thought you had no time for society and yet here you are, in the very heart of it, charming the distinctly uncharmable Countess Lieven. Can you fault me for wondering what you are seeking here?'

'I thought you would be pleased I am engaging in interests other than conspiracies.'

'Are you? There is no ulterior motive to your sudden decision to enter London society?'

'None. You could have asked me that without bothering to invite me to dance and putting your reputation at risk, you know.'

'My reputation?'

'As an unrepentant rake. Being seen dancing with a dowdy northern heiress is bound to tarnish it.'

'My dear, anyone dressed in one of Fanchot's masterpieces cannot be labelled dowdy.'

'You can tell this is made by Madame Fanchot?'

'Is it not?'

'It is, but how—? Never mind.' She cut herself off, feeling a flush rise to her cheeks. Elspeth had let fall that the many fashionable men were known to pay for their mistresses' wardrobes amongst other things. Ever thorough, Mercer's report on Lord Sinclair had included the name of the widow reputed to be his mistress and when she had seen beautiful Lady Ilford at the Barnstables' soirée that woman had indeed been wearing what looked like a Fanchot concoction of black net over a Pomona-green dress and a stunning emerald necklace. Clearly his lordship was generous with his paramours.

'You dance very well, Miss Silverdale.'

'Thank you, Lord Sinclair,' she replied properly and then allowed her pique to make her add, 'You dance moderately well yourself. I hardly notice I am dancing.'

'That is not a good sign. I prefer women to notice when they are dancing with me.'

His hand tightened a little on hers as he turned her in the dance, the other applying the slightest pressure to bring her closer. The shiver of heat that spread from both points of contact reminded her it was not smart to taunt the devil.

He was different in this setting, more like the man she had met that first day in the church than the teasing, exasperated and conscientious man who came to Spinner Street. She wondered which persona was the true Lucas Sinclair. Probably they both held a kernel of truth and even more probably she had not yet encountered the true

Lucas Sinclair. The fact that she wished to was a danger in itself.

'You might want to step on my toes, then,' she suggested. 'I am sure to notice that.'

'I am very tempted to do just that, minx. Is this how you have been talking with all your staid suitors? Since I haven't seen any of them change colour or trip, I presume not.'

'I have been a model of propriety and good manners for Elspeth's sake.'

'At least until you forced her to approve my invitation to waltz.'

'How do you know I forced her?'

'It does not require an occultist to reveal what she was thinking as I approached.'

His fingers feathered an inch lower, gathering her for another turn. It was a blatant lie that she did not notice that they were dancing. She had never been so aware of a dance, of being held, of wanting more...

She cleared her throat and changed the topic. 'Lord Westerby said you rarely attend such occasions. Is that true?'

'The Lievens are particular friends of mine. When I am in London I sometimes attend their entertainments. Why, did you think I came to see you?'

'Perhaps to keep an eye on me and ensure I was not taking advantage of this setting to engage in my investigations. Correct?'

'You are assuming I knew you would be here.'

'Did you not?' she asked. Strange she had not considered he might have been as surprised to see her as she had been to see him. It was not smart to begin thinking of him as omniscient. The music began to fade and he guided her to the edge of the dance floor and her insides coiled tighter—she was not ready to concede defeat, surely there was something she could do...

'People will be curious now,' he said in the same faintly mocking tones. 'If you treat this lightly, it will further your cousin's social ambitions. Best feign ignorance of my reputation, though. You do not want to lose your ingénue's gloss too soon.'

'So I was right and this is a palliative to your conscience for not helping me.'

'I appear to remember I did help you.'

'Not as much as you could, I would wager. Which reminds me—if you care to come to Spinner Street tomorrow afternoon I have something to give you and something to show you. Not before five. Unfortunately Elspeth and I have morning calls.' She turned away before he could refuse.

Chapter Eight

He should know better.

He was well past the age where his actions should be dictated by curiosity and amusement. And certainly by that crudest of motives, lust. He told her he was done and yet here he was, knocking on the anonymous door in Spinner Street because that little slip of a girl dangled a worm on a hook.

Now that he had seen her in the civilised setting of Dorothea Lieven's ballroom her behaviour appeared even more anomalous. In her expensive gown and with her usually haphazardly gathered curls dressed in the latest mode she looked precisely what she was, a well-born, proper and wealthy young woman. He should not even have danced with her. If her chaperon was worth her salt she would have sent him on his way and certainly not allowed her to haunt Spinner Street with no more protection than an elderly, rolling-pin-wielding nurse. For all Lady Phelps knew, anyone seeing Miss Silverdale enter and realising a young woman was all but alone in a house in this neighbourhood might think it a perfect opportunity to take advantage... Or perhaps the credulous Marcia Pendle might uncover Madame Bulgari's ruse and...

He shoved away the thoughts that leapt from catastrophe to disaster and knocked again, resisting the urge to beat on the door. As the silence stretched he cursed and headed to the area door. He had seen enough violence in his life to provide ample material for his imagination. She wasn't his responsibility, but he should have sent word to her family or bound her up and sent her back to Yorkshire himself. Or at least had Tubbs send someone to keep an eye on the house.

No rolling pin was levelled at his head when he entered which didn't reassure him in the least. He went up the narrow stairs and in the descending gloom of the winter afternoon he saw the orange gleam of light under the study door. Without pause or thought he hurried to open it.

She was asleep on the sofa, her cheek pillowed on her palm, her other hand fisted about a scrawled piece of paper and resting on a wooden box on the floor. He bent and slid the paper from her grasp and placed her hand gently at her side. She sighed and stretched, but didn't wake, and he remained standing there for a long moment, fighting back the demand every part of him was making; had been making ever since he had kissed her. Before that. Waltzing with her yesterday had been a mistake, giving his body false hopes of pursuing the instinctual rhythm between them to its natural conclusion.

He told her he had no intention of being led, but this was precisely what he was letting her do. He couldn't even console himself with the thought that she wanted anything from him but his help in pursuing her queries satisfying her curiosity about kissing. Being brought to heel was humiliating enough, but being brought to heel unconsciously was a double blow to his pride.

Not enough to convince him to walk away again, though. He doubted there was much that would convince him to walk away just now.

He touched her cheek very lightly, following the curve of her ear, resting his palm against the side of her neck. He could feel her pulse, slow and steady. Then she shifted and shivered, her lips moving slightly around an indeterminate word, and his own body clenched, hot and ready.

He had no idea what he was going to do with her, but it had to be something.

She opened her eyes and smiled, the candlelight turning her eyes to gold. He remained very still. Any second now she would wake fully and that expression, warm and so intimate he could almost believe it was meant for him, would dissipate. Already it was giving way to confusion.

'Lord Sinclair?' she whispered and he wished he could stop everything, keep her there, in that no-man's land between sleep and waking, before she started thinking. With just that soft, warm expression that looked like longing.

'Lord Sinclair,' she whispered again. 'I fell asleep. What time is it? I thought you were not coming.'

'Shall I leave?'

'No. Stay.' Her voice was rough from sleep and it echoed through him.

Stay.

She sat, pushing her tousled curls away from her cheeks. A blur of movement from behind him made him tense, but it was just Inky, taking advantage of the open door to head for the warmth of the fireplace. The cat curled up by the grate, tucked its paws together like a disapproving judge and fixed its stare on him.

A cat was no barrier to seduction, but the disapproving stare sobered him a little. So did Olivia's next words.

'It is near seven o'clock and the carriage will arrive to collect me soon, but I am glad you came.'

She took the box from the floor and placed it on her lap. On a background of dark wood was a miniature painting of the view out the mouth of the Grand Canal, the delicate tracing of the Uffizi Palace on the left and in the distance, wholly inaccurate but very lovely, a sunset in shades of purple-blue and just a tinge of orange. A single gondola was trailing a grey-white wake as it disappeared into the distance. He had watched many sunrises with that precise view from the roof of his cousins' palazzo. The coolness of morning, the lapping of water below, the fresh and rotten smells of the sea. She couldn't possibly have known that.

'What is this?' he asked.

'A box.'

'Clearly. What is inside it?'

'Your father's letters. I thought they would be safer here. I went with Elspeth to a stationer's shop today and I saw this in the window of a little store just down the road. There was also a lovely magnifying glass with a silver-engraved holder for my brother and…never mind. Do you like it?'

She held it out and he took it without thinking. The letters were nestled on a bed of dark-burgundy silk and the wood was faintly warm, pliant under his fingers. His shoulders felt stiff and there was a pain between his eyebrows. It had been a very long time since he had wished his parents were still alive. Like a fly, grief was sometimes inescapable, but he never allowed it to settle. To wish his mother was there so she could meet the woman sitting before him was… not smart.

'My mother would have liked it.'

'I am glad. I know you want nothing more to do with this, but I wished to thank you for helping none the less.'

'Does that mean you are abandoning your quest?'

'No. I am afraid not. Why did you not tell me your father mentioned the name Jasper Archer in the last letter he sent Henry?'

'So you have overcome your conscience and read them?'

'Actually, no. You left them on the table, remember? Inky scattered them during the night and while I was picking them up that name leapt out at me. I did read the letter then, I admit, but it was all but impossible not to. Not that it revealed anything but that someone named Jasper Archer worked with your father and with Henry.

But I thought it would be worthwhile tracking him and...'

'Richly though you deserve it, I will save you the waste of time. A man named Jasper Archer who worked at Buxted Mallory passed away four years ago. And before you begin concocting more plots, nothing more ominous occurred to him other than succumbing to typhoid fever in Barbados.'

'You made enquiries. Did you discover anything else?'

'No.'

'Oh.' She frowned at Inky and the cat mewled and circled until she found a position that evaded Miss Silverdale's eyes. He waited, watching the flash and flitter of thoughts reflect on her face.

'Your father wrote very fine letters. Very orderly and articulate,' she said at last and he couldn't stop himself from smiling. Relentless.

'It is kind of you to say so, Miss Silverdale.'

Her eyes focused and she smiled. 'Making game of me won't help, Lord Sinclair.'

'I'm aware very little will help at this point. Where is that tortuous mind of yours heading now?'

'I know you want nothing to do with this, but I cannot help wondering if perhaps...no.'

'Coyness doesn't suit you. If I am to be stabbed, I prefer to see the knife coming.'

'That is a very gory analogy. Very well, I was wondering if there are other letters of his in his belongings.'

'What makes you think I would wish to keep any of his belongings?'

'I should not have asked, I am sorry.' Her eyes softened and he could have kicked himself for his childish and revealing words.

He shrugged and went to sit by the table. Inky rose, stretched into a sleek black arch, the tips of her extended claws shivering, and then settled into a ball by his feet. He stroked the raven-black fur, matching the rhythm of the cat's purrs.

'I think there is a trunk in the attic somewhere. I doubt there is anything of interest in it, though. I still think you are tilting at windmills.'

'Possibly. Probably. I shan't walk through walls, but if I see a door I find it hard not to at least peek inside. It is my fault Henry is dead so it is the least I can do.'

He stopped petting the cat. The compassion in her eyes was still there, but the agony he had seen before was back as well, so he approached lightly.

'I am curious how you reach that conclusion, Miss Silverdale.'

'It was because of me that he came to work in London. Something I did, back in Gillingham, caused strife between him and his previous employer and when he took my part they made it all but impossible for him to work in the neighbourhood so he accepted a position in Lincoln's Inn. If not for me none of this would have happened.'

'You should not play billiards, Miss Silverdale. You will become all too caught up in the myriad possibilities of how each ball may or may not be deflected from its trajectory and probably miss all your shots. That is the first time I have heard you voice something that is utter rubbish and you have offered many contenders for that title already.'

Her smile was a little sad. 'It does not feel like rubbish. I wish it did. Even if his death was purely accidental, I still feel I played a part in it. Being away from Mary for extended periods might easily have led him to seek other...well, you know.'

'So you accept his death might be precisely what is appears—an unfortunate accident?'

'Of course I accept that is a possibility. I am not completely naïve. I am also aware it is pure selfishness on my part to try to offer an alternative explanation, but even if that is all this is, I cannot ignore the possibility that arises from Marcia Pendle's words or from his notes about your father. It would be…it would be a betrayal.'

'You are sounding more and more like Don Quixote, Miss Silverdale. Your nurse might have called me a varlet, but I am of no mind to play the page to your misguided knight. What is so amusing?'

'Nothing. Perhaps you are right about me. As a child that was precisely what I wanted to be.'

'Don Quixote?'

'No, a knight errant. My brothers and I devoured Malory's *Morte d'Arthur* and we named ourselves the Knights of the Brown Stable in homage.'

He laughed. 'It doesn't have quite the same noble ring as Round Table.'

'Well, it wasn't meant to. Part of the pleasure was to poke fun at how stuffy they were. At least that was Guy's idea. He was a master at taking the stuffing out of the stuffy, but I was very serious about my calling as a knight.'

'Not a lady?'

'Goodness, no. I don't think I ever fully accepted that women could not be knights.'

'So you were Sir Olivia?'

'No, Sir Olive-a-Dale, after an old broadside ballad about Robin Hood and Allan-a-Dale we found in our library. My brothers always chose silly names. For example, Guy was Sir Silver Sliver because he has this streak of silver in his hair from when he was very young. Carl was Sir Snarl Ballocks, never mind why; Ralph was Sir Half de Staff and Jack was Sir Prudence Primrose, but we took pity and shortened it to Sir Dense. Ralph was particularly furious about his which he said was thoroughly inaccurate and it took me years to understand why they would snigger when he refused to answer to the name. He dubbed himself Sir Sturdy Staff instead. So you see, Sir Olive-a-Dale was quite the most mildly named of the knights.'

'And what did the Knights of the Brown Stable do? Carouse? Joust? Acts of chivalry?'

'Hardly. Acts of devilry more like. We were very wild as children, even with Henry and Mary trying to tame us. Henry was our guardian and trustee, but Guy always insisted he was in charge and he was, for better or for worse. Part of our chivalric code was to stand by each other through thick and thin.'

'Are you still close?'

'Aside from Guy we all moved away from Gillingham, but we are still close. They all visit me when they can and we know we can depend on each other when in need.'

'So why are they not here helping you? With all those fine knights errant at your beck and call, why not summon them instead of blackmailing an unworthy knave into service?'

'I did not blackmail you.'

'You most certainly did. Don't evade the question. Why not convene the Brown Stable?'

'Because if I told them what I was doing they would try to protect me and stop me and I cannot allow that. Guy always said that being a knight meant assuming responsibility for your mistakes. That is what I am doing.'

'Do you know, I have discovered a serious flaw in your reasoning. If this is a conspiracy around my father's death, whether Henry was in London or Yorkshire should not matter. On the other hand, if his death was merely an unfortunate accident because of a weak heart, it could have happened anywhere.'

'Anywhere would have been better than in bed with another woman. And he was hardly likely to have sought other company if he was living year round in Gillingham with Mary Payton.'

'It would have required more subterfuge but it is eminently possible. You are stretching the facts to fan your guilt, Olivia. I am beginning to reassess whether Sir Olive-a-Dale was longer on brawn than on brain and rather short on both.'

'Precisely why I applied to you, seeing as you are so well endowed in both quarters.'

'I am not so easily pressed into service for the price of a few empty compliments.'

'I know that. But if I promise not to proceed behind your back, will you help?'

He went to her Wall of Conjecture, trying not to smile. She might have been the runt of the litter, but he suspected she was accustomed to manoeuvring her brothers at will. Which made her choice to leave her home in Yorkshire all the more peculiar. Something had clearly happened to drive her away and his curiosity was nipping at his heels. He could, of course, use Oswald's resources to make enquiries, but the thought of spying on her and her family made him uncomfortable. She might have dragged him into her world, but he was wary of dragging her into his. He wanted her to confide in him. To trust him.

Fool.

He stopped at the sound of carriage wheels slowing to halt outside. Before either could speak the door opened.

'It's the carriage, miss…' Nora paused, pressing her lips hard together. 'It's you again, eh?'

'I told him to come, Nora. To give him the box.'

'Could have sent it. Here's your cloak, miss. We shouldn't keep them boys waiting in the cold.'

'May I deliver you somewhere, Lord Sinclair?' Olivia offered, but Nora interceded.

'Best not in the carriage, Miss Olivia. Can't trust footmen not to gossip.'

Lucas went to the door.

'Lord Sinclair…'

'I will call on you tomorrow at Brook Street, Miss Silverdale.'

He didn't turn or wait for her response.

Chapter Nine

'Lord Sinclair is coming here? To Brook Street? Olivia Silverdale, you cannot be serious!'

'Why not, Elspeth? A host of men call here with or without their mamas during your At Home hours. When I agreed to attend a few social events I did not take into account heiresses were so thin on the ground in London.'

'I know, is it not wonderful? After all those years in Guilford I forgot how pleasurable it is to go out and about in town. By the way, I am expecting your new gowns from Fanchot this afternoon. I think the bronze and ivory will do for Lady Westerby's soirée.'

'I cannot believe we ordered them all, surely we will not need quite so many? The dressing room is already full to bursting.'

Lady Phelps's eyes slid away and immediately Olivia felt guilty and hurried on.

'I adored the pale-yellow one you chose from the plates, Elspeth. I hope it looks half as lovely on me. And the lavender with the Greek motif on the flounces and at the waist is exquisite on you.

I haven't the eye for fashion you have. I probably would have chosen the blue.'

'Blue is quite out of the mode at the moment, I'm afraid. But you cannot distract me, Olivia. Why is Lord Sinclair coming here? I know I promised I shan't interfere in your other activities, but that was before Lady Barnstable took us up, or rather took you up. Oh, dear, it is all going to go horridly wrong, I can feel it in my bones. My dear, you must never tangle with men like Sinclair. Why, if you have even heard one-tenth of what they said of his grandfather and uncle! And of course his father was killed in a duel over another man's betrothed!'

'It is not very charitable to visit the sins of the fathers upon the sons, Elspeth.'

'Certainly, and I would never consider doing so if not for this particular son's activities. In particular with all those foreign women...' She shuddered.

'I know he is a rake, Elspeth. Mercer's report was most thorough. However, you shall have to trust me that he is not in the least interested in my person or my fortune. Besides, he has been a little useful for your ends, hasn't he? You cannot deny that waltz did more good than ill to enhance my standing.'

'Well, I must admit for some reason men appear to have taken his interest in you as a challenge. And having Countess Lieven approve your waltz herself and publicly announce you will be receiving vouchers for Almack's…well, that was quite a coup.'

'There, you see? And that would not have happened without his good offices, so do try not to worry.'

'But, my dear, how can I not worry when you spend half your days alone with Nora in Hans Town? I do wish now we are entering society again you would put all that aside. I know how devastated you are by Mr Payton's passing, but… My dear, the Sinful Sinclairs are dangerous. You are out of your depth.'

Olivia was spared having to answer her cousin's impassioned appeal by the entry of their butler Pottle with the news that the packages from Madame Fanchot had arrived. Olivia held out her hand to her cousin.

'Shall we go explore our new treasures?'

Elspeth sighed. 'You do know how to distract me, don't you? Very well. But please be careful.'

'I always am,' Olivia lied.

Elspeth's nerves improved dramatically at the sight of the stack of boxes and layers of gowns the maids were arranging in the dressing room and

Olivia meekly agreed to try on the new acquisitions. It was in the middle of this flurry of dressing and undressing and of silks and satins and muslins and gauze that Pottle announced Lord Sinclair's arrival.

'I shall be down directly, Pottle. No, Bessy, help Lady Phelps with her dress. I shan't be long, Elspeth.' Elspeth met her warning gaze with a look that was as descriptive of a heartfelt groan as any Olivia had seen but Olivia hurried downstairs, guilty yet determined. Whatever Elspeth hoped for during her return to society, Olivia had no intention of being deflected from her purpose. She was here to discover the truth about Henry and for that she needed Lord Sinclair's co-operation.

He stood by the mantelpiece, examining the miniature of her and her brothers. As always when she came into his presence she felt the unbidden response of her body, like the striking of a bell—a first sharp strike, discordant and uncomfortable, and then it peaked and settled into a warm hum. It was disorienting, but she refused to allow it to dictate her dealings with him. Eventually it would lose its edge, just as it had with Bertram. She knew better than to trust these feelings—today she could hardly even remember what she found so fascinating about her once betrothed. She must have been blinded indeed. She would not be so again.

He turned at her entry, but did not immediately answer her greeting. She waited as he inspected her, pressing her hands together, wondering what he was thinking.

'A trifle early in the day to be in full battle regalia, isn't it?' he asked at last.

'Madame Fanchot just delivered my new dresses and we were in the middle of enjoying their unveiling. Do you like it? It is a little unconventional, I know, but she said the colours add lustre to my lacklustre appearance.'

'That cannot possibly be a quote from Madame Fanchot. When she lies she does so to flatter.'

She tried not to react to the mild compliment, concentrating instead on matters of business. She sat on the sofa and gestured to the chair opposite, but he joined her on the sofa and touched the fabric at the slope of her shoulder, his fingers lingering on the embroidered gold stars.

'In answer to your question about the dress, I like it very much. Unconventionality suits you. Why is it that such a dress would look utterly reasonable in a ballroom and yet in this very proper drawing room it appears quite decadent?' he murmured, his voice as silky as the fabrics encasing her. 'I am curious, though. I thought in Brook Street you followed the dictates of your chaperon and yet here we are alone together in your drawing room. Where is Lady Phelps?'

'She will join us later, but I wished to have a word with you alone first. She knows why I am in London, but I prefer not to burden her with the details of my activities. You need not worry I shall take advantage of you.'

'I am not in the least worried about that, Miss Silverdale. You made it quite clear you are not interested in my person other than my kissing skills.'

She ignored the taunt. Yesterday he had distracted her by listening to her nonsense about her brothers and the Knights of the Brown Stable with such interest and today she was determined she would not allow him to do the same, though a discussion of kissing would... No.

'Quite. So... Shall we discuss how best to proceed? I know you do not think it a likely lead and I must admit a vicar is an unlikely candidate for a crime, but being a man of God is no guarantee of virtue and perhaps we should after all visit the Eldritches you mentioned.'

'Just a moment, Miss Silverdale. Before you plunge on and start issuing demands I would like to make something very clear—if I agree to proceed down this path with you, we will do so on my terms.'

She hauled hard on her internal reins and the smile that threatened and merely nodded.

'Obviously.'

'It appears far from obvious to you, so let me be absolutely clear about the rules. First and foremost, you will take no step and ask not one question without my approval. I will not interfere with your Brook Street existence as long as you refrain from tainting it with this quest. I understand why you wish to keep your activities cloaked by situating them at Spinner Street, but if you wish to continue your masquerade, there will be some changes.'

'What changes?'

'You sound as suspicious as if I am asking you to sign away your fortune. The first change is that I will send a young man to stay and act as footman there. Perhaps a maid as well. Your nurse can do with the help and you can do with the protection.'

Olivia forced a frown. It would certainly not do to show how delighted she was by this sign of his willingness to deepen his involvement.

'I do not need protection.'

'You are the one spouting on about conspiracies. This is not open to negotiation.'

'Oh, very well. What else?'

'You do nothing behind my back.'

'I already agreed to that. Anything else?'

For a moment he looked a little uncertain and it occurred to her he was younger than Guy, which was strange because he seemed older, or rather, ageless—more an idea than a person. With the watchful and focused intensity gone she could see him as a boy. He would have been twelve when his father died, old enough to be thoroughly aware of death and disgrace. She clasped her hands against the need to reach out. Sympathy would have him out the door faster than she could make a fool of herself. Finally, he spoke.

'Tubbs, my butler, found a trunk with my father's belongings, or rather whatever was sent from Boston after his death. It has been gathering dust in the attic. I haven't looked… I haven't had time to inspect it yet, but Tubbs tells me there are books and papers in it. If you wish I can have it brought to Spinner Street. You may do what you want with it and then consign the contents to the fire. I doubt they are good for anything other than kindling. As long as you do not disclose anything you find there to anyone.'

'Lord Sinclair, are you certain...?'

He stood and went to the mantelpiece, nudging the miniature further to the centre. 'Do you or don't you want to look through the contents of that trunk, Miss Silverdale?'

'Yes, but...'

'Don't expect me assuage your conscience as well as give in to your requests. Choose.'

A decent person would step back, Olivia told herself. Would respect the pain he was not willing to voice, but was so evident. Henry himself would probably tell her she was stepping deeper and deeper into moral murkiness. But if there was even a slim chance of finding the truth, she had to take it. It would be foolish to forgo this opportunity merely to protect sensibilities she was not at all certain Lucas Sinclair possessed.

Choose.

'I promise to respect the contents of the trunk, Lord Sinclair.'

He didn't answer and guilt tightened its talons about her, but she held herself from retreating.

He returned to the sofa and in those short steps she saw the transformation back to Sinful Sinclair. He did not sit, which put her at an even more distinct disadvantage to his substantial size. He smiled and once again flicked the trim of her sleeve with his finger, causing another shiver of awareness to snake up her shoulder, but this time it merged with the ache of her heart and her conscience, leaving her strangely breathless.

'You will do very well in London if you are careful, Miss Silverdale. I can see why Dorothea was taken with you; she must have seen the echoes of her own ruthless streak. Very well, I shall have the trunk delivered to Spinner Street tomorrow. Tell your combative nurse that Jem, one of the boys delivering it, will be staying. You needn't worry she will be too upset, he will soon charm her and I think she is sensible enough to know you will be safer with someone reliable in the house.'

'Lord Sinclair...'

'No, don't ruin it with an insincere show of conscience now that you have what you want. Enjoy rooting through my father's remains. Now if you will excuse me, I have more important matters to attend to. Unless you wish to convince me to remain?'

There was no flirtatious warmth in his dark eyes, no mocking knowledge of his power. The question was an attack, defying her. When she didn't answer he laughed and left.

Chapter Ten

'Good Lord, again?'

'Perhaps the rumours are true after all? I did not credit it, but twice in one week... My dear Lady Barnstable, it is quite unprecedented.'

'What rumours, Lady Westerby?' Elspeth asked and the little clutch of matrons leaned closer together.

Olivia shook open her fan, wondering how much longer she and Lady Phelps had to stay before it would be considered polite to leave the soiree. It was not a good sign that she was already tiring of these occasions, but they did appear to be rather repetitive. Listening to Bertram's enthusiastic accounts of London society it had been the pinnacle of her ambition to go there one day as his wife. Yet here she was, with a slew of titled gentlemen vying for her attention, even if primarily for pecuniary reasons, and all she could think of was her mistake regarding Lord Sinclair. She kept assuring herself this was no time for scruples, but she still felt as slimy as a slug and about as appetising.

She forced her attention to the whispered discussion around her.

'What other reason could there be?' Lady Barnstable was saying behind the protection of her purple-silk fan. 'This is his second appearance at a social function in a week. It is quite unprecedented, I tell you. Just look at him, as cool as the devil himself. As if there is nothing at all untoward about it.'

That caught her attention, and when the women looked as directed Olivia knew what she would see. Lucas Sinclair was standing just inside the main entrance to the ballroom, in conversation with a group of elegantly dressed gentlemen. He stood in the group and yet utterly apart. It wasn't merely his height and the hint of the Latin in his dark looks. Despite the humour in his hooded eyes, there was something too aware in his stance, as if he was incapable of relaxing his guard. When the blow came, he would be ready for it while the rest of those in the room might not even realise it had been struck.

Her conscience tugged at her again, as it had hourly since he'd left Brook Street earlier that day, and she quashed it again. Lord Sinclair had not achieved his reputation by accident and it was ludicrous to tiptoe around his feelings. If there was even a chance she might discover something pertinent to Henry's death in Howard Sinclair's papers, it was worth the cost. The only reason she had sought association with the earl was to redeem Henry's reputation; to baulk now would be disloyal.

Lucas turned his head and met her gaze and she realised he knew precisely where she was. As his gaze lingered on her, the voices of the women by her fell as if an announcement was pending. Clearly they were wondering whether Sinful Sinclair would repeat his performance by acknowledging the northern heiress. Olivia could almost feel the tension of their expectation quivering the air around her.

He turned away, without even the perfunctory nod of recognition, returning to the gentlemen at his side. Olivia clenched herself around the all-too-familiar sensation of humiliation and rejection. For two whole months after refusing to marry Bertram she lived with these sharp waves of mortification as the residents of Gillingham turned their backs on her one by one.

'For your own good,' Bertram's aunt told her after another matron failed to nod to her in the square. 'You've run too wild all your life, Olivia Silverdale, you and your brothers. Maybe now you'll come to your senses, marry my nephew and start behaving as a proper young woman ought.'

For two months Olivia held her ground before she indeed came to her senses and left Gillingham to live with Elspeth rather than marry the man who betrayed her or bow to the people who rejected her. Only her poor brothers and Henry Payton took her side, accepting her decision though she told no one but Henry the truth. It was unfair that Henry's kindness and unstinting loyalty cost him and his family everything.

It was a salutary reminder of what mattered. Not what these shallow people thought of her, but repaying the trust and lifelong care of the Paytons. She would not lose sight of her objective. Lord Sinclair was angry with her at the moment for revealing a weakness of his, but though he was a rake he would stand by his word and help her and that was all that mattered.

When her dance partner came to claim her she smiled brightly and brought to bear every skill she had learned by wheedling her brothers into allowing her to take part in their activities. By the time the dance was over she had made another conquest and was exhausted and thoroughly depressed.

'Isn't Mr Bolton charming?' Elspeth whispered to Olivia. 'He is very eligible. It cannot even be said that he needs your dowry, he has a very nice property in Sussex, you know. And so handsome.'

Olivia frowned. Had he been handsome?

'He reminds me of Colin,' she replied.

'Colin? Oh, Colin Payton. You really should not refer to young men in such familiar terms in public, my dear, no matter how close a family friend. Besides, Mr Bolton is much more handsome and the Boltons are among the finest families in England. Lady Barnstable noted it especially and I foresee even more attention from her son now. Who is your next partner? Oh, it is a waltz. I did tell you it was not a good idea to dance with That Man. No one dares follow in his footsteps and invite you to waltz. See, they are all watching to see who will be brave enough to step forward. It is truly most bothersome. When we attend Almack's next week I must secure you an unexceptionable partner.'

Olivia unfurled her fan and toyed with it as she half-listened to Elspeth—Almack's, Mr Bolton, Lord this and Mr that—while her other half closed the door of her study and stared again at her Wall of Conjecture. But it wasn't Elspeth's chatter or the first bars of the waltz that brought her to the surface, but the sudden awareness of being watched. She glanced up and again met Lucas Sinclair's gaze. This time he did not look away—he clearly was aware of the quandary facing her suitors and probably enjoying her discomfiture.

She resisted the urge to make one of her brother Ralph's favourite gestures of disdain, but some of her intent must have been evident because a glimmer of amusement lightened his gaze. She raised her chin with a slight shrug and resumed her contemplation of her fan, but the heaviness on her shoulders lifted a little.

'Oh, no!'

Elspeth's exclamation gave her a moment's warning and she glanced up to see Lord Sinclair standing before her.

'I feel I should assume responsibility for your predicament, Miss Silverdale.'

'By compounding it, Lord Sinclair?'

'It is my gambling nature, I am afraid. I tend to double down on a losing streak.'

'If that means what I think, it is very poor financial thinking.'

'Strange, you don't strike me as the kind of woman to cut her losses.'

'I am not. In the event of a loss I would reassess my initial considerations and try to make a decision based on a firm foundation, not a vain whim.'

'Olivia…' Elspeth pleaded and Lord Sinclair laughed, his gaze skimming over the silent matrons who were watching their every move.

'You are in danger of not only compounding your predicament, Miss Silverdale, but embellishing on it. Come, you will do less damage dancing.'

He held out his hand as the music swelled into the silence that settled around them and she stood.

'Good,' he murmured as he led her among the dancing couples. 'I should not have been so petty as to snub you earlier, but returning the snub would have served no purpose.'

'I was not tempted to, Lord Sinclair. You have every right to be angry—'

'One stipulation,' he interrupted. 'We will not discuss your machinations in these settings. I make the rules, remember? A key rule is that as of this moment we draw a firm line between those two worlds. In this world we are precisely and only what the world sees. Is that clear?'

She nodded and his hand shifted again, pulling her closer as they turned. It hardly made sense that this was only the second time they had danced.

Dancing with him was like the kiss—fiercely exciting and yet familiar. Her body moved with his without thought, adjusted, turned and adapted in a manner wholly unlike the other dances that evening. Perhaps it was because it was the waltz, or the way his hands moved on the fabric of her glove and gown. Probably this was evidence of precisely what made this man so dangerous.

'I shall have to enjoy this unaccustomed obedience to the full, Miss Silverdale. Like that foolish fairy tale, it clearly doesn't survive into the light of day. So will none of your hopeful suitors dare waltz with you?'

'They certainly won't now that I am waltzing a second time with you. Elspeth is likely succumbing to despair, poor thing.'

'You will come about. Lord Barnstable has very expensive habits, you know. And Bolton is hanging out for a country wife to take back to his mother in Sussex. He has already mentioned his mother, hasn't he?'

She frowned. She hadn't paid very close attention to all of Mr Bolton's comments, but now that Lucas mentioned it…

'I think he did. Is that bad?'

'I return the question to you. Is it bad that a

man contemplating marriage makes it a point to tell a prospect how perfect his mother is?'

'It could be a sign that he is a caring, considerate man.'

'It could.'

'And I don't care to be labelled a prospect.'

'Well, that is unavoidable. You have firmly entered the marketplace, Miss Silverdale, so *caveat emptor*—beware what you are purchasing.'

'I am surprised you are willing to dance with me, then, Lord Sinclair. A second waltz will mark you as much as it will me.'

'It is always amusing to rattle the London cage a little by acting out of character. Besides, I enjoy waltzing with you, Miss Silverdale, though I am surprised you have not yet been ripped from my rapacious arms. Your chaperon looks likely to cut out my heart and kick it to the gutter for the dogs to fight over. Dancing with rakes does not suit her plans for you.'

She wrinkled her nose.

'That is a revolting image. Besides, Elspeth would never do anything so crass. She knows I am in no danger of being swayed by a rake's empty charm.'

'Then she is a fool. Don't overestimate yourself,

Miss Silverdale.' He was smiling, but the amusement was gone from his eyes and she flushed.

She flushed 'You misunderstood… I was not referring to you. I know you aren't in the least interested in me, not like that.'

'Not like what?'

'You know. In any serious manner. I meant that I am in no danger of being caught by a rake because I am not in the least interested in matrimony.'

'At all?'

She shook her head.

'You know why I am in London. This…all this is to make Elspeth happy while I go about my business. And she is.'

'So all this finery and flirting is to buy domestic peace? You do not enjoy it in the least?'

She shook her head, but the lie stuck. *This* she did enjoy—only too well.

That thought brought a bite of heat to her cheeks and it sharpened as she realised she was watching his mouth. She forced her eyes up and met the taunting heat in his.

'It is good you have no taste for gambling, Miss Silverdale, because you are a poor liar. Those honey-and-moss eyes hide a great deal, but they fail you when you need them most. Right now they reveal you have no clear idea what you are doing here or why.'

'Must I?'

His thumb skated over her gloved palm and she couldn't prevent her hand from curling, almost closing over his finger in a manner wholly prohibited in the dance. She was breathless suddenly, but not from dancing. She heard the music enter its final flourish and wanted to protest. She did not want it to be over. Ever.

He did not immediately lead her back to Elspeth, but drew her to the wall where the windows were covered with deep-claret curtains. Against their lush background he looked the image of what he was—dark and dangerous and out of her league.

'If you plan to continue on this wilful path, then, yes, you must. I know this world, unfortunately, so let me explain something to you. Right now everyone is wondering what I said to make you blush so charmingly. They will presume I have been my sinful self and absolve you of anything but youthful vanity in accepting my second invitation. But next time they will begin to stack the deck against you. They will peel back the layer provided by your golden dowry and begin to find your flaws. And then, if there is even a hint that you are merely toying with them and their ambitions, they will be merciless…'

The words struck her like hailstones, the skin at her nape turning cold and clammy. She touched her fingers to her cheek, but it felt numb, distant. Even his voice was muffled, like the boom of thunder while hiding under a blanket. She stared at the snowbound landscape of his cravat, like the rise and fall of the winter ground in the moors just off Silverdale land, a cold crust over unforgiving, infertile ground.

'Olivia?'

She shook her head, but his hand closed on her arm, both drawing her to his side and propelling her forward. Within a moment the noise and music was back. The colours and the press of people, and the clamminess faded. She put some distance between them, firming her step.

'I am all right.' Her voice still sounded shaky and she cleared her throat.

'What the devil happened?' His voice was pitched low and it rumbled through her like a storm moving away. She shook her head and laughed.

'I had forgotten how much I hate these fashionable corsets.'

His fingers tightened again and just as they

approached Elspeth he bent and whispered in her ear.

'A very poor liar, Olivia. And never mention corsets in public unless hinting you would like them removed.'

With a slight bow he left and she sank into the chair beside Elspeth. Her cousin did not speak and Olivia was too tired to placate her. But she ensured she was a model of maidenly virtue for the rest of the evening, dancing and smiling with whomever Elspeth approved of, though when the second waltz began still no man approached her and Elspeth sighed in relief as Lord Sinclair led a lovely brunette in a gossamer-thin jonquil-yellow gown on to the floor. He left soon after with a group of men and Elspeth heaved another sigh of relief. Olivia did as well. She needed the quiet.

Chapter Eleven

Lucas hesitated before approaching the door of her study.

Six hours. Jem and Davie had delivered the trunk to Spinner Street that morning and while Jem stayed to settle in at Spinner Street, Davie returned with the information that Miss Silverdale was at the house. Jem knew to send word when they left for Brook Street, but as the hours ticked by no word had come.

Which meant she was still there, in her study, and no doubt she had already festooned that wall of hers with whatever titbits she extracted from the remnants of his father's pathetic life.

What would she do if he walked in there and tore the whole thing down, packed her into a post chaise under armed guard and sent her back north where she belonged? Probably wait until he was out of view and talk her way out of the post chaise and start all over somewhere else. The girl was relentless. From the beginning she got her own way on every front. Every concession she appeared to make was just another net tugging him along in her wake.

Relentless.

He looked down at the faded and scuffed floorboards outside her study, remembering the strange interlude at the ball last night. For a moment he had been certain she would faint, but whatever she said it was not her corset that drained her face of blood and her eyes of expression, but shock. Something he said had pulled the world out from under her and that was eating away at him just as much as her violation of his boundaries.

This was pointless, as useful as railing at the moon. *Just go in there and see the damage, man.*

She was watching the door when he entered, like an animal alert to a predator's presence. But she must have known it was him because there was no fear on her face and no sign of discomfort. Her mouth was just hovering on the edge of a smile, between welcome, embarrassment and, worst of all, compassion.

Damn the girl. He was not an object of pity, no matter what she had found.

'Well?'

'Well what?'

'Have you unearthed some dastardly plot? Perhaps a secret billet from Napoleon himself?'

'I haven't looked,' she replied.

'I beg your pardon?'

She indicated the closed trunk.

'I haven't looked.'

'Why the devil not? It isn't locked.'

'I presumed it wasn't, but I didn't want to open it in your absence.'

He controlled himself with an effort.

'That was the whole point of my sending it here. You wanted the blasted thing.'

'Yes, I know. But I'm afraid you will either have to do this with me or take it back. Would you care for some tea?'

He had no idea what to do. Shake his fists at the sky? Walk out? Laugh? Kick the damn trunk into toothpicks and kindling and toss it into the fire? Take her upstairs and do what his body was clamouring for ever since that blasted kiss?

He sat on the sofa and ran his hands through his hair.

'Brandy?' she asked and he nodded. The scent of cinnamon permeated the whole house and he realised he hadn't eaten in hours.

'Is there anything to eat?'

'Of course. I must admit I wasn't quite certain I would approve of Jem, but Nora's knee is bothering her, it always does before a frost, so it is quite useful to have someone who can help us with the fetching and carrying. He is helping her fix the window catches in the small back parlour so I shan't bother him. I will go and ask Nora to prepare us a tray myself. Here.'

She handed him a glass of brandy and was gone before he could react. Something buffed at the back of his legs and grey eyes glinted at him as Inky slunk out from under the sofa and went to sit by the trunk like a sculpture of the Egyptian cat god Bastet beside a sarcophagus.

'I think you're the only sane one in this house,' he said, but Inky merely widened her eyes and, very deliberately, inched the empty china bowl where Olivia sometimes dropped titbits for her towards Lucas's boot. They viewed each other for a moment and then Lucas gently nudged the bowl back towards its owner. The sleek dark fur above Inky's liquid grey eyes gathered together into a look that would have separated a beggar from his last rag, and again, even more slowly this time, the paw nudged the bowl, this time tapping it gently on the floorboards a few times before settling it against Lucas's boot.

'My God, did you take lessons in relentlessness from your mistress?' Lucas muttered. 'I don't have anything but this brandy and I doubt I will be forgiven for encouraging you to tipple.'

Before either could continue their stand-off, the door opened and Olivia slipped back into the room.

'There. Jem will bring it when it is ready.'

She went to stroke Inky and placed the bowl back in its place. She did not look at him as she moved towards the wall and then back to her desk. She was nervous, but for all her lack of artifice he had no idea what she was thinking this time. Nothing that boded well for him, no doubt.

'I keep changing my mind,' she said at last. 'More than anything I want to help the Paytons, but not at any price. So I have been trying to think of other ways to go about this and I decided I shall visit the vicar, Mr Eldritch. Perhaps he can help me after all. I told Jem to take back the trunk when he has finished helping Nora.'

He put down his brandy and went to stare at the trunk. It sat and sulked and the thought of hauling it back into the attic at the Mausoleum felt...wrong.

'Not everything can be tucked back into place, Olivia. Come. Let's see what treasures we can unearth. At the very least a skull or perfumed billets from my father's mistresses. Open it.'

It was cowardly to make her do it, but she didn't question his command. With a brief look at him she sank to her knees by the trunk and raised the lid.

It was surprisingly neat for a trunk that stood untouched for twenty years. He wondered if Tubbs had dusted it inside as well as out before bringing it downstairs. Probably.

She touched one of the books with the tip of her finger and he felt a prickling on the back of his neck. He had given his father that volume of Hume's *The History of England*. He could remember the feel of the cherrywood-coloured leather when he had chosen it at the bookstore in London the last time he had been there with his family, the year everything went wrong.

She looked at him and he crouched by the trunk as well and opened the book. The edges of the paper were a little frayed, soft from frequent reading, and the inscription on the front page was faded but legible. Even at that age his handwriting resembled his father's. A little rounder, bold and large, to make a point.

She read his inscription, her voice fading at the end. *"'I couldn't find Volume One, but I shall buy it for you when I do. Mr Marley assures me you can begin here. Happy birthday, Papa.'"*

He closed the book and put it on the carpet.

They took them out one by one. Most of them were books his father acquired in Boston and told him nothing but that his father loved history. Halfway through the process she went to the desk and brought back a notebook and pencil and began making a list of the books with the seriousness of a quartermaster-general facing a protracted siege.

'Another list for the wall?'

She glanced up from a cumbersome copy of Burton's *Anatomy of Melancholy*. 'Lists help me think. If it bothers you I shall stop.'

'Not at all. Pray continue; there should be some record of what my father left behind aside from more unwanted Sinclairs.'

She ignored his comment, which was probably for the best, and he returned to examining the books, handing them to her as he took them out. Beneath the books were sheaves of papers that looked like shipping documents and accounts.

He sighed and took a pile over to the sofa.

'I will look through these, though I doubt there is anything of interest. You see if anything catches your eye in there. If you find evidence of his mistresses, feel free to toss it in the fire.'

'What memorabilia do mistresses usually leave behind? Under duress Mr Mercer informed me that the only blatant signs of Henry's mistress were embroidered pillows, a pot of dying flowers and some feminine garments which I hope Mr Mercer disposed of before Colin's arrival. You are probably better versed in the tell-tale signs of a mistress given your substantial experience in those quarters. What evidence should I be looking for? Requests for baubles? Complaints about being used and then cast aside when they were no longer sufficiently entertaining?'

Her voice was light, almost funning, but it couldn't conceal her bitterness and it took the sting out of her comments. Knowing how disappointed she was in her godfather, he should have been more careful.

'I apologise for ever mentioning the word. Shall we agree to proceed without discussing mistresses?'

'That might prove difficult. They seem to be rather at the centre of this conundrum, at least on the surface.'

'You are the one arguing your godfather's death wasn't about mistresses at all, so take a leaf from your own book. Besides, I do not have a mistress.'

It wasn't a lie. Still, he should have kept quiet. He didn't look up from the papers he was examining, but could feel her watching him with the alert, curious look that portended ill.

'What of Lady Ilford?'

'For pity's sake, Olivia! You cannot just ask a man outright about his private life. It is none of your concern. Besides, depending upon gossip for your information is not reliable. Lady Ilford and I are no longer...associated.'

'You are right, Lord Sinclair, I apologise. It is none of my concern.'

Her tone was so proper he risked looking up, but she was bent over the contents of the trunk quite as if they had been discussing nothing but the weather. A lock of her hair fell over one shoulder, one curl shaping an inverted question mark over the modest bodice of her dress. She swept it back as she shifted position, settling more comfortably by the trunk, her skirts moulding to the shape of her backside and thighs. His imagination extrapolated from the memory of her waist during the waltz to what it would feel like to skim downwards, over the lush curve of her hip, but this time without gloves, without clothes...

He tightened his hold on the documents to counter their conviction they could already feel those curves, warm, pliant... He schooled his breathing, just as he did before facing danger, forcing himself into a controlled rhythm. He shouldn't be surprised his mind was showing distinct signs of softening. It was a form of madness to be sitting here at all, going through the documents of a dead man, alone with a respectable if eccentric young woman who was subverting his life without even realising it.

'Oh! Look!'

Her exclamation didn't even register until she rose to her knees, holding a packet wrapped in string. Her gaze was wary as it met his and he felt a sting of embarrassment along his cheekbones. She couldn't possibly know what he was thinking merely by looking at him, could she?

'They are letters, but it looks like a woman's hand. Would...would you like to see them? Or shall I put them back?'

'No.'

She hesitated. 'No, you don't want to see them, or, no, don't put them back?'

Just no. No to all of this.

He stood and went to uncork the brandy. 'Who are they addressed to?'

'To Howard. They are dated 1801.'

'The year of his death. Does it say from whom?'

There was silence and then the rustling of paper. 'From Tessa.'

He hadn't expected to be relieved, but he was. Relieved and a host of too many other things.

'My mother. Theresa.'

'I will put them back.'

'No. You wanted this. You read them.'

'This is personal.'

He turned to face her. '*This* is personal? You have a talent for understatement, Miss Silverdale. Have we finally reached the limits of your audacity? Read the blasted letters.'

He had expected, *wanted* to shame her or make her angry, but her expression softened further. The insult of her pity and compassion was almost too much for him to bear, but before he did something he would regret further she looked away.

'Very well.'

'Aloud.'

'There is no point trying to punish me for this, Lord Sinclair. It isn't I who is likely to be hurt.'

'Read.'

'Very well,' she said again, breathed in and began.

Dear Howard,

After my long letter just two days ago I have little of import to add and I do not even know if this will reach you before you sail, but I cannot resist just a few more words to speed you on your way back to us and to tell you that Lucas is home safely.

I am including a more visual greeting from Sam, who insists the green blotch in the centre is your boat being carried on the back of a dragon. A good dragon, apparently. It is to be hoped you do not encounter any such beasts, good or otherwise, on your way home.

We have been busy indeed on our side of the high seas. Now Lucas is down from Harrow he has taken on the task of preparing Chase for those hallowed halls next year.

I eavesdropped unashamedly on these lessons and you will be relieved to hear that they include not merely demonstrations of pugilistic skills, but also pointers on surviving mathematics and Latin, two areas in which Lucas appears to excel, though I have no idea how since neither you nor I are particularly skilled in those arenas and it is all I can do to make the household accounts balance. Perhaps he is, as you said, a little like your brother Oswald. Not in spirit, though, I am relieved to say.

I worried that the events of the past couple of years might change him, but it is not so. Sam ran to him and for a moment I was afraid he might consider himself too old for such displays, but in a moment the three of them were no more than a bundle of limbs and laughs rolling on the lawn.

Chase is in heaven. I think he has missed him most of all, but will show it least.

I decided not to tell them about your father's and brother's death. Even without discussing the less than flattering circumstances—wholly appropriate as far as I am concerned—I am only glad at least the females they were entertaining escaped unharmed. I felt it best to wait until your return. I hope Oswald's letter informing you of the circumstances was not too great a shock but I cannot bemoan their loss. This can mark a new beginning for us.

I am near the end of this page and in a hurry to see it off to you. Hurry back, but above all be safe. Do remember to wear the flannel belt I made under your coat. It will be chilly on the ship and you must keep warm.

*I daresay I should call you Lord Sinclair
now, but I shan't. And I dare you to call me
Lady Sinclair.
    My love with you always.
All our love,
Your Tessa*

She was right. It hurt.

He remembered that day. Strange. He remembered precisely that image: Sam running towards him from the house, his mother on the steps of the little cottage. He didn't remember rolling on the lawn, just the hesitation now that he was all grown up, battling with joy and relief that he was home. That little house in Burford had been more of a home than ever Sinclair Hall or the Mausoleum in London. But it lasted all of two years, perhaps less.

Lucas sometimes wondered if his memories of those two years were a childish fantasy, but his mother's words were too vivid and real. To her it had been real. Whatever his father had done, she had been happy and still in love after more than a dozen years with his father.

He should give these letters to Chase and Sam. That would be the right thing to do.

Olivia sat with the packet on her lap, her finger touching the scrap of paper with Sam's attempt at a boat. Then she folded it and put it back on the stack and secured the string and returned it to the trunk and walked out of the room.

For an instant he was too surprised to react. He caught up with her on the stairs to the upper floor.

'Where are you going…?' He stopped in shock. Tears were pouring down her cheeks.

'I am so sorry,' she whispered. 'I never should have read that. You are right. About everything. I am so sorry.'

He wrapped his arms around her and because he wanted nothing more than to take her upstairs he led her back down. But he didn't release his hold on her when he sat with her on the sofa. He handed her his handkerchief and she buried her face in it. Her shoulders were shaking and felt surprisingly frail. He risked touching the honey-brown curls loosely gathered into a knot that was in constant danger of slipping loose. They were feather soft and the scent of peaches reached him. He was particularly partial to peaches, to all summer fruit, but especially peaches, lush and juicy, almost too sweet but with a tart undertone. He resisted the urge to unfasten that knot and burrow into her.

Her voice was muffled as she pressed the handkerchief to her face.

'She sounds so lovely. Your mother. I'm a horrible person to have forced this on you. This is all wrong.'

He didn't answer. There was no point in denying the obvious. It was peculiar that this of all things should affect her so.

Before he could answer, the door opened and Jem entered, bearing a tray and followed by Nora. Olivia went to stand by the desk, her back to them, and Nora directed a murderous look at Lucas.

'Anything else, my lord?' Jem asked and Lucas shook his head.

Nora did not immediately follow Jem out. 'He's a good boy. He can stay if he likes. Good manners,' she said, adding in a voice that carried a distinct snap, 'You harm a hair on her head and I'll have yours. My lord.'

He sighed as the door closed behind her. Olivia had at least emerged from the handkerchief, but she was staring at the wall with a distant look that didn't reassure him in the least. The teapot clicked against the cup as he poured and she started, wiped her eyes and blew her nose, then came to the table and took the pot from him.

'You are right—I am throwing myself at a wall

and there is nothing behind it. I am only causing damage. I will miss this place.'

'Why? Where are you going?'

'I don't know. I cannot return to Yorkshire and I cannot imagine returning to Guilford. Poor Elspeth. It seemed right at the time but now… But London isn't right either. You are correct about me. I am not made for ball rooms and drawing rooms.'

'I did not say that.'

'You meant it. In any case, it is true. I will cause damage there, as well. I must find another way to help the Paytons. I should marry Colin. At least that way they will never have any material concerns.'

He kept silent and watched her pour the tea. Sometimes her movements were so fluid, unhurried, as if there was someone inside her just waiting for an invitation to let go. Be. She needed an outlet for all that pent-up energy, something other than making lists, playing knight errant and masquerading as a proper young woman. But those were dangerous thoughts and not appropriate at the moment. In fact, none of the thoughts that were crashing about in his head were worthy of being voiced. Still, he couldn't prevent the return of the memory of her standing with young Payton in the church, her eyes closed as she raised her face to be kissed—tense and resigned. It was all wrong.

'I don't think you should act hastily,' he said.

Some tea sloshed out of the cup she placed on the table by his side.

'Abandoning my quest is acting hastily? You have been trying to convince me that this is precisely what I should do all along.'

'I still think you will uncover no dastardly plot, but I don't think you should make momentous decisions about your future based on grief and guilt and a conviction you have no alternatives. A woman of your character and means has quite a few alternatives. I suggest you explore them before you do anything rash like marrying a man for whom you have no more than a sisterly affection.'

He wasn't even certain she was listening, her mouth still a downward bow as she inspected her wall.

'I will put everything in the trunk by tomorrow and you can send someone for it.'

'I think we should compromise.'

'Compromise how?'

'I have a constitutional dislike of leaving a task half-done. I don't believe your suspicions are correct, but I still want to look at the letters my father sent to Henry Payton and I think we should finish reviewing the documents in the trunk. I am also willing to accompany you to visit that vicar, Eldritch. Once we have done that we can reconsider if we are chasing ghosts. Agreed?'

Olivia turned towards him. The fire chased away the green from her eyes, turning them into molten honey. Her face was as expressive as always—it reflected surprise, relief, a little fear, a gathering of resolution through the weight of weariness. But nothing he was searching for. No gratitude for a reprieve from the life she had described. No excitement, no...passion.

Not that it mattered. Whether she fully accepted it or not, those choices—either spent in social rounds with her ambitious chaperon or as Mrs Colin Payton—were wrong for her. Someone like her doomed to become a provincial matron in Yorkshire or a plodding peer's wife in London... The mind boggled. It was just wrong. If merely by agreeing to continue he could postpone that fate, his choice was simple. Whether he wanted to or not he had assumed a degree of responsibility for this morass and its perpetrator and, whatever people said of him, he never shirked his responsibilities. Well, rarely.

She sipped her tea and put her cup on the table. 'I think I shall have some brandy instead.'

'Celebrating?'

'I think so. Yes, yes, we are. You are quite correct; I am not ready to admit defeat. Thank you for being willing to see this through.'

He moved towards the sideboard. 'Whatever you do, don't thank me, Olivia. I only ever act out of self-interest. Don't forget that.'

She shrugged and smoothed out her skirts. 'I won't. I shall even write it down. Lord Sinclair is irredeemably selfish. Perhaps even put it on the wall. That way I shan't forget.'

'I am serious.'

'I know you are. You are very serious for a rake. I shall have to reassess my definition of the term. Or find a more appropriate label for you. Is that mine?'

'No, this is yours.' He handed her one of the glasses.

'That is less than half yours!'

'Because you are less than half my size.'

'Nonsense. I would estimate I am just over half your weight and probably some three-quarters of your height. Besides, it is *my* brandy.'

'If you finish this and can still compose a sensible list, you shall have more.'

'I *am* twenty-four, you know.'

'Almost. And I am thirty-two, so I still outstrip you. Now take your brandy and sit down so we can return to our business. This compromise is conditional upon you not arguing with me over everything.'

She sat and smiled up at him and he had the absurd image of going down on his knees for that smile. Putting brandy and lists and death aside and continuing what he had started, stripping her of her worries and controls and thoughts about the future and just…

He turned away, grasping for something to do to escape himself, and remembered the packet in his coat. He extracted it and tossed it on to the desk before going to warm his hands by the fire.

'I forgot. This is for you.'

'What is it?' she asked as she went to pick up the packet.

'New pencils. You are using the stubs. These are from Keswick, apparently—Borrowdale graphite. The stationer said they are best.'

She untied the string and smiled. 'A dozen?'

'Too few?'

She touched her finger to one of the wood-encased pencils. 'No, this is perfect.'

He turned back to the fire and didn't answer.

'Thank you, Lucas. For all of this.'

'You are welcome. I am merely contributing my share to our wholesale destruction of stationer's supplies here. Now I want to look at those letters between Payton and my father. You mentioned you made a list of names mentioned in the letters and documents you have read so far. May I see it?'

'Yes, I have a list where they are by order of number of times mentioned and a list by their connection to his different activities, and another by their chronological appearance, the latest first. I also marked all those I had heard him speak of at any point with an X. I presume most of those people are unrelated to our concerns so I made another list only of those who have the most points of connection...' She stopped and looked up with sudden suspicion. 'Are you laughing at me?'

He mastered his smile. 'Not in the least. I am merely thinking how much my uncle Oswald would appreciate your methods. Show me that last one, please. We shall have to make similar lists for my father's papers. See if anything ties them together.'

'Do you think...? No.'

'No, what?'

'Nothing.'

'Out with it, Olivia.'

'Did your mother keep your father's letters? These are just her letters to him.'

'I don't know. She might have destroyed them after what she learned. She was very upset. I don't know.'

'Never mind. I'm sorry. It was silly to ask.'

'No, it wasn't, but I don't know. Even if she didn't destroy them, they might have remained in Venice or even been lost. We left England soon after for Italy.'

'Was her family from Venice?'

'My grandmother's family, yes. They have a monstrous old palace right on the Grand Canal. My cousin transformed it into a casino since we left so it is probably in better shape than what I remember.'

'I would love to see Italy.' She sighed. 'It seems strange that my parents travelled everywhere, but I have only been three places in my life—London, Yorkshire and Guilford. I always thought it was terribly unfair they never thought to take any of us with them on their travels.'

'Very unfair. Perhaps one day you will go there.'

'Probably not. This is likely the most outrageous thing I shall ever do with my life. Never mind. Well, we shall make do with what we have here.'

She sounded so determined he smiled. He had a peculiar urge to put his arm around her and comfort her. He had no idea what for, but he knew it would probably lead down the wrong path. He was within a hair's breadth of offering to take her to Venice. Best stick to business.

'I'll split this stack of letters with you and we can start writing down names and anything else of interest. I want you to list whatever information you have about your godfather. Anything at all you can think of. Can you do that?'

She nodded, her eyes lighting. He hated giving her false hope, but if he was going to pursue this phantom conspiracy of hers he might as well do it thoroughly. Besides, he wanted to know more about the man she so blatantly adored. Not clever, but there it was.

Chapter Twelve

'Is this where he lives?' Olivia asked, her breath a puff of silvery smoke in the freezing air. She gathered her cloak more closely about her as Lucas helped her alight from the carriage and he tucked her hand against his arm.

'Not quite. At least I hope not. These are St Stephen's burial grounds. I am still not quite certain it was a good idea for you to come with me, but since you appear to enjoy visiting consecrated locations, I thought you would enjoy the excursion.'

'To a cemetery?' She wrinkled her nose, but he could see the sparkle of interest in her eyes.

'I am introducing variety. The church itself is just beyond those walls and the building just at the end is where Reverend Eldritch works and lives with his father. He might be disconcerted if we confront him together and therefore more likely to be revealing, but you may wait in the carriage if you are uncomfortable.'

'I most certainly shall not. I agree confronting him together is an excellent idea, Lord Sinclair.'

'You are too kind, Miss Silverdale. Where are you going?'

'I wonder if we can find the third Eldritch's grave. I am curious.'

He sighed and followed her. The ground was hard and crisp beneath his boots and by the low-hanging clouds, they might see snow soon. He looked around the tumbled, mossy headstones. Some had been gathered and piled against the walls like slate for roofing. The chances of finding anyone's particular grave in this chaos was slim. He wondered if the families of those people whose tombstones were being set aside so brutally knew of their fate. He hoped not.

'What fascinating stories must be buried here,' she murmured as she bent over a cracked tombstone.

'I would much rather pursue less fascinating stories in more comfortable venues,' he replied. 'I suggest we arrange our next meeting at Vauxhall or somewhere equally bright and garish.'

'Vauxhall.' She turned, her eyes lighting, and he couldn't stop his reflexive smile.

'It is too early in the year, but you might convince your chaperon to organise a party there come summer.'

She shook her head. 'I cannot imagine still being in London by then.'

'If it is left to your cousin, you will be wed by then.'

'My cousin is a sensible woman and, though she may hope I shall wake up one day biddable and sheared of my oddities, she probably knows I am not likely to fulfil her fantasies.'

Again he heard the echo of something in her voice and pressed back at his curiosity. The girl's fault lines were not his business.

'You should perhaps adopt some of her faith. London is large enough to accommodate like-minded oddities. There are benefits to size.'

She was peering at a badly chipped tombstone, but she turned at that, her elfin smile flashing. 'My brothers would make a lewd comment here, but I shall refrain. And may I inform you that no chivalrous man would agree I am odd.'

'No chivalrous man would agree to be alone with you in a graveyard. I thought my usefulness hinged precisely on my lack of chivalry.'

'That is a good point.' She planted her hands on her hips and surveyed the graves around them. 'I don't know if we shall find Eldritch's grave in this chaos. What if his tombstone is one of those uprooted ones?'

'Well, he died three years ago. Take a look at the newer stones. Over there. See?'

He indicated the far end of the burial ground next to a row of bare plane trees where the stones were still grey and relatively intact.

'Sound thinking, Lord Sinclair. I shall take the left side, you take the right.'

He ignored her directive and followed her. It was foolish, but he didn't feel comfortable leaving her on her own, even if she was in plain sight. She frowned at him, but didn't comment as she began her search.

Halfway up the row she stopped. 'There are too many children. This is horrible.'

He took her hand without thinking. 'This is life.'

'Then life is horrible. Look—this tombstone is for five children from one family. Not one of them is older than three years old. How could their mother bear it, Lucas?'

'What choice did she have?'

She didn't answer, her hand stiff in his. She had not noticed her use of his name, but he had. He placed his other hand over hers and a snowflake settled on the back of his glove. She touched it with her free hand.

'It is snowing.'

'Are you cold?' He tightened his hands as hers shifted in his. He didn't want her to pull away, not yet, but he let go none the less.

'A little. Are you?'

'A little,' he lied. 'But after spending the past few winters in Russia, this is very mild. I doubt this snow will settle. Come, let us go find Reverend Eldritch and put this issue to rest and then I will return you to the warmth of Brook Street so you can thaw out ahead of whatever entertainment your cousin has in store.'

'She doesn't, not today at least. Tomorrow Elspeth and Lady Barnstable have arranged a party to visit Bullock's Museum in Piccadilly to view Napoleon's travelling carriage and the preserved animals. Lord Barnstable is an avid student of zoology, apparently.'

'Scintillating.'

'There is no need to mock him. He is a very worthy young man and I am looking forward to something other than morning calls. I have always wanted to visit the museums and see the antiquities. I cannot imagine why I did not ask Elspeth to go with me sooner.'

'Possibly because you were obsessed with your conspiracies?'

'Possibly. What were you doing in Russia, by the way?'

What would she do if he told her the truth? If he laid himself bare and told her all about being Oswald's errand boy and ferreter of political secrets? It was so tempting, just to see how she reacted. Most upright women of his acquaintance would react either with shock and distaste that he actually engaged in what they might term 'trade' or indulge in titillated excitement that he lay outside the pale. He didn't want Olivia to react as those other women might.

'I was running errands.' He chafed her hands, but she didn't appear to notice. Her eyes narrowed.

'Does this have something to do with your uncle?'

'My uncle?' He tried to recall precisely what he'd mentioned regarding Oswald.

'Mercer told me you are related to Sir Oswald Sinclair.'

'Did he?'

'He did. Mr Mercer is often very useful. He says Sir Oswald holds no official capacity, but that Canning is completely dependent on him on foreign affairs. Is it true?'

He turned over her gloved hands, catching two

snowflakes on her palms, but they melted almost immediately, leaving faint damp spots on the pale-yellow kid gloves.

'We should continue before we freeze to death.'

'I see.'

She canted her head to one side and drew her hands from his, proceeding to the next tombstone. He resisted the urge to recapture her hand, feeling a little foolish. He couldn't remember ever having an urge to walk hand in hand with someone. It was childish.

He glanced up at the bare trees, all knotty and patched with damp. 'Shall we proceed?'

'I dare say we... Oh!' She paused in front of a headstone. 'Well. You must at least admit it was worth the trip, Lord Sinclair. Arthur Septimus Eldritch. That answers one question and raises quite a few others. I doubt Septimus is a common name, so what is the chance that there is no connection with the Septimus mentioned by my godfather? Now we *must* see Reverend Eldritch.'

He sighed and cursed the fates. 'I hope he is in because I'm dam...dashed if I'm going to drive out to this depressing part of town again any time soon.'

She turned at the gate leading out of the burial grounds and smiled up at him. 'Are you annoyed

I was right? Or annoyed at yourself for not doing a better job investigating the Eldritches?'

'Neither. I am cold and hungry and I doubt your Reverend Eldritch will be in the mood to offer us sustenance when we come enquiring about a man's death and accusing him of colluding with a doxy. In fact, perhaps I should wait in the carriage while you charm him.'

'I don't think I am very good at charming anyone.'

'You could badger him into revealing the truth, then. I can attest to your skills on that front.'

'Again, a chivalrous man would have disclaimed my self-deprecating comment, you know.'

'I dare say he would. Here, have a sip of this before you beard the lion in his den.'

She eyed the flask he extracted from his coat pocket. 'Brandy?'

'Much worse. Try it.'

She sniffed it, wrinkling her nose. 'It smells like horse ointment.'

'It tastes worse, but it will warm you. Be adventurous.'

She took a careful sip and her grimace gave way to a gasp. 'Oh, lord, it *burns*!' She coughed, wiping her mouth with the back of her glove.

He laughed and took the flask. 'Tell me you aren't warmer now.'

'I'm on fire! It is *awful*. My God, do people actually like this?'

'A whole nation of them. It is vodka, a Russian specialty and an acquired taste. Very useful when you are lost in the snow.'

'I am not lost and a few flakes do not merit the name *snow*, and certainly not such an abuse of my palate.' She wiped her brow, setting her bonnet askew and allowing some coppery curls to escape its confines. 'Do you like it?'

He put it back into the pocket of his greatcoat and reached up to straighten her bonnet. 'Not in the least. I never managed to acquire a taste for it beyond its survival value, but I keep a flask in the carriage and I thought it might be useful in this frozen wasteland.'

'Then why on earth give it to me? Are you punishing me for dragging you here?'

He crossed his arms and smiled as she fanned herself with her muff, setting the escaped curls fluttering. Damn, he wished she would take the bonnet off; he wanted to see those curls freed, tumbling over her shoulders. He wanted to gather them in his hands, pull her to him, feel them brush against him as he...

'Lucas? You aren't truly angry at me, are you?'

'I am not angry.'

'You look angry. Well, tense.'

'Does it never occur to you that the greatest risks you incur are in my company, not out of it?'

The muff stopped its fanning.

'I know you will not do anything to actively harm me.'

'How the devil do you know that? Sometimes I think you must be the most naïve person I have ever encountered. You are alone with me in a graveyard halfway across London. I could do whatever I wanted and you would have no recourse.'

She considered him, two lines forming between her brows as they did when she was concentrating on her lists.

'Whatever you think, I am not a complete fool, Lucas. It is a little late in the day to convince me I should be afraid of you. Any risk I run by being in your company is because of who and what you are, not what you might do to me. You might not like my saying this, but I trust you.'

'Blast you, Olivia.'

Her smile twisted. 'I knew you wouldn't like it, but there it is.'

There it is. He should do something to prove

her wrong. Force her out of her complacency…
Damn her. It was futile. He could no more act
against her trust than he could kick a puppy. Her
trust should at least be an antidote to desire, but
it had the opposite effect. He hadn't drunk any
of the vodka, but his body was humming with
heat and need and frustration. Any more of this
and he would…he had no idea what he would do.
He was completely outside familiar territory. He
might as well have been sent on a mission to the
moon. He had no idea what to do to keep her in
her place and keep his own rebellious desires in
theirs. If he had an ounce of sense he would stay
away from her and wait for rationality to reas-
sert itself.

He took her arm and led her out of the graveyard and towards the grey building at the end of
a narrow alley.

'Let me do the talking, Olivia. I doubt the Reverend Eldritch will appreciate your style of inter-
rogation.'

In the end his strictures were unnecessary. The
housekeeper, a short, round and cheerful woman,
informed them that Mr Eldritch, Reverend Eldritch's father, passed just last week and his son
was honouring his request to have his body buried in Cumbria where they originated and was not

expected to return before month's end. Lucas felt Olivia's disappointment in every line of her body.

'Were you acquainted with Mr Eldritch's brother?'

'Not well, sir. He and his wife were not frequent visitors to the vicarage. Well, Mrs Eldritch did visit not a few weeks ago, but that was the first time in many a year.'

'*Mrs* Arthur Septimus Eldritch?' Olivia asked.

'That's right, miss. Poor soul. All alone in the world now but for her little dog. Such a pity there were no children. I have six myself and, though they run you ragged, they fill you from within is what I always say.'

'Do you know where she resides?'

The housekeeper showed the first signs of suspicion. 'No, miss. I never asked. Now I really must be on my way. The man taking Mr Eldritch's place is sadly scatter-brained and we are woefully behind on parish duties. If you have anything else you would like to ask, you may return tomorrow and speak with him yourselves, not that he knows much about the Eldritches. He's from Sussex!'

With that condemnatory statement she bobbed a curtsy and went to the door, ushering them out into the cold air.

They hurried back through the graveyard, eyes narrowed and heads lowered against the rising wind.

'My feet are frozen,' Olivia said as they climbed into the carriage. 'I need my moor-walking boots.'

'No, you need to forget about your plotting and stay inside where it is warm. And so do I.'

'Will you find her or shall I ask Mr Mercer to do so?' Olivia asked and he didn't even bother objecting.

'I will find her. But not now. It is time to take you back to Brook Street, it is beginning to rain.'

She glanced out the carriage window and sighed. 'I knew it wouldn't really snow. I wish it had, though. I think London would look much nicer under a layer of snow. Gillingham certainly does.'

'Do you miss it?'

'I miss walking on the moors. I miss my brothers.'

Again there was that undercurrent in her voice, a tension that spoke either of pain or anger or both. It wasn't his concern, but against his better judgement he shifted across the carriage to sit by her.

'It is cold,' he said and she nodded and picked up the edge of the rug covering her legs, rearranging it to cover his as if he was no more than a child. He took her gloved hand and held it, waiting out the wave of pressure in his chest. Under the cover of the blanket he could feel the warmth of her thigh just an inch away from his. For once it wasn't lust that was torturing him at her unconscious acceptance of his proximity, but an equally fierce need to encompass her, hold her to him and tell her everything would be well in the end. Whatever it took to chase away the melancholy tension in the droop of her mouth.

She was so full of life, she should be smiling, laughing, even crying…feeling…not gathered in and preparing herself to be immured again. She deserved more from life. Certainly better than anything he himself could give her. But life didn't deliver on what one deserved.

'I will find Mrs Eldritch. If we are in luck she lives somewhere in London. Don't expect any grand revelations, though.'

'I don't. Thank you, Lucas.'

'And don't thank me, either. I am between… occupations at the moment. This is keeping me out of trouble.'

She turned and smiled at him, but there was still sadness in her eyes and the ache just went deeper.

'You remind me of the Big Bad Bogus Wolf,' she said.

'The what?'

'Have you heard the morality tale of a young girl who foolishly listens to a strange wolf and she and her grandmama end up as his dinner? Well, in Guy's version the grandmama tells the wolf sad tales of how badly she and the girl are treated by the hunters merely because they are women living alone and so instead of eating them, the Big Bad Bogus Wolf befriends them and they protect each other from the hunters and live together in harmony.'

Lucas thought of the wolf statuette that once stood in the entrance hallway at the Mausoleum. When he asked his parents about it, his father told him how wolves were hunted to the last one in England, leaving him to wonder whether that last wolf had any awareness of its species' fate or had merely gone about its solitary business, a little lonelier each day. He liked her brother's version better. He didn't even mind the implied insult.

'Your brother sounds like a good man.'

She pressed her hand to her eyes. 'He is. The very best. He will be angry with me when he discovers what I am doing.'

'Will you tell him?'

'Of course. Eventually. Poor Guy, we tell him everything. Well, almost everything. It is hardly surprising he doesn't wish to marry; he had to care for other people most of his life and he only tasted freedom for the first time when Jack and I came of age.'

Lucas wondered suddenly what Sam was doing. He was due to go to Sinclair Hall before he left for St Petersburg. Except he didn't want to go anywhere; he wanted to stay right here. In a freezing carriage sharing a rug with the most unpredictable female he had ever lusted after.

Chapter Thirteen

'He coming today as well?' Nora asked, placing the newly baked cake on the kitchen table with a grunt of satisfaction at her creation. Nora might not approve of Lucas's presence, but she was certainly outdoing herself since he had become a frequent visitor to Spinner Street, and the tang of citrus wafted throughout the house above the earthier scent of cinnamon.

'He didn't say, but I think so, Nora.'

'First you said we'd only be in this house a time or two, now we've a footman and a maid and him coming when it pleases him…'

'He comes at my request, Nora. He is helping me.'

'Is he? Helping himself more like.'

'He has been a perfect gentleman.'

'Gentlemen don't sit alone with young women with no chaperon noon till night.'

'He leaves well before night, Nora, so do not exaggerate. And though you are not in the room with us, your presence and that of your rolling pin are felt most keenly. I told you he has done nothing that even the most exacting chaperon could take exception to.'

'You don't sound happy about it, Miss Olivia, and that's trouble enough. Men like him are trouble whether they mean to be or not. I've known you before you knew yourself. How much longer will we be?'

'I do not know.'

Nora didn't bother responding and Olivia went to her study and stared at her wall. After a few moments there was a soft knock at the door and her heart kicked, but it was only Jem.

'May I, miss? I have a tray of tea and cake from Mrs Jones and something from his lordship.'

Her heart, already much abused, gave a protesting thud and sank.

'Yes, Jem? I gather he will not be coming today?'

'I don't know about that, miss. He said I was to purchase a foot warmer.'

'A what?'

He looked as surprised as she felt. He placed the tray on the table and went to fetch a wooden box with an ornate handle from the hallway.

'A foot warmer. Surely they have them in Yorkshire, too, miss? To keep feet warm. Here, I've already put in coals from the kitchen.'

'I know what a foot warmer is, but…never mind. Why did he tell you to purchase a foot warmer?'

'His lordship said as you might find it useful.'

'Did he?'

'He did, miss. I'll just put it under the desk, shall I? Oh, and he said that since Nora has taken to my sister, Abby, it is best she come to stay at Spinner Street as well to help Mrs Jones with more than just the dusting.'

'Did he?'

'She's a good girl, don't you worry. Here, you may sit down now, miss, and see how well it will serve.'

Olivia sat as directed, simply because it was easier and more dignified than stamping her foot and demanding to see Lucas immediately so she could make it clear to him…

She tucked her feet against the wooden box. She hadn't realised how chilly the floor was until now. Blast the man.

'The carriage that brought the foot warmer is still outside and Mrs Jones asked if I could accompany her to the drapers. Apparently they delivered the wrong bolt of cloth this afternoon.'

'Cloth? For?'

'I fixed the windows in the back parlour, but

the damp got to the curtains. His lordship said...'
He trailed off at her expression, cleared his throat
and continued. 'I did offer to go myself, but Mrs
Jones says I haven't an eye for colour. Abby is
downstairs with the linen if you need anything,
but if you would rather we wait until you leave
for Brook Street...'

'No, I shall be quite all right, Jem. Go with
Nora.'

'Very well, then. Is there anything else I can
fetch for you, miss?'

*Yes. Your master's head on a platter. Or at least
his presence.*

'No, Jem. This is truly delightful. Do please
convey to Lord Sinclair my supreme gratitude
for all his generous arrangements on my behalf
and inform him I shall of course be defraying all
related costs.'

Jem nodded and grinned. 'In those words,
miss? I don't know if I'll remember them rightly.'

'You may phrase it as you see fit, Jem. So long
as the sentiment is clear.'

'Oh, very clear, miss.'

As Jem left the study, Inky darted inside and
made straight for the foot warmer. After rubbing
against it, the cat curved her lean body around it
and closed her eyes.

Olivia listened to the quiet of the house, her feet absorbing the warmth emanating from the new addition to her study.

'You might think this foot warmer is unadulterated bliss, but it is not so simple, Inky,' she informed the cat purring at her feet. 'Every time I turn my back he has made some new inroad into my life. Soon he will be finding you a companion cat.' Inky blinked and yawned, a flash of sharp teeth and pink tongue, then turned and wrapped herself the other way, tail flicking defiantly. 'I've become a responsibility, Inky. And he is wrapping me in cotton wool so he can walk away from this with impunity.'

'I should have known you would find a way to read some dastardly motive into a foot warmer.'

He hadn't even knocked, she thought, trying to muster up some resentment to stifle the now familiar wave of joy that attended his appearance.

He went to the fire, extending his hands to the flames. 'So. Tell me why you are peeved.'

'I am not peeved,' she replied. 'I am merely wondering how many more additions you plan to make to my household without consulting me.'

He cast a look at her over his shoulder and she shivered, but his answer was matter of fact.

'Nora appears quite content with having Jem

and Abby here to help and they enjoy being of use. There isn't that much to do for all members of the Tubbs clan at the Mausoleum.'

'That is not the point and you know it.'

'You wish me to ask permission next time?'

'There should not be a next time.'

He shrugged and went to sit by the table. Inky unfolded herself, stretched and padded towards Lucas. It was typical that Inky, who almost never regarded anyone other than Nora and, rather grudgingly, Olivia, would show such an appreciation of Lucas though he rarely did more than bestow a casual stroke or scratch. It was precisely as Nora had said. He didn't even mean to seduce, but he did. It was unfair.

She was worse than Inky—at least Inky didn't think of him between strokes.

'At least someone here appreciates me,' Lucas said affectionately as he bent to give Inky her due. 'Shall we start over? Good morning, Miss Silverdale. Good morning, Inky, you pestilential feline.'

'Good morning, Lord Sinclair. Should I draw parallels?'

'I would deem you more terrier than feline. What has Nora supplied today?' he asked as he uncovered the plate on the tray.

'Do you not eat at home?'

'The Mausoleum isn't a home—it is a furnished cavern. But, yes, I did eat though I left some room for Nora's cakes. I am glad she found use for the oranges, this smells wonderful.'

'Are you responsible for the oranges as well?' she demanded.

'Mrs Tubbs, I believe. I have found Mrs Eldritch, by the way.'

She almost bounced out of her chair.

'Have you? Why did you not say so immediately? Where is she?'

'In the back parlour.'

She did bounce out of her chair and promptly sat back again. 'Lucas Sinclair!'

'Olivia Silverdale?'

'Well?' she asked. 'Does she live in London? We must speak to her!'

'We will, tomorrow. There are limits to my depravity and I draw the line at interrogating widows on a Sunday. My rules, remember?'

She squirmed in her chair. 'Elspeth has arranged for us to join a party to the British Museum tomorrow at noon, but I shall tell her...'

'No. As I said, we will keep these two worlds separate and that means you will not change your plans. Besides, I am also otherwise occupied tomorrow morning. I will find some excuse to make an appointment with the widow that won't raise her suspicion, but will ensure she is at home and I will inform you of the place and time tomorrow. Who is in this party to the museum?'

'The Barnstables and the Westerbys, I think. Elspeth mentioned some other names, but I cannot remember.'

His mouth curved, but it was the mocking smile that he wore in public. 'The noose draws tighter. The money in the clubs is on Barnstable, but Westerby is close behind.'

'Are you serious? People are wagering they will offer for me?'

'No, Sir Olive-a-Dale, they are wagering you will accept. There is no doubt they will offer so no one will give odds on that possibility. There are other contenders, like Bolton, but the odds are much longer. There was even some consideration about adding my name to the betting books after our second waltz.'

'This is unbelievable.'

'Apparently your disbelief was shared by the *ton* since no one was willing to take the other side of the bet, so interest dwindled.'

'I meant I cannot believe people wager on such nonsense. Have they nothing better to do?'

He raised a brow. 'Is that a serious question? You ask whether a group of people whose sole purpose in life is to be entertained has something better to do than find new ways to titillate themselves?'

'Oh, dear, do you think Lady Phelps knows anything of this?'

'Of course she does. Your chaperon is no fool and she has your interests at heart.'

'What she believes to be my interests.'

'Don't discount her opinions because they don't march with yours.'

She watched as he poured and placed a cup of tea on the desk by her hand. Concentric rings quivered on the surface of the liquid and she touched the rim of the cup, trying to quiet the sting of tears in her eyes. Her brothers hadn't poured her a cup of tea since she was a child. Giving her tea and a foot warmer and pencils was unfair, especially when she wanted so much more. She expected nothing else, but when he had so casually dismissed the possibility of adding him to the list of her suitors the sting had been sharp and deep.

She took one of his pencils, sliding it between her fingers. They were so finely made it was almost a pity to use them. She should put one aside to remind her for ever of these strange days and the even stranger man who she had trapped into helping her. Perhaps one day she would tell her grandchildren, if she had any: this was given to me by the man who changed my life. She didn't quite know how, but he had.

This was given to me by the man I love.

'What is wrong?' he asked abruptly.

'Nothing is wrong.'

'Liar. Are you upset with me, Lady Phelps, yourself or the world at large?'

'Myself,' she replied, forcing herself to retreat from the topic that could lead nowhere but to more pain. 'I've been making lists of everything I find in the letters, but I'm afraid if we learn nothing from Mrs Eldritch I am out of ideas on how to advance.'

'That is probably because there is nowhere to advance, Olivia. No, don't answer, just give me your latest lists while you return to reading my mother's letters. If you find anything embarrassing, don't tell me.'

She surrendered her lists and opened the Venetian box where she kept his parents' letters.

'You know, you don't have to wait until I am here to read them,' he said, watching her.

'Yes, I do. Eat your cake.' Olivia unfolded the

next letter and concentrated on Lady Sinclair's lovely writing. He was right—it was silly to wait until he was present to read them. It wasn't that she wasn't tempted to continue when he was not there and it wasn't merely that she felt it wasn't right to read them behind his back. She enjoyed his presence as she read about him, layering the tales of his young self on the man.

She didn't know whether to be glad or sorry he refused to read them himself. If he did, he might not allow her to continue. But he *should* read them. They were so full not just of love and longing, but of all the intricacies of life—the frustrations and fears of being a mother who for the first time was away from her husband and coping with three growing children who tested her and each other. There was a beauty in the honesty with which the woman wrote to Lucas's father. Longing was followed by anger which was followed by contrition in a flow that made Olivia's heart ache.

She didn't have Howard's letters, but there were enough clues in Tessa's responses to show he wrote her very different letters than those he addressed to Henry Payton. Whatever he had done in Boston, his letters to Tessa Sinclair appeared to be full of love, interest, admiration and concern for her and his children. But then if he was anything like his son, he would obviously be very adept at manipulating people. There was nothing to show he had not also applied precisely that charm on the women of Boston and the young woman who purportedly had been the cause of the tragic duel.

She picked up another letter, casting a quick glance at Lucas. His concentration reminded her of her brother Carl when he was in the middle of one of his experiments and she wondered what it would do to break his focus on Henry's legal papers. He was ploughing through the stack far too quickly for her peace of mind. Her eyes moved over the sharp lines of his profile and the overly serious curve of his mouth and settled there.

He was so very beautiful it made her heart ache.

Beautiful was utterly the wrong word, but it wasn't. It wasn't merely that he was handsome, that was undeniable, but she could see him now, the man inside the impressive shell. He was deeply flawed, but despite that he was a good man. She never would have believed she might come to that conclusion when this had all begun.

For a moment she indulged the image of going over to him, slipping on to his lap, putting her arms around him and pressing her mouth to the tense line of his lower lip and…and then he put her aside and told her not to be a fool. Even her imagination was unforgiving. She sighed and fixed her attention on the letters, allowing the images raised by Lady Sinclair's writing to draw her in and away.

'What are you laughing at?' His question broke through her concentration.

'I wasn't laughing.'

'Yes, you were.'

'I didn't make a sound!'

'You didn't have to.' He approached the desk, planting his hand on the surface as he leaned over her. She resisted the urge to cover the letter. She didn't want him to find any excuse to take it away.

'Your mother was describing Sam's intervention on behalf of a goose.'

'A goose? Lord, I remember that. It was Landry's, a farmer who lived close by.'

She let him read over her shoulder, breathing in his scent as her body mapped the warmth of his proximity. Was it too much to hope that when she married it would be just like this? This mix of comfort and tingling heat just at a man's presence? She would lean back against his chest, touch the tips of her fingers to the large hand resting on her desk, trace the roughened ridge of his knuckles and the softer sweep of skin between his thumb and forefinger. Place her hand over his...

'Poor Sam, she was miserable for weeks after that,' Lucas said, his voice warm and indulgent, and surprise penetrated her pleasant and painful fog.

'She? I thought... I was certain Sam was a boy!'

'So was she for a while. She wanted to be like Chase and me and was furious when she realised she couldn't. She still has a hard time accepting reality, rather like you. The two of you would probably deal very well together.' He picked up the next page of the letter, his brow rising, and she held out her hand to take it back.

'I am still reading that.'

'There isn't anything here that pertains to this case.'

There was nothing she could say because he was right. She watched his hand reach for the packet of the remaining letters and she clutched her hands in her lap against the need to stop him.

'Please don't take them, not yet.' The words rushed out of her and he hesitated.

'They are just foolish anecdotes.'

She didn't answer or move.

'What on earth do you see in them?' he asked.

'My mother is hardly the most scintillating correspondent. Not even village gossip, just a repetitive recounting of the scope of her very limited life.'

'You have no idea how lucky you are.' She hadn't meant to say that, certainly not with that sulky voice.

'I beg your pardon?'

'Nothing.'

'No, not nothing. If you want these letters, you will have to explain yourself.'

She didn't look up. She was so close to tears and she didn't even know why.

'You will say it is foolish.'

'I doubt it. Even if I do, that hasn't stopped you from telling me what you think thus far. Tell me.'

She resisted the urge for all of ten seconds. When the words came they were rushed, tumbling over themselves like sheep hurrying to pass through a closing gate.

'My parents were naturalists and they travelled around the world and left us in Yorkshire with a succession of wet-nurses, nursemaids, governesses and tutors. The Paytons were our legal guardians while my parents were away, which was sometimes for fifty weeks out of each year. The only letters they wrote were occasional accounts of their adventures. They never asked questions about us or referred to anything we wrote in our letters and eventually we stopped writing. Jack and I invented outrageous tales of our exploits just to see if there was anything that could elicit a response. I once sent a letter saying I was performing in Drury Lane under the name of Shady Nightingale. When they died of a fever in the Dutch Indies I remember Jack being suddenly furious with them now that it was too late. I don't remember feeling much at all. Between the ages of two and fourteen I had seen them for all of what amounts to less than a year.'

She paused, her side aching as if she had been running.

'You are right that the letters probably have nothing to do with discovering what happened to Henry, but they aren't merely foolish stories. *I* might be foolish, but *they* aren't. I know what happened afterwards must have been horribly painful for all of you, but in these letters it all seems so…so full of love.'

He didn't answer. She could hear her breath in the silence and the soft swish of Inky's tail on the floor beneath the desk, rhythmic and soothing.

Lucas went to the sofa, dropping on to it with a thump and linking his hands behind his head. 'I'm doing it again,' he muttered.

'What?'

'Falling into line. Do you know I reached the rank of major in the army?'

'No, I didn't. That didn't appear in the gossip columns. It is very impressive.'

'Is it? None of the skills I acquired commanding hardened soldiers seem to amount to much around here. I win more battles going head to head with my uncle and hardened politicians than I do with you. You might not have been able to control your wayward parents, but I would warrant you are very used to getting precisely what you want from everyone else.'

'Hardly everything.'

'I would damn well hope not. Very well. Keep the letters for now. Just don't… Never mind. Keep them.'

He picked up the document he had been reading, but after a moment he put it down again.

'You are right, we were lucky. Up to a point. Those letters tell you nothing of my parents' life before we left the Sinclair household. Believe me, you wouldn't have liked my mother's voice then. My grandfather was a vicious bastard and my uncle John, the eldest of that mixed brood, was even worse. They didn't dare touch Oswald because…well, they just didn't and no one touched my aunt Celia because she was the jewel in the crown, at least until they sold her to a neighbouring lord for a respectable title, but my father was treated like dirt because he wasn't the spitting image of the Sinful Sinclairs.'

He laughed, but it wasn't a pleasant sound. When he continued his voice was as hard and cold as a diamond.

'His nickname was Howard the Coward. That's what they called him to his face, every day. My grandfather would ask me—where's Howard the Coward hiding today? Up to his tricks with that papist bitch of his? That was what he called my mother because my maternal grandmother was a Catholic. Until they left.'

His eyes fixed on hers with the same taunting humour that she knew now was nothing more than a cloak over his pain.

'Why did your parents leave?'

'When I was ten my uncle, who is no doubt having a grand time in hell, tried to rape my mother while drunk. She beat him off and my father challenged him to a duel, but even drunk my uncle got the better of him. When my father recovered he went to work for his friend Buxted in Boston, hoping we could follow once he was settled there. That never happened, obviously.

Ironically, my grandfather and uncle were killed in a fire in their hunting lodge in Leicestershire so my father should already have been on his way back to England to claim the estate when the duel took place.'

Inky crept up and buffed at his legs, and he stroked her.

'Once I was old enough to think clearly about it I realised his taste of freedom was too much for my father, but he lacked the experience to cope with his late foray into Sinful Sinclairs' antics. So before you go idealising other people's lives I suggest you scrape the surface a little. You can't drape a silk cloak over a tub of offal and expect it not to reek to high heaven.' He rubbed his face and stood. 'Hell. I know it is still early, but I need a drink. Do you want some?'

She joined him by the sideboard, wishing it was acceptable to put her arms around him. Foolish. He wouldn't accept her comfort. She touched his sleeve instead.

'I'm sorry I brought it all back. You probably don't believe me, but I really am. I don't want to hurt more people.'

He handed her a glass. This time he had been more generous. 'I'm not blaming you. No one is forcing me to come here.'

'Then why do you?'

He raised his glass. 'Because I want to bed you.'

By some miracle only a few drops sloshed over the rim of her cup on to the carpet. She took a step back, her heart beating like a fist battering to escape her chest.

'Do you mean you are doing all this just so you can bed me?'

'And if I am?'

'I don't believe you.'

'Why not?'

'Why not? Because I'm not... You cannot possibly... You spent hours alone with me and not done a single thing that would give credit to that statement. Not since that kiss. If this is a joke, it isn't amusing.'

'If it were a joke, it still wouldn't be amusing. Despite my well-deserved reputation I draw the line at seducing virgins. Let us just call this...an exercise in self-restraint. Abstinence is supposed to be good for the soul and mine could use some cleansing. Stop backing up, you'll trip over Inky. I'm not about to pounce on you.'

'I'm not worried you will pounce on me. I think this is another tactic to distract me from the letters and my investigation. You're trying to scare me off.'

His mouth twisted and he put down his glass.

'You are hell on a man's vanity, Olivia. That is my cue to leave.'

'I didn't mean…'

He raised a hand and she fell quiet, her heart thumping painfully, her cheeks stinging with heat.

'I will tell you where and when to meet me tomorrow. Goodbye, Miss Silverdale.'

Chapter Fourteen

'I have been to Greece, my dear Miss Silverdale, and I assure you the marbles are in much better hands here in the museum than back there suffering the ravages of time and weather, not to mention possible pillagers.'

'Apparently they have not survived the ravages of pillagers, Lord Westerby, since they are here in the museum rather than back where they survived some two thousand years of time and weather…'

'Oh, there you are, Olivia,' Elspeth called cheerfully from behind them. 'Do come and look at a lovely urn I have found. I declare I have never seen such exquisite detail; it has given me a marvellous idea for an evening gown. Please excuse us for a few moments, gentlemen.'

Olivia was only too grateful to be drawn away. When they were safely at the other end of the large gallery she sighed.

'I know, I know. It is merely that he is so very certain of himself. I hate it when people don't even wonder if they might be wrong.'

'Dear me. Do you?'

Olivia grinned at Elspeth's tart response. 'I am *not* as opinionated as Lord Westerby.'

'You might not be as opinionated, but you are far more stubborn. Now behave. You have done exemplarily well for the past hour. One more hour and we shall be done. Is it so very painful?'

'No, of course not. I love it here. Could we return, just the two of us, at some point? I would love to see everything without the accompanying lectures as Lord Westerby and Lord Barnstable try to outdo themselves in proving their erudition and improving mine.'

'Of course we may. Now, stroll with me while your temper cools.'

'Where are the Ladies Barnstable and Westerby and the others?'

'Resting their weary feet and gossiping on the benches in the small gallery over there. Another group has wandered off to see the Elgin Marbles again. I think they are happy to leave you to the devices of their sons, but I thought it best to come see how you fared.'

'Thank you for rescuing me. I shall take advantage to seek the withdrawing rooms. You needn't come with me.'

She did not wait for her cousin's response, but hurried away. She needed a moment purely alone so she wandered towards the Townley Gallery. She wanted to see the bust of Ramses without receiving another lecture from her hosts.

'That is the oldest ruse in the book,' a voice purred behind her and she barely had time to turn before a hand closed on her arm, firmly turning her back to face the large reddish-brown carved granite head and torso of the Egyptian pharaoh. 'No, don't turn. This way we are merely two casual viewers of this marvellous specimen of Egyptian history.'

'What ruse?' she asked, her heart hammering so hard at the surprise of Lucas's appearance she was certain it could be heard in the hush of the gallery.

'The visit to the withdrawing room while the matrons doze on the benches and the men pontificate on the importance of pillaging the treasures of other cultures. You should know better than to argue with people like Barnstable and Westerby. You are more likely to convince our rotund Prince to become a Methodist priest than dislodge those barnacles from their sense of superiority.'

'Were you spying again, Lord Sinclair?'

'Hardly. I went by Brook Street to inform you we have a meeting with the widow this afternoon and that you are to have your carriage stop just north of Putney Bridge at five o'clock. When your butler said you were still at the museum I decided to deliver the details of our meeting in person. Something tells me your cousin would not approve of my leaving you another note with details of an assignation which any industrious servant could open.'

'Probably not,' she admitted. 'She is rather sensitive about my dealings.'

'I sympathise. Ramses the Second was an impressive-looking fellow, no?'

He indicated the statue and she forced her attention to the pharaoh.

'He looks far too nice for a man with such a dubious reputation.'

'Most rulers who are remembered tend to have dubious reputations if they are not to leave history indifferent. Having seen some of his larger legacies in Egypt, I can imagine he had to exert quite a bit of force to achieve what he did and made a few enemies into the bargain.'

'You have been to Egypt as well?'

He smiled at the awe in her voice. 'We spent many winters there after we moved to Venice. A cousin of mine is a famous antiquarian. Is Egypt also on your list?'

'Should it be?'

'Certainly. After Venice, though.'

She shook her head at the absurdity. 'Neither is likely, unfortunately.'

He remained silent for a moment, then indicated the bust. 'So. What do you think of the human god and almighty ruler of the two Egypts?'

She turned back to Ramses. 'He looks rather… sweet.'

'Sweet,' he repeated with an edge of disgust.

'Well, he does. The way his mouth curves just a little. It's in the eyes, as well.'

'For heaven's sake, this man was considered an actual god. He ruled one of the most powerful empires ever to exist and built some of the most enduring monuments ever constructed. I doubt he would have achieved that by being *sweet*.'

'But he didn't build them, did he? He must have had scores or hundreds or even thousands of minions to do that. My ancestors didn't personally mine the ores that made us wealthy. They paid others to do it. At least I hope they did.'

'Precisely. And those people weren't persuaded to risk their lives in the mines because your ancestors were sweet.'

'True. If you saw any of their portraits the last word you would associate with them is *sweet—*

they look like they might have set the Vandals and Goths running for their mothers. But Ramses would be different, wouldn't he? If he was regarded as a god, he would want people to consider him a father figure, someone they would want to love and who would love them in turn. I amend my assessment—he looks benevolent, not sweet. Is that more acceptable, my lord? Is that the only reason you came? Have you learnt something new?'

He sighed. 'Do you ever lower it?'

'Lower what?'

'That lance you tout about with you to tilt at windmills. For once put aside your knight's quest and accept this moment is nothing more than what is called "a visit to a museum" and serves no other purpose but to entertain and perhaps to educate. In that light I will show some of my favourite pieces which are luckily at the opposite end of the galleries from the Barnstables and the Westerbys.'

'I must return soon or Elspeth will be concerned.'

'Tell her you became lost.'

She smiled. 'You have an answer for everything, don't you?'

'I could say the same of you. This way…'

Olivia didn't resist as he guided her towards a series of marble statues. With each amazing creation they passed her mind slowed, emptying of concerns. There were beautiful reliefs of men and animals in silvery marble, statues of women draped in marble gowns of exquisite detail that must have taken years to execute, a host of Roman busts with milky-blank eyes and serious expressions, as if blinded and depressed by being frozen in time.

And it was quiet. Not the quiet of Spinner Street or the hush of the moors in winter, but a silence that amplified the images of a hundred worlds and tales that stretched out from each work of anonymous art.

'We don't know their names,' she blurted out.

'I beg your pardon?'

'The people who created these. Can you imagine? Men, and perhaps even women, with such amazing talent and yet we have no memory of who they were. Invisible people.'

'Are they? These men, and perhaps women as you say, were probably valued very highly for their skills at the time. You didn't trust just anyone with your chunks of precious marble and with the decoration of your temples. If you believe in ghosts, imagine what they would feel if they saw people basking in the beauty of their creations thousands of years after their death.'

'Well, I don't believe in ghosts any more than you do. But you are probably right; they were unlikely to qualify as invisible.'

'You often hark back to invisibility though I have no idea why. You are one of the least invisible people I know, Olivia Silverdale.'

'You needn't say it with such exasperation, Lord…'

She stopped, her words fading at the sight of a life-sized statue of a naked man clasping a discus poised before the throw, every muscle sculpted into frozen tension. His left hand was resting on the side of his right knee and was missing a finger and somehow that loss made the whole more magnificent and even reassuring, that the two thousand years that passed this statue by cost it only a finger. Like many of the other statues, it was positioned to provide some cover of modesty, but in this case it failed utterly. She stared in amazement at the full-scale depiction of a beautiful, naked male. She held her breath, half-expecting all that tension to be released in a flinging of the discus and then it would straighten and turn to present itself in all its naked glory.

'I don't understand society in the least,' she said at last, her voice hushed in the silence of the gallery. 'My godmother was once offended because Colin rolled up his sleeves in my presence when we had to rescue Twitch from a bog, yet this is perfectly acceptable? I distinctly saw a matron with two very young women in the previous gallery.'

Lucas inspected the statue, his hand curving over her forearm as if to pull her away, but he didn't.

'No doubt she will shield their eyes as they approach, while she looks her fill, of course. For some reason society is less exacting about its expectations from history than it is from its members; another example of hypocrisy and at least this is one we should be grateful for. This statue is called a discobolus. Do you like it?'

'It is amazing. I wonder if the sculptor's model looked quite so magnificent or whether he, or she, embellished. I could almost believe his skin would be warm if I touched it.'

'Why don't you try? There is no one in the room but us at present. Be daring.'

Be daring.

'You are quite mad.'

'In a sense. Go ahead. It is only stone, after all. He won't bite. Or kick.'

Looking at the sinewy stretch of calf and thigh, the corded tension of the arm and the ridged surface of its chest, she tried to repeat those words. *It is only stone. Be daring.* Any other thoughts would be fanciful.

Be daring.

She shrugged and extended her hand, intending to touch only the cold marble pedestal. For some reason she reached the ankle bone and it was cold and hard as expected, but instead of drawing away, her fingers clung to the marble, trailing upwards. The glassy grain rasped against her finger pads and without warning another image interposed itself into the space between her and the discus thrower. It was a fictitious image because she could not have seen it or anything like it. It was not the statue, but Lucas. Except his skin was warm and as her hand lingered there the heat expanded through her like burgeoning fire, making it hard to breathe. She watched in utter bemusement as her fingers moved up the statue's calf, tracing the bulge of muscle, then up over the thigh...

Lucas's abrupt move caught her off balance. Suddenly she was two steps away from the discus thrower, Lucas's arms pulling her back firmly against him, her body outlined by his, her bottom pressed hard against his thighs. She felt the soft brush of his lips against the side of her neck just below the ribbon securing her bonnet, his arms close around her breasts and waist, holding her for an agonising second that sent all the heat inwards like raging furies closing in on their prey. Then she was free and he was inspecting the melancholy bust of a woman bursting out of a flower.

She stood there as the room reasserted itself, only moving when an elderly couple she had seen earlier drifted in and, as they caught sight of the discus thrower, hurried through rather precipitously.

'You are a menace, Miss Silverdale,' Lucas said without turning.

'*You* told me to touch it,' she replied, as annoyed with him as she was with herself and her unaccountable reaction.

'I said touch it, not make love to the blasted thing. You're worse than Pygmalion; at least he only mooned over his statue. At least I think that's all he did, my Ovid is rusty. Come, you should find your chaperon before I forget again that we are in a public space.'

'Why? What would you do if we weren't?'

He turned and she wondered if indeed some ancient magic had infested her through contact with the statue. She did feel daring, powerful…she could feel the blood moving through her, a surge and ebb of life, heat, need. She didn't want to lower a veil over the powerful sensation of touching him. As frightening as it was, she wanted to cling to it, explore it in her mind. He had felt it, too, at least for that moment. It was obvious in the way he had pulled her to him and in the distance he now set between them, in the grooves of tension bracketing his mouth. His words came back to her. *Because I want to bed you…* Such urges were probably trivial for a rake but right now she wasn't bothered by being one of many. Because right now he desired *her*; she felt that desire like a live flame between them, threatening to burst into a blaze.

'Were you jealous of Mr Discus Thrower?' she murmured, moving closer.

'Olivia…' His voice held a warning, but the unconscious use of her name was an admission in itself—she noticed he employed it when she crossed a line. Most often it was to warn her away from his affairs, but now she could hear a rough scrape under the liquid sound of her name. But then the cynical smile returned, erasing that momentary bridge.

'I have not sunk so far as to be jealous of a lump of stone. You should return to your party before they begin to beat the bushes in search of you...'

'Olivia! I have been looking everywhere for you!' Elspeth hurried towards them, her mouth falling open as she noticed Lucas. 'What on earth is going on here, Olivia Silverdale?'

Olivia's cheeks stung with sudden heat. Thank goodness Elspeth had not seen that brief embrace.

'Nothing, Elspeth. I became lost on the way back and encountered Lord Sinclair.'

Lucas laughed.

'An atrocious liar, Miss Silverdale. I think you had best stick to dignified silence and I will remove myself before you are required to make any further implausible excuses. Good day, Lady Phelps. Five o'clock, Miss Silverdale.'

They watched him leave the gallery and Olivia waited for the inevitable.

'Olivia Silverdale.' Elspeth's voice was barely a hiss. 'We will discuss this later. Right now we must return to the others and you will be as charming as you are capable to Lord Barnstable and Lord Westerby.'

'Elspeth, I did not arrange to meet him here.' That at least was the truth.

'Later. I do not wish to hear his name mentioned until we are home and then perhaps you will explain what madness has possessed you to risk—' Elspeth cut herself off as they caught sight of Lady Barnstable. 'Later. Now smile and prove to me you have not completely lost your mind.'

Olivia smiled and knew that, too, was a lie. Her mind, and heart, and all else were well and truly lost.

Chapter Fifteen

Lucas touched the panes of his study's window. The glass was sharp with cold. Perhaps Olivia's nurse was right and a frost was coming. It would be fitting to his mood.

The mews below was empty and what little colour left by winter's claws was leached away by the darkening clouds. The earth didn't look capable of spring. He was struck by a fear that perhaps this time it wouldn't come. That some action of his would lead to disaster. It very nearly had.

Why the devil had he gone to the museum? Jem could have delivered a note later. He should never have gone to Brook Street himself in the first place. Her quest might be the centre of her existence, but he should not allow it, or her, to become the centre of his.

He knew that and yet as he summoned a hackney on the street outside her home that morning he gave the museum's direction rather than the Mausoleum's. On a whim. A whim which had come close to costing Olivia dearly. He had many sins to his name, but he had never ruined a woman's reputation.

It was one thing to risk the titillated interest of the *ton* by dancing with a debutante in the setting of their ballrooms and quite another to actually embrace her in the staid setting of the museum. If her chaperon had arrived just two moments earlier, he would even now be on his way to Doctors' Commons for a special licence.

A month ago…a week ago that thought would have made his blood run colder than the Baltic in January.

Now…he had no idea any more.

Perhaps he had spent too many years playing Oswald's games, living in a world where one never trusted one's senses and rarely one's mind. Emotions did not even come into play. Outside his lifelong care for a tiny group of people—a few relations and a handful of friends—he had never considered emotions at all.

He wanted to believe his confusion was only the result of what she had dragged out of the graveyard of his stunted emotions along with the memories of his parents and the undeniable warmth of his old life. Once those emotions settled back into their rightful place the others would lose their potency. She would lose her potency.

It was a worrying sign that he didn't want that to be true.

He turned away from the window and wandered downstairs, his boots echoing in the cavernous silence of the absurdly grandiose entrance with its double-arced staircase that had once been lined by paintings of generations of Sinclairs. He had consigned them all to the attic when he returned from the War. It was one thing taking reluctant custody of the Mausoleum, but quite another to have to climb every night to his rooms under the baleful glares of the hordes of Sinclairs before him. Could this monster of a house be redeemed?

Could he?

He reached the entrance hall and looked around, trying to take stock. It had been decades since anyone had entertained here—if one could call the salacious excesses his uncle and grandfather indulged in entertainment. Polite society had certainly not seen the inside of these walls in his lifetime. Unlike some houses this floor was dominated by a ballroom to the left of the stairs and on the right was another room, almost as large, called the Great Hall, which his grandfather used for fencing. As a boy he had spent many hours there being tutored by an Italian master of the art, but he had not entered it since that day over two decades ago. It had just been a lurking entity to the right of the stairs, like an arthritic joint, occasioning a twinge when his mood was low, but something to be ignored and passed over.

Well, it could be ignored no longer.

The enormous room was surprisingly clean, which said a great deal about Mrs Tubbs's pride, even if not much about his own. There was no sign of the fencing strip he remembered, but at the end of the hall under a holland sheet was the unmistakable shape of a rack of fencing foils.

He breathed in and out, sounds and smells returning of that horrific day his uncle had returned, drunk, and tried to force himself on Lucas's mother. His mother's shrieks of fury had drawn them all into the Great Hall, but he remembered most the clash of steel as his father and uncle fought, the smell of sweat and blood. He remembered taking Sam in his arms and pushing Chase outside on to the pavement. That was his last time in this room until today.

He twitched back a sheet covering a side table and picked up the bronze statuette of a standing wolf. So this was where it had been hiding. The Big Bad Bogus Wolf.

'So you have finally decided to brave the dreaded Great Hall. I forgot how big it is.'

Lucas turned with relief. 'Chase! You're back. I was actually thinking it looks smaller than I remembered. Perspective is everything, isn't it?'

'Very true. Do you think those are the same foils Uncle John and Father used that day?' His brother moved towards the rack of foils Lucas was inspecting.

'Probably. How is Sam?'

'Hard at work, surrounded by her quills and paints and notes. She asked when you are coming to the Hall. Strangely we discussed precisely that night. She remembers it though she was just a babe.'

'So do I. She was terrified.'

'She wasn't the only one; I thought Father was dead.'

'Uncle John did as well. That was the only time I've seen him exhibit a commendable emotion, even if it was fear of what Grandfather might do to him.'

'Bastards, both of them, the world is a better place for their absence. Fitting they died in a fire while inebriated. A sound preparation for hell.'

Lucas selected a foil, testing its weight. They were tarnished with age, but the quality was excellent, just a little too heavy at the hilt, though. After a moment Chase spoke.

'I came across Alvanley on Piccadilly.'

'So?'

'So he asked me if you were finally hanging out for a wife. Said he had a niece with a handsome dowry you might want to consider if the leopard was tiring of his spots.'

'Charitable of him.'

'That is what I said. Naturally I was curious what led to that burst of generosity and he enlightened me you had begun to attend society parties and waltz with wealthy heiresses. Or rather one particular heiress. Alvanley is usually highly reliable, but naturally I was sceptical. Until he mentioned the name of the heiress. A Miss Silverdale. What is afoot, Lucas?'

Lucas chose one of the foils and tested its balance. Trust his grandfather to have chosen only the best when it came to weapons.

'You know what is afoot, Chase. I told you before you went to the Hall.'

'Yes, but that does not explain why you would seek her out in public or why Tubbs tells me two of the Tubbs clan were assigned to her household. I can think of three possible explanations, none of which is reassuring.'

Lucas raised the foil. 'Entertain me.'

'Very well. First, you are worried about something she has unearthed and are spying on her. Second, she has uncovered something and is blackmailing you into serving her ends. And third, you are contemplating defusing the threat by seducing her.'

'Interesting that you do not credit Alvanley's theory might be correct.'

'Unlike Alvanley and the rest of the world, I happen to know the condition of your finances and that you have no need to marry an heiress.'

'I might have other reasons to contemplate matrimony.'

'Are you serious? You are toying with me, aren't you? I know you have no wish to populate the earth with Sinclairs any more than I do. Another explanation does present itself.'

'This should be interesting. Enlighten me.'

'Did the jade entrap you? I never thought a woman would get the better of you. The sweet Yorkshire lass must be damn good between the sheets.'

Lucas's hand tightened on the hilt, holding back the urge to act. He turned away, returning the foil to its place as he counted out his anger.

'Damn,' Chase cursed. 'I'm sorry, Luke. I spoke out of turn.'

Lucas shrugged. 'No, you spoke out of experience, but do not do so again. She is not my mistress, she is not blackmailing me and at the moment she has uncovered nothing incriminating and I doubt she will. With any luck a meeting we attend today will mark the end of her quixotic quest and she will be leaving her Spinner Street fantasies behind.'

'For?'

'As long as they do not involve the Sinclair name, that is hardly our concern, is it?'

Perhaps he had not achieved quite the right tone of disinterest. He could feel Chase's gaze on him and he took another foil just to occupy himself. For a moment he was tempted to share his confusion with Chase, except that he was the big brother. It just did not work that way. Besides, what would he say?

I embraced a woman in the middle of the British Museum.

I worry her feet might be cold so I sent her a foot warmer.

The thought of her marrying Colin Payton or Barnstable or Westerby or anyone...

Chase would think him fit for Bedlam and perhaps he was.

'It will be over soon,' he said instead. That at least was true. One way or another it would be over soon because he was approaching the end of his endurance. The intelligent course of action would be to put some distance between himself and his unwitting nemesis so he could consider his options. Calmly.

He returned the foil to the rack. 'I must leave for a few hours, Chase.'

'Miss Silverdale again?'

Lucas didn't bother answering.

Chapter Sixteen

The carriage slowed, but barely stopped before the door opened and Lucas jumped inside. He tossed his hat on to the seat and chafed his gloved hands together. His cheekbones were reddened from the cold and for a moment Olivia could see the boy described in his mother's letters, returning home from an escapade with his brother and sister in the woods behind the house, cold, muddy, happy. Not that he was muddy, but as his eyes met hers with a hint of a smile she could see the remnants of that happiness. It was so different from the first time they had shared a carriage ride together and she wished it was her right to reach out to him, but she sat quietly, her muff hiding the tension in her hands.

'This won't do, Miss Silverdale,' he said after a moment. 'You are five minutes early. You must learn the art of fashionable tardiness.'

Her mouth did not ask her permission to smile. 'I escaped early. Lady Phelps was not happy about my disappearing this afternoon when we are invited to the opera this evening.'

'Ah. Then it was not out of concern that I might freeze my…freeze out there, but because you were being frozen back at Brook Street. I am sorry you are suffering for my transgression. I should not have come to the museum.'

'Nonsense. It is as much my fault. Besides, I do not see why it is different from dancing with me in a ballroom.'

'Don't you? For someone so intelligent you can be singularly obtuse, Olivia. Or perhaps just wilfully so. I may be a rake, but I still have two siblings whose future I would not wish to contaminate any more than I must.'

She frowned, genuinely confused. 'I don't understand.'

'I mean, Olivia, that even I must be willing to accept responsibility for certain transgressions. Do you even realise what would have happened if any member of your party had come into that gallery just then?'

She flushed, more at the memory of that strange moment than at what might have happened. But she did realise. He might walk a fine line on the edge of society, but the only reason he was helping her was to protect the tarnished Sinclair

name. If someone had seen them, he would have
offered the *amende honorable* and she would find
herself betrothed. Again.

To a rake. Again.

To Lucas.

'Once this visit is over I draw the line, Olivia.
There will be no more investigations. You are
old enough and intelligent enough to face the unpleasant reality that life does not offer neat solu-
tions to your problems. You will end your lease in
Spinner Street and tear down your Wall of Conjecture and resume your life as Miss Silverdale.'

'I know you are upset with me, but I will not
allow you to dictate to me, Lord Sinclair.'

'I won't bother trying. But this time I will not be
dissuaded from having a word with your brother
and trust to his superior powers of persuasion.
He might find your recent activities of interest.'

The heat in her cheeks began to sting. 'You
shoot to kill, do you not, Lord Sinclair?'

He looked a little heated himself. 'When it is
necessary, yes. This is no longer a game, Miss
Silverdale.'

'It was never a game. If you are angry at me,
I give you leave to tell me so directly, Lord Sinclair.'

'I am primarily angry at myself, Miss Silverdale. I should know better than to have set down this path in the first place. Once this meeting is over you will do better to focus your efforts on charming your way through London.'

'I have no interest in doing such a thing, even if I were capable.'

He laughed, but it was the harsh dismissive laugh she disliked. 'It does not suit you to be coy. What the devil do you think you have been doing these past weeks?'

'Acting.'

The anger faded. 'It is not all an act. Your admirers would not linger if that was all it was.'

'My admirers would linger next to a week-old ham if it were possessed of my fortune.'

His grin doused the annoyance in his eyes. 'You underestimate yourself. I won't deny your wealth was the draw for people like Lady Barnstable and Lady Westerby, but, believe me, Countess Lieven would not have sponsored you on the strength of your wealth alone. She has no more patience for the likes of the Barnstables and Westerbys than I do. By the way, I think it would be as serious a mistake for you to marry either of them as it would be to marry your tame Colin.'

'I have no intention of marrying Lord Barnstable or Lord Westerby.'

She did not bother mentioning Colin. She had not decided what she should do about Colin and she didn't want to discuss him with Lucas. He did not answer, but though he sat with the same stillness that was so typical of him, she saw his thumb pressing down on the knuckles of his other hand one by one, as if they were prayer beads. She had noticed that habit before, but never realised it for what it was—he was tense and holding himself in check.

'You omitted Payton from that denial. Do you think you would be doing that boy any favours by marrying him?'

'Certainly the favour of removing his and his family's financial concerns for the rest of their lives. Concerns that were precipitated by my actions.'

'You keep saying that. What the devil did you do that would merit a lifetime of misery by shackling yourself to someone wholly unsuited to you?'

'I told you, it was my fault Henry fell out with his employer and could no longer work around Gillingham. If not for me he would not have died, or at least not in such circumstances, and the Paytons would not now be facing financial ruin.'

'Why was it your fault? What did you do?'

'Does it matter? I thought you were not interested in petty details.'

'What did you do, Olivia?'

She looked out the carriage window, her heart thumping, everything rushing back. Agony, humiliation, fury.

'I can uncover it for myself, you know,' he said into the silence and she arched her shoulders back. No doubt he could.

'I was betrothed.' Her voice wavered, so she cleared her throat and continued. 'Three years ago. But I refused to marry him and his family sued me for breach of contract. I settled with them. Bertram's…my betrothed's father Sir Ivo is the local squire and Justice of the Peace in Gillingham and after Henry took my side Sir Ivo ensured no one there would seek Henry's counsel. Henry was already engaged on some briefs in London, but he gradually spent more and more time here. I wanted to recompense Henry for the damage I caused, but he was far too honourable. He said he would have taken more work in London anyway since he enjoyed it a great deal more than what he did in Gillingham, but I think he was placating me. Colin assumed some of Henry's work in the area and I thought it was not so very bad after all. But then he died.' Her lungs felt tight, heavy at the top, but she continued. 'After his death Mr Mercer dealt with the legalities and arrangements in London as a favour to me and he told me everything. But he was not the only one who knew what happened in Henry's leased house. Sir Ivo heard the gossip from a fellow magistrate in London and spread the news throughout Gillingham.'

'Were you forced into the betrothal with this... Bertram?'

'No. I was in love with him.'

The same stillness remained, nothing but the rhythmic motion of his thumb pressing down knuckle by knuckle.

'Then why did you refuse to marry him? What did he do?'

'Why presume he did anything? Perhaps I merely fell out of love and decided he did not suit me?'

'Is that what happened?'

The misery returned, hot and hard, and she pressed the heels of her palms to her eyes. She shook her head. The silence stretched and his hands closed softly on her wrists and drew down her hands. His touch was gentle, but he looked as cold as the first day she had met him.

'What *did* happen, Olivia?'

'I discovered he didn't love me.'

He sat back and nodded, slowly, but his expression didn't shift.

'There is more to it than that.'

'Yes. I think I could have borne that, convinced myself it would come in time, but I heard him…them. We were three best friends—myself, Phoebe and Anne—and we all fell a little in love with Bertram when he returned from London, even Anne though she was already married to a nice young man. I was amazed when Bertram began courting me, but he was so charming he convinced me he truly cared. Then a few days before the wedding I passed the orchard and overhead him and Anne… She was crying. She didn't want him to marry me. She said that it was already horrid betraying John and that she did not even know if the child she was carrying was his or John's and now all of us would be miserable. And then he…he assured her they would continue just as before except that now he would have all the funds he needed.'

She steadied her breathing and continued. 'I needed to think, so for three days I hid and told everyone I was ill. Then I summoned Bertram. I don't know what I expected. He didn't show surprise and certainly not remorse. He said I was making a mountain of a molehill and that no one would believe me because he and Anne would deny it and he would put it about I was suffering from female complaints. He even told me tales of what they did to women who suffered from nervous prostration. Then…then he told me not to worry, he was capable of satisfying two women. He even tried to kiss me, but I couldn't bear it and I told Twitch, my wolfhound, to chase him off. Bertram was furious and later he stormed in with his parents and even my brothers tried to make me explain, but I couldn't. I just said, no, I had changed my mind.'

'Why not tell the truth?'

'Because I knew my brothers would be livid and prove just how wild the Wild Silverdales could be and that could hurt them even more than Bertram. And besides, there was Anne. Do you have any idea what would have happened to her? To the child? Even if everyone believed Bertram, they would still doubt her. It would devastate her life. But that was not the worst of it…'

'Henry Payton was the worst of it.'

'Yes. I was so desperate to have someone hear me and foolishly I told him everything. He took my side but could not defend himself to Sir Ivo because I had sworn him to secrecy. I should have tried to help him, but I was already living with Elspeth and then Jack was killed and I kept my head down and tended to my narrow little world. Then Mercer came with news of Henry's death and I realised none of it would have happened if not for me. So I had Mercer hire a Bow Street Runner and told Elspeth we were coming to London. That is why I am here and that is why I will consider marrying Colin if all else fails.'

Again the future stretched out ahead of her. Long and flat and desolate, like the worst of the moors in winter when they had nothing to offer but muddy patches and faded heather. Soon, all too soon, she would have to abandon her quest because no doubt he was right, she was tilting at windmills.

'Are you still in love with this... Bertram?'

The question surprised her—of all she revealed, surely that was the least relevant?

'No, of course not. Looking back, I doubt I knew what that meant. He was so dashing it was fashionable to sigh over him and for the first time in my life I was an object of envy and not merely for my dowry and so I dare say I wanted it to be true. As painful and humiliating as the truth was, I think I am very, very lucky to have escaped him.'

Her fingers played with the rug covering her legs and she wished Lucas would sit by her again as he had on their return from the vicarage. But he remained where he was, his thumb moving from knuckle to knuckle until the carriage slowed to a halt in front of a modest row of houses.

A young maid ushered them through the small house to a parlour in the back and a woman rose at their entry. She was not the elderly woman Olivia expected, but a handsome woman of forty or fifty years, dressed in a modest grey dress, a tiny terrier peeking behind her skirts. Her eyes focused on Lucas and a frown, almost of recognition, played across her pleasant face.

'You are… Mr Tubbs?'

'No, Mrs Eldritch. My name is Sinclair and this is Miss Silverdale. We were hoping you might assist us with some enquiries we have about a Mr Henry Payton.'

The effect of his words was alarming. The woman did not completely lose consciousness, but she turned ashen, her hand closing on the back of a winged armchair as she wavered. Lucas hurried forward and took hold of her shoulders, but before he could speak she took a couple of harsh breaths and straightened.

'Do you have smelling salts, Olivia?' Lucas

asked as he pressed the widow gently on to the armchair and Olivia shook her head.

'I will fetch the maid.'

'No, please don't,' Mrs Eldritch whispered. 'Please. It was merely a moment's weakness.' The terrier gave an agile leap on to her lap and she gathered it close, her light-blue eyes fixing on Olivia.

'Olivia? Olivia Silverdale? From Gillingham?'

'Are we acquainted?'

'No. I have heard of you, though. From Henry... from Mr Payton. And you...' She turned to Lucas. 'I thought there was something familiar. Are you related to Howard Sinclair?'

'His son. I apologise for the subterfuge in using Mr Tubbs's name, but we... Never mind, may we sit, Mrs Eldritch?' Lucas asked and she blinked, pressing her hand to her forehead.

'I...yes. Do please sit down. Would you care for some refreshment? I haven't...'

Her voice trailed off and she looked at them again as they sat on a faded brown sofa on the other side of the fireplace. 'Why are you here?'

Olivia met the widow's eyes and there was such pain there she could think of nothing to say, her mind suddenly scrambling away from this confrontation as from a snake. It was Lucas who answered.

'I think you know why we are here, Mrs Eldritch.'

Olivia only realised Lucas's ruse when the woman sank her face into her hands, her words muffled.

'May God forgive me, I know I never shall.'

Olivia must have made a movement because Lucas covered her hand with his. He need not have worried, she was too stunned to speak, but she was glad for the warmth of his hand on hers.

'Tell us what happened. All of it, from the very beginning.' His voice was soft, inviting, and the woman gathered the terrier closer, turning her tear-filled eyes on Lucas.

'It is all my fault. It was never meant to go beyond a…a friendship. Henry… Mr Payton and I knew each other years ago. My husband worked for Lord Buxted in Boston and Henry came on business and… He never said anything, he was far too honourable, but I knew. I saw it in his eyes, and he must have seen it in mine. Then…' Her eyes focused on Lucas. 'Then there was that duel. My Septimus and another man, Mr Archer, acted as seconds. I am so dreadfully sorry about your father, Lord Sinclair. He was a most pleasant man, I never understood how…well, that is neither here nor there. After our return to England I did not see Henry until four years ago. He heard of Septimus's death and my difficulties and came to offer assistance.'

'And you became friends.' Lucas supplied and she flushed.

'That was all it was. At the beginning. We truly did not see anything wrong with it.' She glanced at Olivia, her mouth twisting. 'You might ask, if there was nothing wrong with it, why did we meet in secret? But then society has no forgiveness towards friendship between men and women, particularly if the woman is unwed or a widow. But in truth I dare say we were both aware those unspoken feelings were still there despite the passage of years…' She breathed deeply and ploughed on. 'When I told him I must leave London to stay with my sister's family in Ireland he suggested the…change in our relationship. He leased a house and we met when he was in town and then, that day… I came as always, but the next morning… I woke, but he didn't. Somehow I found myself at my brother-in-law's vicarage and told him everything. He was naturally furious, but he assured me there would be no talk.'

'You are not aware of the nature of the arrangements he made?'

'No, he said he had a parishioner who might know of someone who could help. I do not suppose he will speak to me ever again and, anyway, I depart for Cork soon.'

The little terrier shivered in the woman's lap, whining a little as it rearranged its front paws. The woman petted it, cooing softly.

'Perhaps it was a judgement on me—if so, I can never forgive myself. We had become so sanguine about meeting Henry even came here once when I asked him to help me sort through Septimus's papers and see what should be kept and what discarded. It was the first time he met Galahad.'

Olivia blinked. 'Galahad?'

Mrs Eldritch patted the terrier. 'This is Galahad. He took to Henry immediately. It gave me hope that it was not such a terrible thing to be doing. But obviously it was beneath contempt. Do you despise me?'

The words escaped Mrs Eldritch with force, as if pressed out with bellows. Olivia met her gaze, the light-blue eyes of a pretty woman left with very little too early in her life. Olivia searched for some anger or disgust, but found none. Perhaps it would come later, but all she could find was regret for this woman and for Henry.

'No. I think I am glad he had your friendship. He was a good man.'

She hadn't meant to make the woman cry. The terrier whimpered and danced on his mistress's lap, and Olivia went to sit on a narrow chair by the widow. She didn't know what to say so she clasped the woman's hand and stroked the terrier until the weeping stopped.

'I'm so terribly sorry,' Mrs Eldritch said, drying her eyes and cheeks, and Olivia gave the terrier a final pat and began to rise, but she sank down again, avoiding looking at Lucas.

'Did Henry ever discuss Howard Sinclair with you?'

Olivia saw Lucas shift in his chair, but the widow shook her head.

'No, though he knew him through the Buxteds.'

'You heard of the scandal, though?' Olivia prompted.

'Well, naturally I heard the gossip after the duel, though I never quite understood why Septimus and Mr Archer had to leave Boston simply because they acted as seconds. I admit I never thought it of your father, Lord Sinclair, but I was not of his or the Buxteds' social circle and Septimus himself never shared the details of that day; it was not a topic suitable for...' She stopped, clearly aware of the irony of her utterance.

'Never mind, it was merely a thought. Thank you for speaking with us so openly, Mrs Eldritch. Goodbye.'

She rose, but the widow reached out and clasped Olivia's hand, drawing her back down beside her.

'He spoke of you often, you know, Miss Silverdale. That is how I knew your name. I felt he loved you and your brothers quite as much as his own children. He was deeply saddened by what happened with your betrothal, but said it was all for the best.'

'How could it have been?' Olivia burst out. 'He would not have had to seek employment outside Gillingham if it were not for my actions.'

Mrs Eldritch flushed. 'That is not quite correct, Miss Silverdale. I do not wish to evade culpability, nor to spare Henry his share of it. He sought employment in London because of me and when the opportunity arose to take additional cases in London he did so. That decision predated your betrothal. It was quite the opposite—he even delayed taking up that employment because he felt you needed his presence after you ended your betrothal. He told me later how brave he thought you were to assume the burden of guilt. Though he himself felt it was better the world knew that young man for what he was, he felt he was in no position to preach morality. Forgive me, but I envied his affections for all of you. I always wanted children of my own, but God did not bless me. Perhaps if I had had children I would have found it in me never to start down this path. So you see, if anyone bears the burden of guilt for his death it is I. Sometimes I believe his heart would not have given out if it had not such a burden of guilt to bear. I do not ask you to forgive me, but please do not hate Henry for this. I could not forgive myself for that.'

'I am not here to judge Henry or you, merely to understand. Henry was like a father to me and I will always love him, whatever mistakes he made. If there is anything I can do for you, you can always write to me care of Mr Mercer at Thirty-Two Threadneedle Street.'

Lucas took her arm and they walked out into the cold.

'I told the carriage to wait for us further up. It would draw too much attention standing on her doorstep.'

She nodded and tucked her hands deeper into

her muff as they walked. The cold air stung her cheeks and when he took her arm, pulling her a little towards him on the narrow pavement, she had to resist the urge to go further, lean utterly into the comfort of his warmth.

The carriage was moving slowly along the edge of the common at the end of the road, but the horses came over at a trot when the driver spotted them. Inside Lucas took a rug and placed it over her legs almost cautiously, as if she was an invalid. Then he turned to look out of the window, his arms crossed over his chest, his mouth a stern line.

'You were very kind to her,' he said, breaking the silence.

'It was not her fault.'

'Most people would disagree. She would have accepted whatever accusation you chose to level at her.'

She shivered. She wanted to sink into his kindness, his approval. Sink into him. But she couldn't. She hated that he thought her ruthless, but to have him praise the other side of that coin was unbearable.

'Don't make it a virtue in me. Please. I was not being kind. It was all I could do not to throw my arms around her and thank her. A voice inside me kept saying—it is not my fault. You heard what she said. It was not truly my fault he was in London. I need not bear that burden, because she is carrying it. So it isn't kindness, it is relief. I have not redeemed Henry, but she has redeemed me and it is terrible of me to feel relief, but I cannot help it. I thought I began this to relieve Mary's pain, but it was mostly to assuage my guilt. Oh, God.'

It struck her then, a wave of such grief, it felt like it would drag her to her knees.

'Henry doesn't exist any longer. Jack doesn't exist any longer. I will never ever hear them again and they will never hear me. They just…aren't. I can't bear it.'

His arm was warm and hard around her shoulder as he moved her towards him. She realised she was still shivering. It was a strange shivering, like a wet dog, or jelly—mindless, purposeless shivering. It wasn't hers, really, this shivering, because her body felt suddenly foreign to her, small and emptied and hollow…

She felt the scrape of her ribbon just under her ear as he pulled it loose. Her hair snagged on her bonnet, but he pulled it free and tucked it behind her ear, his knuckles resting for a moment on the pulse galloping beneath her jawline. Then he spoke her name against her hair, slowly moving his mouth back and forth on the sensitive skin just at the crest of her temple. It was soothing, she recognised that, some little arm inside her reached out like a monkey in a cage, scared but beckoned by a treat. The rest of her stayed in the dark where it was safe.

A terrible fear struck her—she might be disappearing, too, just like them. She had to stop this. Take action. She could not slip back into those years in Guilford. She straightened, dislodging his arm.

'We still haven't answered the question regarding his comments about your father—'

'It ends here, Olivia!'

His voice was reasonable but brutal in its finality and she wanted to raise her hands and stop it before the inevitable happened. She had tried to prepare herself, but to no avail.

'But surely you can see this doesn't negate...'

He was the one to raise his hands and she stopped again.

'It ends here. We will not be chasing down any more vicars and widows, not even so you can grieve properly. You will have to find another way. You are no fool and you know your lists aren't the real world, Olivia. What we saw today is the real world—people trying to go about their lives and mostly muddling through and making mistakes and living with them.'

He breathed in, turning towards the window. 'This is not what I want to deal with; I deal with men who know what they are doing and the prices they might pay for it. *That* is fair play. This...this was the equivalent of stepping on a kitten's tail or penning a wolf in with a herd of sheep. There are repercussions to every step we take. For all we know even by visiting Mrs Eldritch in that little town where everyone is watching everyone we have done harm. This is the last time we play Bow Street Runner.'

'But what am I to tell Mrs Payton?'

'Good God, you tell her nothing, of course.'

She knew it made no sense to argue with him, but she wanted, no, she *needed* him to understand. 'How can I allow her to continue to believe Henry died in the arms of a courtesan? You don't understand—that lie made Henry a stranger to his family. They not only lost the man they loved, but they lost him doubly. The way he died put everything into question. Not just their future, but their past, who *they* are. So, if I could, just a little, bring back who he was to them, even with his flaws, but who he really was, someone they recognise, then that *is* something. I don't want to hurt anyone along the way, but I can't help wanting to repay them.'

'Do you honestly believe this will be an improvement on Marcia Pendle? Would you prefer to learn your husband had a relationship with a woman he had a *tendre* for twenty years ago and was meeting in secret for years? That he cared for so deeply he changed his life to be close to her? I doubt your godmother will find any solace in this revelation.'

He was right again. The truth might, to a certain extent, relieve her own guilt and salvage her perception of Henry, but Mary would be devastated to learn it had not been merely a carnal connection, but something that transcended what she shared with her husband of almost thirty years. Lucas was right and the decent thing to do was stop before she caused even more damage. Her dreams of saving Henry were just that, dreams. And not just Henry—she would have to abandon her desire to be a saviour for Lucas. She was no knight in shining armour. Sir Olive-a-Dale couldn't even save herself and shouldn't that come first?

'It is over, Olivia. Do you understand?'

'I understand.'

I understand you are done with me and I don't want you to leave. I know you will eventually, but not today.

At least the shivering had stopped, but the darkness inside her was spreading. She sat, helpless and scared. Not of him, but of the distance forming between them. He was right to hate what they were doing and right to disdain her. Now he would leave, not like last time when he had been afraid of what he would find in himself, but because he disliked what he saw in both of them. She could not remedy that.

Her eyes devoured his profile, its hard lines and the tension in his mouth. His words were calm, but now that he was no longer touching her she saw the tell-tale movement of his thumb over his knuckles. He was not calm.

As if to confirm her realisation he shoved a hand through his hair, breathing deeply. She sat still, but her own hands prickled with the need to touch him, to relieve some of the barely leashed pressure inside him. She clasped them tight against the need to touch the hair he had disarranged. She remembered how it felt from the time he had kissed her, sliding against the soft skin between her fingers, silky and then feathering away against her palm. She shivered a little and before she could think she moved closer and took his hand, holding it between hers.

'Careful, Olivia. I've expended my last ounce of nobility for the day. Don't test me.' His voice was flat, but hers shook a little as she answered.

'I do not know what else to do.'

He breathed in again and she waited for him to draw away, but his other hand closed over hers, larger and warmer, but still rigid.

'You don't have to do anything.'

Yes, I do. I must stop you from leaving. I'm not ready yet. I never will be.

'You must have had a very peculiar upbringing,' he added, shaking his head.

'Don't make excuses for me.'

He pulled his hand from between hers and she tried not to cling to it, but he merely stripped off her glove and gently turned her hand palm up in his. He traced the stain of ink along her index finger and heat hissed up her arm, so vivid she thought she could hear it. The hairs on her arm rose in its path, all the way to her nape, reaching round to close a fist around her throat. It was all she could do not to visibly press her legs together as the flush of heat spread there as well.

'Are your fingers ever free of ink?' he asked. It was an innocent question, but either her internal fire or the rough gravel in his voice warped it in her mind. Still, she tried to answer it as given.

'Rarely. Only when I run out of ink and must rely solely on pencils.'

'You are no Lady Macbeth, scrubbing away at your sins.'

'You're wrong if you think I do any of this lightly, or that I don't feel any guilt about my actions,' she said, a little too fiercely, trying to pull away, but his hands closed hard around hers, gentling immediately as her resistance faded.

'Oh, I know you do. I don't think you do anything lightly. It would be far better if you did. But you are a very uncompromising person, Olivia. You want the world to work, but you have low expectations that it will do so of its own accord. Which means it must have worked very ill indeed for you in the past. I am glad this gives you some modicum of relief, but as you have just discovered it can fix nothing. Not in any meaningful way. You will have to face that you are only clinging to this so you can escape deciding where to go next. You're running, Olivia. That's all this is.'

'Well, then so are you. Isn't that what your whole life is about?'

'The difference between us is that I embrace

my running, I don't try to put a grand name on it like seeking the truth or justice or redemption or any of that rot.'

'You are right. I will stop.'

She untangled her hands, raising his left hand to her cheek, turning her mouth to the warmth of his palm. She acted without thought, but the moment his skin brushed across her lips it took her over and she froze, everything froze.

'Olivia. I warned you.' His voice was low and tense, but as she felt the curtain fall on her time with him she knew she could not allow him to leave without at least... She tested it again, mapping his palm with her mouth, her breath coming back to warm her lips, slip between them and out again. At the juncture between his fingers she felt a mirrored shiver just at the same spot on her own hand, could almost see him bend his head to press his mouth just there. To taste... So she did, her tongue dipping into that V, gathering the sensation of the roughened pad at the base of his finger, then the sudden soft satin of the sheltered skin, the tension of the muscles and sinews...every surface had a different flavour of his taste. Musk, earth, life, something as familiar as her childhood, but wholly new.

'Olivia. Hell and damnation, we cannot do this.

Listen to me!' His voice was harsh, but he did not pull away, his fingers even curved, slid over her lips, sending a shiver of heat and anticipation through her.

'I'm listening,' she whispered. And she was, to the tension in his hands, his voice. She felt it in every inch of her body, telling her to act, to grasp this, take what she wanted, to give... Without thought she caught the tip of his finger between her teeth and pressed gently. He groaned, dragging his hand away only to grasp her shoulders.

'Listen to me. We cannot do this, not here, not now.'

'Then where and when? You said this is the end for you. There is no other time.'

She didn't know if it was courage or fear that made her act. She just knew she didn't want him to leave. It no longer had to do with Henry Payton or his father. It was him. It was terrifying. She turned, half-rising on one knee, grabbed the lapel of his coat and canted her head to press her lips to his.

He caught her arms above her elbows, as if to steady her or push her away, but she felt his indrawn breath against her mouth, a tremor in the convulsive tightening of his fingers on her arms. His lips were firm, but so smooth, like gliding over polished, sun-warmed marble. She pulled at them gently with her own, testing their pliancy, reminding herself how wonderful his kiss had been, how it lingered and taunted and plagued her since. It was impossible to consider he might leave. That this was, as he had said, the end.

Don't think, Olivia. Think, and he'll leave.

Her hands slid up, caught on the transition between his waistcoat and the linen cravat, softer and warm, her fingers just curving over the edge, poised to touch him. She softened her mouth against his and without conscious thought her tongue touched his upper lip, tasting and testing. Her fingers sought him, too, rose to curve over his neck, to his nape, everything inside her expanding, warming.

'Olivia.' His voice was harsh, a warning, but one of his hands rose to curve about her nape as well and in the tension she felt the tearing forces inside him and for the first time she believed he meant what he said.

He wanted her.

'Yes,' she whispered, leaning against him, forcing him to take her weight. His hand captured her waist, tugging her against him in time for her to feel the shudder run through him, the faint protesting groan that she felt more than heard. Her body arched into the hard planes of his body, sliding her fingers deeper into his hair, catching on the vulnerable indentation at his nape, threading through the silky midnight of his hair, much softer even than it looked. Everything about him was extremes, confusing, alluring, devastating.

'Kiss me again, Lucas.'

Finally he obeyed. He kissed her deeply, transforming her tentative caresses into a plundering exploration, his lips burning hers, his hands moving over her body as if plotting its downfall inch by agonised inch. Her skin itched and burned to be bared to his touch and, when his hands slid under her behind, raising her so that she straddled his legs, she arced her back, trying to move closer, to mould herself against him. He drew her lower lip between his, suckling it, his teeth scraping at it, his breath cooling and heating the pulsing, sensitised flesh. She moaned, her fingers pressing deeper into the warmth of his hair, begging for more.

The swaying of the carriage around a corner rode her body hard against his and his fingers dug deep into her buttocks, his hips rising to press the hard muscles against where she was burning to feel him. She might be inexperienced, but she knew what that ridge of heat pressing against her meant. She remembered Bertram moving against her, grinding his hips against her thigh, his face red and heated. She had not liked it much then, it felt unconnected to her dreams of soft kisses, but now that sign of desire shot flame through her, focused all her senses on it—she wanted to feel it again, she wanted to bare it against her, feel it, possess it…him…

She moaned, shifting and spreading her legs as much as her skirts allowed, trying to fit him against her. He groaned, too, grasping her hips and raising her off him, but he did not let her go, pulling her on to his lap and holding her close, his face buried in her hair.

'This is madness. We are in a carriage, for heaven's sake.'

He sounded tortured and it finally penetrated enough for her to really look at him. His eyes were as dark as midnight and her heart stumbled as she absorbed the devastating mix of desire and contrition in them and the tension in the grooves that bracketed his mouth. She didn't doubt he wanted to bed her, but then he had probably wanted to bed dozens of women. He was probably well trained at walking away from temptation when necessary. All too soon this would be over and she would be left with…what?

She leaned her head against his shoulder, her hand against his chest. 'Will you come to Spinner Street with me, Lucas? I shall think of something to tell Elspeth. Just for tonight. I'm not asking for anything else.'

'You have no idea *what* you are asking for.'

'Well, that is rather the point, isn't it? I wish to find out and I would like you to show me. It is unfair of you to start this and then just leave me wondering. It is like being alight from within, like a hot air balloon, filling and rising, but not knowing which way to steer. I can't imagine not knowing now. You must have had hundreds of women, why not one more?'

He cupped her face and leaned his forehead against hers.

'That is a gross exaggeration, but even then you aren't one more woman, Olivia. You are not someone I wish to trifle with. You deserve better than…this. One day you will fall in love with some young man. Not your proper and boring Colin, but someone and then you might regret…'

She pulled away and sat back in her corner. Her fingers shook as she refastened her pelisse.

'Just tell me you don't wish to, Lucas. Don't start spouting mawkish nonsense you don't even believe in.'

'Olivia…'

'No! I'm tired of being lectured about what is right for me and good for me. First my brothers and the Paytons and Elspeth and now you. I didn't take it from them so I certainly shan't from you. I decide what is right for me. You want to go, then go!'

'Olivia, listen to me!'

'No!'

He knocked on the carriage wall and it slowed.

'Perhaps not here and not now, but you will listen to me and we will settle this once and for all. Tomorrow at noon I will come to Brook Street. Be there.' He did not wait for her response, but opened the carriage door and disappeared into the gloom.

Chapter Seventeen

It was a familiar sensation.

In the rumble of noise that filled Haymarket Theatre Royal she looked up from her seat in Lady Westerby's box and met Lucas's gaze. He was standing in one of the scarlet-draped boxes opposite theirs with a group she recognised from Countess Lieven's ball, several of whom wore elaborate foreign uniforms glittering with decorations and silk sashes. This time he bowed very slightly, but did not smile, and she was not certain that was an improvement on being utterly snubbed.

She turned her attention to Lord Westerby, trying to subdue the burn of confused pain and resentment and confusion plaguing her. Lord Westerby was explaining the lyrics of the upcoming opera and she smiled and uttered something empty and tried to stop her hands from toying with her fan and her mind from acting like a barrel filled with billiard balls rolling down a hill—thoughts crashing and bouncing off each other and not one of them settling.

What was she to do now? She could not return to Gillingham. And for all her brave words about marrying Colin, the mere thought of the enormity of that sacrifice sent her heart into a panic of rejection.

Lucas, blast him, was right. She could not do it. Before she had met him...perhaps. Then, her naïve little mind regarded marriage to Colin as form of legal friendship that would be as much a haven for her as for Colin and the Paytons. Now the idea struck her as absurd, even cruel—both she and Colin deserved better. She would find some other means of helping the Paytons; she was nothing if not resourceful. Henry had made his choices and now she must make hers.

If only she knew what they were.

She refused to return to Guilford, either. The most logical choice would be to remain in London with Elspeth and enter society wholeheartedly. Have men dance attendance on her and vie for her favours and her fortune.

Her eyes moved of their own volition back to the box opposite. A tall woman stood very close to Lucas, her fingertips almost brushing his sleeve and her hair so pale it shimmered like silver in the light of the enormous chandeliers suspended above the pits. His profile was a sharp sketch against the curtains drawn away from the door to the box and he was smiling at the beauty. Black sludge threatened to overwhelm Olivia and she looked away, only to meet the gaze of a man looking directly at her. He might easily have been Lucas's twin, but he wore his hair longer and she thought his eyes were lighter. This must be his brother Chase, she thought. As their eyes met he smiled, a wholehearted, direct grin. She was so surprised she smiled back.

'Olivia. I am afraid I dropped my fan,' Elspeth said sharply. 'Do help me find it.'

'Here you are, Cousin Elspeth.'

As she handed her cousin the fan, Elspeth's voice hissed in her ear.

'Flirting with one Sinclair is bad enough, flirting with two of them is the definition of madness.'

'Hush, the opera is beginning.' Olivia admonished with much more composure than she felt.

The cover of music did not bring the calm she hoped for, because nothing had prepared Olivia for Mozart. It was nothing like the modest concerts she had so loved in Gillingham. Those were like peeking into a window of a lovely home while being jostled by crowds on the pavement. This was to step into a new world and leave everything behind that was wrong. The future, her fears, her failures—all faded. She forgot all about proper posture and the edict of not displaying eagerness or emotion in society, and utterly ignored her host's attempt to flirt with her under the cover of the music. She leaned forward and gave herself wholly to the magic. If she could have climbed out of the Westerbys' box and curled up at the foot of the stage and wrapped herself in the music and begged them never to stop she would have. For the first time in weeks she felt simply, uncomplicatedly alive.

In love.

She did not look at Lucas, but she felt him. The music cleared the world of everything but him and the deep core of need inside her that reached out to him. It made everything so simple. It spoke for her, a love letter without words: it said everything she felt and would never say.

When the music faded she felt a physical ache in her chest, her eyes burning. She might not know where to go next, but she knew she wanted to feel.

Again without thought her eyes turned to the box opposite. Lucas was in the back of the box, cast in the dark shadow of the drape, but she could make out the sharply carved planes of his face, could feel the tension in every line of his tall, lean frame. The bustling theatre pit was nothing more than an empty chasm between them, echoing with everything that was inside her and wanted out.

Then people were rising and she had no choice but to become Miss Silverdale again.

'You did not tell me the half of it, Luke. That is one hot burning ember.'

'What the devil are you talking about?' Lucas asked, scanning the crowd in the foyer.

'Miss Silverdale. She was listening to the music as if her very life depended on it.'

Lucas had noticed that, too, unfortunately. He had noticed little else during the opera. The music became a backdrop for the living painting of her taut, entranced figure as she all but absorbed the theatre with the sheer force of her pleasure. By the end of the act he felt exhausted, defeated and elated all at the same time.

'And here I thought we came to the Opera so you can keep tabs on Razumov,' Chase continued. 'I did not know this was not business, but pleasure. But on the surface it looks like Westerby is in the lead. The odds will shorten on him in the clubs after this show of primacy,' Chase remarked.

'Wasted money. She won't marry him.'

'Shall I put my money on Barnstable, then?'

Lucas finally turned to his brother. 'You wager one penny with her name attached to it and I will break your perfect nose.'

Chase grinned. 'I consider it one of my most notable skills that I always know how to get an honest answer out of the impenetrable Lucas Sinclair. Ah, there is my future sister-in-law. I think I shall introduce myself.'

'Chase!'

'Then you introduce me. Come, don't be shy.'

'Damn you.'

'Yes, yes, later.'

Lucas was not surprised by the succession of surprise and antagonism on Lady Phelps's face as he and Chase approached their party, nor by the subtle stiffening of the Westerbys. He would very much have preferred not to face Olivia right now, but it was better than allowing Chase to go alone which he undoubtedly would. Besides, if there must be gossip, and unfortunately there must, introducing his brother to her might give it a different direction. Perhaps. He had no idea what was about to happen since this was utterly new territory for him. But whatever qualms had survived that carriage ride, watching her listen to Mozart had made it eminently clear there would be no Westerby, no Barnstable and no blasted nice boy Colin in Olivia's life. There would be only him.

It was as simple as that.

Olivia's smile was tentative as they approached, but her eyes were still bright with pleasure. He read contrition there, too, and the same wariness as when they met in public, as if unsure who she was and who he was outside her little world of Spinner Street. He was no longer certain himself.

The two parties acknowledged each other like warring factions discussing a ceasefire and then he turned to Olivia.

'May I introduce my brother, Mr Sinclair. Charles, you have not met Lady Phelps and Miss Silverdale, I believe.'

'I would certainly have remembered,' his brother said softly as he bowed. Lucas did not bother listening to the rest of his brother's flirtatious nonsense or even to Olivia's laughing responses. He watched her face, warm with life and interest, the flashing of gold shards in the green of her eyes as they narrowed in amusement, her gloved hands moving as she spoke, as full of life as the rest of her. She needed an expanse to live, to experience. He would build an opera house just for her so he could watch her come alive to the music. Then he would...

He was well and truly lost.

'Do you agree, Lucas?'

'What?'

'La Fenice is an experience every music lover should indulge in.' Chase said. 'It isn't only the music. The interior is like stepping into a music box.'

Lucas couldn't help smiling at the growing awe on Olivia's face as Chase described the famous Venetian music hall.

'Did you often attend concerts there?' she asked, envy dripping from her voice.

'Our mother adored music so we had little choice,' Lucas replied. 'Twice a week during the performance season she would herd us into formation and make us sit through hours of Corelli and Scarlatti.'

'Ah, yes,' Lady Westerby interjected. 'I remember Lady Sinclair's family was Venetian. Such a fine, noble people, though I never did understand quite why they chose to build a city on the water. Only think of the damp. I'm afraid my constitution would suffer.'

Chase nodded. 'You are quite right, Lady West-erby. Venice would definitely not agree with you. Best remain on English soil.'

'I don't know about that,' Lord Westerby said with a smile at Olivia, a flush rising on his pale skin as he spoke. 'I would not mind seeing the ruins and all that. Palminter just took his new wife to Greece, didn't he?'

Usually Lucas would have felt a little sorry for such an awkward and revealing statement, but even knowing this pleasant but slightly dense young man had no chance of attaching Olivia, he could not prevent a surge of jealous resentment that he would even be contemplating it.

'Could find some nice pieces for the family pile in Derbyshire,' Westerby added hopefully and Lady Westerby took the torch and began expanding in some detail about the Westerby estates. Olivia listened politely, smiled and once again settled into Miss Silverdale. He could almost see how she meticulously tucked away the remnants of the Wild Silverdales, like strands of escaped hair tamed into her fashionable coiffure. He didn't want her gathering herself in. He wanted her as she was in Spinner Street, with the plain muslin gowns, her fingers stained with ink and her hair slipping its pins. He wanted her frowning at her lists and pinning them on walls while he made himself useful keeping her feet warm and her body satisfied and her mind occupied with living.

He wanted her.

'Should we not depart, Lady Westerby?' Lady Phelps interrupted.

'You are not staying for the second act?' Lucas asked.

'I am afraid not, Lord Sinclair. We are promised at Lady Hazelmere's soirée, are we not, Lady Westerby?'

'And there is the Countess beckoning to us, Lucas,' Chase added. 'It was a pleasure to make your acquaintance, Lady Phelps, Miss Silverdale. I look forward to furthering it.'

Chase waited until they were safely out of earshot before addressing Lucas. 'That set the cat among the pigeons. You did notice we were being watched most avidly from all corners? I wonder what will be made of you introducing your brother to Miss Silverdale.'

'I did not introduce you; you were the one to force that meeting.'

'They don't know that. What the world saw was one Sinful Sinclair presenting himself and his brother most properly to a gently nurtured young woman. Poor Westerby, I think he is actually fond of her, it isn't just the money,' Chase said as they approached their box.

'His mother will find him some other heiress to moon over.'

'No doubt. So. What are you planning to do about it?'

'I am certainly not planning to discuss it here with you.'

'Point taken. Too crowded. Do you know what I found fascinating?'

Lucas sighed. 'No, what?'

'I have no idea what she was really thinking. Too many layers. She lets slip the society layer and you see all that curiosity and laughter, but then that is still a layer and there is something behind it and for all I can tell behind that as well. It's like a hall of mirrors; keeps you guessing which is the real one, you know?'

Unfortunately he did.

'I know she likes me. I just don't know why,' Chase continued.

'How do you know she likes you?'

'I just do. I like her, too. What's more important, I think Sam will. Any chance you can convince her to marry you before I must depart for the Continent? I want to see the spectacle with my own eyes. Will you do it at the Hall chapel?'

'Chase.'

'Sorry. I should not be enjoying your downfall so much, should I? I'm glad I agreed to attend tonight. Until I saw your face this evening I had no idea how serious it was.'

'Chase!'

'There. I'm done. It will be interesting to see how quickly the betting books take a turn tonight.'

Chapter Eighteen

Whenever Lucas thought he had reached the bottom rung of this particular ladder of discomfiture, something proved him wrong.

Attaching himself to the Lievens when they mentioned they were expected to make a stop of courtesy at Lady Hazelmere's was sinking low indeed. He should have gone with Chase to Cribb's Parlour or returned home, but neither the noise of Cribb's or the silence of the Mausoleum were bearable at the moment.

In any case, he should not be here at another perfectly innocuous, utterly boring and wholly respectable entertainment. Unlike Olivia's hapless suitors, he had the advantage of knowing precisely where and when he would have her to himself and precisely what he intended to do when he did. However unsuitable he might be as a bridegroom to a proper young woman, he was a damn sight better for her than any of her current prospects and, however properly she was acting under Lady Phelps's aegis at the moment, she was as unsuited to becoming a London socialite as Sam. He could no longer consider whether it was a mistake. He could no longer consider much of anything that didn't involve Olivia and it was time to accept this was not merely a fleeting, if particularly brutal, attack of lust or some peculiar effect brought about by the unearthing of his past.

The only problem, which Chase had identified with his usual brutal acumen, was that he did not know what she was thinking.

He did not doubt she desired him—she had been entrancingly open about that in the carriage, almost disastrously so. He also didn't doubt that she liked him, that she enjoyed being with him, even that she trusted him, up to a point. But though he was glad for all of these he did not know whether they amounted to what he wanted from her. He couldn't even label it love because there was surely something wrong in depending on an emotion that only two weeks ago he would have sworn either didn't exist or, if it did, was beyond his ability to experience. If it was love that had him firmly by the heart and mind and groin, it was a damnable affliction and he understood better why the poets thrashed on so much about it.

More than anything he wanted to be as necessary for her as she was to him. And he had not the faintest idea if he was.

So here he was, standing in Lady Hazelmere's impressive ballroom with its three massive chandeliers casting the light of hundreds of candles on a world he had done his best to avoid, searching the sea of fashionable silks and plumes and flitting fans for the warm brown curls of the most impossible woman of his acquaintance, his heart thudding as if one of the Tsar's Cossack assassins had a knife held to the base of his spine.

'The Silverdale chit? The odds are shortening on Westerby, but now that Sinclair looks like he might want to get riveted, I wouldn't waste my blunt. I heard he came to speak with her at the Opera. Introduced his brother to her, no less.'

Lucas stiffened but did not turn at the murmurs coming from behind an arrangement of potted palms to his left that marked the entrance to the card rooms.

'Did he? That is daring of him, given his brother is just as much a rake as he. Fascinating, but I have just heard an even more titillating titbit, my dear Forsyth. Apparently, the heiress baulks at the fence.' The voice of Rodney Paget, ageing roué and gossip, was unmistakable. Lucas carefully moved closer.

'What's that, Paget? You have a tip for us?' Forsyth asked eagerly.

'I do, indeed. A most interesting piece of news fresh from the countryside. I came across Hamilton at Stultz today. Poor fellow just returned from a conjugal visit to his wife somewhere in the wild north and we were discussing the latest wagers at Watier's. Apparently, the Silverdale heiress is from the town next to his. Got a name for her, too. The Gillingham Jilt.' He paused for effect and there was a shuffling as his audience drew closer. 'Left some poor sap at the altar and the fellow's family sued her for breach of promise and won.'

'What's this about the Silverdale heiress, Paget?'

'It's true. Engaged to some fellow, but gave him his marching orders the day before the ceremony. Her family sent her away to a cousin to wait out the scandal. Looks like they think it's safe to let her out and about. Pity. For an heiress she's an appealing little thing. Still, can't be too cautious. Someone should tell Barnstable to shy off before he's burnt.'

'And Westerby. Blast. I'd best go change my wager. If the girl's a flirt…'

'Stands to reason. I've seen her casting out lures to Sinclair. Aiming high. Perhaps she thinks he's done up and needs her blunt.'

'I doubt it, took two ponies off me at White's

the other week. Still… Can't see her daring to jilt *him*.'

'He won't have her. Likely he's bored.'

'More likely feeling his age. Even the Sinclairs need heirs. If this is true and she is a deep player, I just might take a visit to Watier's. The Gillingham Jilt, eh? Has a nice ring to it. Might make the Almack tabbies reconsider that voucher, eh? How long d'you think before that makes the rounds?'

Lucas did not wait to hear their assessment on the speed of London gossip. If Hamilton had spouted his news at his tailor's that afternoon, it was a miracle they had not heard it at the opera.

He spotted Lady Phelps before he did Olivia. She sat very straight beside Lady Barnstable, but by the rigid smile stretched across her face it was obvious London gossip was already working its magic. He didn't bother with subterfuge but walked directly to her.

'Lady Phelps, may I have a word?'

She directed a harried look at Lady Barnstable, but as that lady was staring ahead determinedly, she rose, a little flushed.

'Where is Miss Silverdale?'

'Dancing with Sir Frederick Whitby, but…'

'I presume you have heard that Hamilton has brought back news from Yorkshire?'

'Yes. I...'

'Has Miss Silverdale?'

Her shoulders sagged. 'No, I do not think so. I heard this very instant. Mrs Fitzherbert very kindly came seeking enlightenment.'

'I am sure. I heard Paget spreading the word near the card room. Well, we shall just have to nip this in the bud.'

'Paget! It will be all over London by tomorrow. How can it possibly be nipped in the bud?'

'Quite easily. It is one thing to enjoy themselves at the expense of Miss Silverdale, it is quite another to do so at the expense of my betrothed. The only way to combat gossip is through fear or the promise of an even juicier titbit. We will exercise both tactics.'

Her eyes widened. 'Lord Sinclair...'

'Just keep her with you when she returns from the dance. I will have a word with Paget and then return.'

He did not wait for her response, but sought out one source of the problem. 'Paget. A word.'

'Sinclair. It is quite marvellous how you have begun to come among us mortals. Are the rumours true? Are you indeed hanging out for a wife?'

'No. I have already found one. Which is why

I want a word with you. I hear you are enjoying yourself at her expense. I don't like that.'

The fashionable smirk disappeared, as did the colour in his florid cheeks. 'I... I did not...'

'Yes, you did. If I hear from anyone that you repeated that charming epithet you spouted earlier, I will have my friends come demanding their vowels from you. That will be the opening salvo; you will relish what follows even less. So keep a leash on your tongue and on that of your feckless friends. Enjoy the rest of your evening.'

He strode back to Lady Phelps, making a quick stop by the orchestra on his way. Olivia was already there, standing with her back to him, but she turned as he approached. Her eyes were large, more green than gold, and very bruised.

'Have you told her?' he asked Lady Phelps, but his eyes held Olivia's.

'I had to, but...'

'I will explain the rest. That is our cue, Miss Silverdale. Come.'

He held out his arm and she placed her hand on it almost blindly.

'Where?'

'To the dance floor, of course. They are striking up a waltz.'

'But...it was to be a country dance.'

'Was it? I think the orchestra leader found the waltz to be a more lucrative choice.'

'But why?'

'We are celebrating.'

'I don't think I want to celebrate gossip at my expense. Do you honestly think dancing a third waltz with you will overshadow the satisfying ring of the Gillingham Jilt? What a pity I hailed from Gillingham. I don't think there are many towns in England who would have worked quite so satisfactorily with the word jilt. I always knew this was a mistake. I told Elspeth it was. There is no point in staying in London in any case.'

Her eyes dipped, but he had seen the burn of tears there and pulled her a little closer, stroking her palm through her glove. A faint pink flush rose over her pale cheekbones, but she kept her eyes downcast.

'It was not a mistake; this is merely *ton*nish nonsense and will blow over in less time than it took to surface. It is best to face it head on. It is not in your nature to run.'

'Yes, it is. I ran last time.'

'That was different. You are different—you are the woman who has forced Sinful Sinclair to become her lowly page and run errands for her.'

The edges of her mouth wavered upwards. 'That was easier than it might appear.'

'Do not tell anyone, please. I would rather not have the moniker Sinful Sinclair exchanged for Spineless Sinclair.'

'Perhaps Sensitive Sinclair?'

'You are enjoying my downfall far too avidly, Olivia.'

Her lips curved, her eyes crinkling at the corners, the golden lights sparkling, and some of his tension began to dissipate. Whatever happened, of all the options he could imagine for her future, marrying him was at least not the worst and he would do everything in his power to make it the best. If she ever forgave him for what he was about to do. No, what he had already done.

'I have something important to tell you, Olivia. I need you to listen to me and not react for a moment. Can you do that? No, don't frown. Just tell me whether or not you feel you can take another shock. It is best done out in the open, but we can go find a quiet corner if you prefer.'

'Has something happened to my brothers or the Paytons?'

'No, it has nothing to do with them. This is about us.'

'Us?'

'Us. The gossip is about to die a swift death because in good Venetian tradition I have just made it clear to a key member of the worst of our society that if he insults you, he insults me. It is not quite a declaration, but will no doubt be interpreted as such.'

'Are you mad?'

Yes.

'No, I am very sane. This has been on my mind for a while now, but I thought it best to wait until we resolved our other problem as best we could before I broached this topic with you. Which I hereby do.'

'Lucas, you cannot possibly be serious. You cannot offer for a woman simply to scotch gossip.'

'It is done all the time, but...'

'Perhaps, but this gossip has nothing to do with you.'

'If it affects you, it affects me. Now that your quest is put to rest, I want to make that very clear. It was my intention to offer to you before this nonsense surfaced, but I thought it best to wait so we could become better acquainted, or at least acquainted in more normal surroundings. But I won't stand by and have that bottom-feeding catfish make hay at your expense. Before you tell me again that I am mad, I want you to consider the benefits of my proposal. Aside from the prospect of travelling to Egypt and Venice and exploring the ramifications of kissing, I believe we are compatible on quite a few levels. I have the utmost respect for your intelligence and your integrity and I think you have a fair assessment of my faults, which is always useful in a spouse. I know you need freedom and space and I am willing to accommodate those needs...' He took a breath, aware that he was beginning to babble as she remained silent, her eyes still wide with shock. Any more of this and he would start begging. The music was beginning to wind down and he was beginning to feel desperate.

'Olivia. Say something. Other than "you are mad".'

'Lucas, you mustn't do this. This is wrong. This is what you told me not to do with Colin. You do not wish to be married. Right now I have become a...a responsibility, but even if you wish to...to, well, I cannot say it aloud here, but even then you should not... Oh, what have you done?'

He kept moving in the dance, a little stiffly now, gathering his resolution against the pain.

'It is done, Olivia. Just...trust me this time.'

'Of course I trust you, Lucas. But I cannot

allow you to make such a sacrifice. And merely for some mean-spirited gossip. I would have weathered it.'

He glanced towards Lady Phelps who sat watching them anxiously. He wondered what was to be done now. Though it was too late for that.

'It is done, Olivia. Is it so very terrible?'

Her hand tightened on his. 'Of course it is not in the least terrible, Lucas. I think… If you really do not mind… Did you mean what you said? Were you truly thinking of offering for me before this?'

The tightening knot in his chest eased a little. 'I would not lie about that. Does that mean you will marry me?'

'You *are* mad, but, yes.' The words came out in a rush and she stopped and smiled at him, her cheeks flushed in the light of the candles. '*I* must be mad, too. Yes, Lucas, I would like to marry you.'

The music died and for a moment he stood there, his hand still on her waist, his other hand clasping hers, fighting the puerile urge to hug her to him, reassure himself with her warmth that he had not taken terrible advantage of the situation. Instead he pressed her hand on to his arm and led her towards Lady Phelps.

Chapter Nineteen

Olivia jumped to her feet at the sound of the knocker, her heart leaping from trot to gallop as it had again and again throughout the very, very long night.

It was only ten o'clock and they had arranged for Lucas to arrive at one o'clock, but perhaps his night had been as fitful as hers and he had come earlier. She hoped so.

She had slept at some point, but woken at dawn with an abruptness usually reserved for cries of 'fire' and every time she remembered the events of the previous evening, alternating waves of hot and cold rushed through her, a mix of joy and terror. Of all the eventual scenarios she had explored for her future, she had not contemplated marriage to Lucas, but now that it was done she could hardly imagine it could be otherwise.

The thought that he might actually *wish* to marry her was peculiar, but somehow she did not doubt it. It was not that he loved her as she obviously loved him, but she could see why if he must marry eventually he would consider her a suitable wife, despite his frequent frustration with her wilfulness. They shared affection, humour, and then there was the attraction he had never hidden from her. Perhaps even in time all this would coalesce into the same intense need she felt for him, but even if it did not, she would count herself lucky to have secured as much.

She felt guilty to feel so happy when she had failed the Paytons so utterly, but perhaps together they would find a way to help them.

Together.

She squirmed again at the rush of joyful warmth and the rising thud of her heart as the drawing-room door opened.

'Mr Mercer, Miss Silverdale,' Pottle announced.

'Mr Mercer. You are here early!' Olivia said brightly to hide her disappointment. 'It is not yet turned ten o'clock. This cannot bode well. Have you gambled away my three per cents on the "Change"?'

Mercer, never blessed with a sense of humour and certainly not about matters financial, frowned.

'Certainly not, Miss Silverdale. This is not about our affairs, but I nevertheless felt it to be pressing enough to call upon you myself at the earliest opportunity, given your recent interests.

I received a letter addressed for you from one Mrs Eldritch, I—'

'What? Where is it?' Olivia demanded impetuously. She snatched the sealed letter Mr Mercer extracted from his leather case. It was brief, but it brought her to her feet.

'Oh! I must send for Lucas... No, this may be nothing and I cannot keep summoning him... Mr Mercer, I must beg your company for an hour or so. Can you escort me to Putney?'

'Putney? But why?'

'I cannot say. Have Pottle hail a cab and I shall fetch my bonnet and cloak and join you in a moment.'

It was one o'clock and snowing by the time Mercer helped Olivia descend from the cab at Brook Street. Heavy, slushy flakes gathered in the cracks on the pavement and she hurried inside when Pottle opened the door.

'His Lordship's here, miss. He arrived soon after you left, miss. He is...he is a trifle concerned, miss. We did not know where you went, you see,' Pottle said in a hushed and hurried voice as she struggled to untangle the damp ribbons of her bonnet, his expression giving her a second's warning before the door to the drawing room opened.

She didn't respond to the warning in Pottle's voice or to the expression on Lucas's face, focusing on removing her bonnet and cloak and unbuttoning her pelisse. As Pottle removed the cloak from her grasp and melted away she considered requesting a pot of tea, but thought better of it. Refreshments would have to wait until she weathered this storm. Lucas stood aside, indicating the drawing room, his face blank, but the intensity of his fury obvious, so she entered without a word.

'Three hours,' he said as he closed the door behind him. 'Pottle said you left over three hours ago without a word to anyone. May I be so bold as to ask where in *hell* you have been for three hours in the middle of a snowstorm?'

'It is hardly a storm, more a flurry.'

'Olivia!'

'There was no need to worry. I was not alone. Mr Mercer was with me.'

'That is no answer. You cannot just—'

'Mrs Eldritch sent me a letter care of Mr Mercer.' She rushed ahead. 'I probably should have left a note explaining, but I didn't think and I was certain we would be back well before noon. But then there was an overturned cart and our cab could not pass and we had to walk for miles to find another and then on the bridge...'

'I don't give a damn about overturned carts and bridges! You should have consulted with me before haring off on one of your misbegotten missions. Those were the blasted rules!'

'Lucas, calm yourself. There is no need for histrionics.'

'Olivia, if you knew how calm I am compared to what I might justifiably be at the moment, you would be very careful about issuing cautions. For all we knew Mercer ran off with you.'

The thought of Mr Mercer abducting her was so amusing she almost burst out laughing.

'Mr Mercer has a specific vest for every day of the week and his housekeeper only varies his menu on Sundays. The thought of abducting me would likely send him into an apoplexy; he would as soon be devoured by wild boars. It was quite the other way around, I abducted him.'

'Don't split hairs with me, Olivia! I have permitted you to pursue these enquiries—'

'Permitted! May I remind you that you have no authority over me, Lucas! It is not for you to permit or otherwise. Now, do please stop trying to play the outraged guardian and listen to me.'

'Hell, I am not playing! You will not go anywhere again without a proper escort and without informing someone of your destination. Am I clear?'

'Crystal. But you are outside your authority, my lord...'

He didn't wait for her response, but stalked out, the door bouncing against the wall. She remained standing there, a whole maelstrom of unsettled emotions battling for prominence. She had been so excited to see him and tell him what she discovered. It never occurred to her that her absence might even be noticed, let alone have an impact on anyone. Still, he had no right...

She was still standing there when Lady Phelps entered with uncharacteristic diffidence.

'You should at the very least have taken me along, Olivia.'

'I didn't want to force you out in this horrid weather, Elspeth. There was no need. Mr Mercer is perfectly proper...'

'Lord Sinclair doesn't know that. I told him you would be safe enough, but he is a worrier. He even went to Mercer's offices in Threadneedle Street, but that was more than an hour ago and time kept ticking... Well, he didn't say a word, but I tell you I could feel it in the walls. Men do not know how to worry properly, it is all shoved down and then the only way it can get out is in a burst of hot air. He is like my husband in that respect. I believe he thought you were so unnerved by the events at the ball, you convinced Mr Mercer to take you home to your brothers. He even sent his servants to the major posting houses to see if anyone by Mr Mercer's description hired a post chaise.'

Olivia groaned. 'I never thought...'

'I know you didn't, Olivia, and that is part of the problem. I told him you would not run and I think part of him believed me, but the other part must have worried even more, because we were out of ideas and he thought perhaps something terrible happened. I may not have approved of him, but, whatever his reputation and his past, I can see he takes his responsibility towards you very seriously. You are no longer on your own.'

'Enough, Elspeth. I know you are right. I must apologise.'

'Not right now. Give him time...'

'No, it is best he fume at me rather than at the walls. There is something important I must say to him and it cannot wait. I am sorry to force you out into this weather, Elspeth, but we must go to Sinclair House.'

Chapter Twenty

'Go away.' Lucas snarled at the knock on his study door. Tubbs knew better than to knock twice. And Oswald or Chase never bothered knocking anyway.

A second knock sounded and he glared at the blank wood. 'I said go—'

Olivia slipped in and closed the door behind her, a hesitant smile curving her lips. For a moment his rumbling fury just stepped aside, making way for the same slap of gratitude, relief and heat that had struck him when she returned to Brook Street earlier. It left him shaky and even angrier.

She stayed for a moment with her back to the door before moving forward, the firelight warming the soft ivory and bronze tones of her skirts and accentuating the curves that plagued his dreams at night.

He had felt ten times a fool for haring over to Brook Street at an ungodly hour in the morning simply to reassure himself she had not changed her mind about the betrothal. Discovering she was gone was bad enough, but with each passing minute his mind embroidered and embellished and his heart ripped itself to shreds and shoved the remains into a dark, dank hole in the ground. It had only been three hours, but it felt infinitely longer and more desperate than any siege he had ever lived through.

He wanted to hate her for reducing him to this state, but as she moved towards the desk his simmering anger migrated south, settling into the familiar thudding tattoo of desire and the deeper pull of need. What remained of his anger turned against his own fallibility.

He could tell by the excitement in her eyes that she was intent on enlightening him about whatever she uncovered that morning. She didn't even realise the effect she had on him. She could send him into a panic, into a fury and into thorough lustful frustration without even distracting herself from her latest foray into conjecture and conspiracy.

'I realise you are burning with the need to share your latest findings with me, Olivia, and I'm impressed you managed to subvert Tubbs sufficiently that he did not even see fit to inform me of your arrival, but I think it is best we postpone all discussions until later. I am not in the mood.'

'I didn't come about Mrs Eldritch, Lucas. I came to apologise. It is no excuse, but I honestly never thought anyone would notice my absence, let alone worry. It was dreadful of me.'

'Let me guess. Lady Phelps lectured you.'

She clasped her hands in front of her and smiled ruefully. 'She did, but she merely hurried the process along. I would have realised you were right eventually. Next time I promise I shall consult with you first.'

He felt peculiarly raw, like the skin after a scab had fallen off—tender and wary. He should put the whole episode behind him, but the memory of those hours when his mind leapt from one scenario to another, alternating between anger and sheer terror, wouldn't be put aside.

When she had walked in to the Brook Street hallway, her cheeks red from the cold and her eyes bright with excitement, he had been slammed simultaneously by such joy and such fury he had strangled them both into cold submission. He still didn't know what to do with either of them. Desire he could, and would, deal with. The moment the legal seal was placed on their union he would indulge every lustful dream she roused in him and then he would finally have some peace from that aggravating frustration. Everything else...he just didn't want it. It was all too much at the extremes. He might deal in risky situations, but not when it came to his internal dealings with himself. There he very much liked remaining in the stable centre. But today her disappearance had made it clear just how far outside that centre he had ventured.

Damn her.

'Just don't do it again,' he said sternly, shifting some papers on his desk. 'I gather from your meek demeanour Lady Elspeth came here with you?'

'Of course. She is waiting downstairs in an enormous drawing room. This place is gargantuan.'

'You should not keep her waiting, then. I will come by later this evening and we can speak then.'

'Won't you at least kiss me goodbye?'

The heat that swept through him was so swift and so extreme he leaned his hands on the desk, resisting the urge to leap over it and put a categorical end to this torture.

'Even in light of our betrothal you shouldn't be in this room alone with me.'

'Just on my cheek and I shall leave. To show me you forgive me.'

She stopped at the corner of the desk and tilted

her face, just touching her cheekbone with her finger. His muscles contracted in outrage that he was even contemplating abstention. He could already feel the softness of her skin, warm and fragrant against his mouth. That close her curls would tickle his own cheek, feathery and begging to be let loose, her scent would wrap around him, taking him back to their carriage ride when she had leaned in to him, promising everything.

Just hours ago he had been convinced she had disappeared, that, as mad as it felt, he might never see her again and it had been terrifying. Now she expected him to kiss her on the cheek like a little girl and let her go...

Hell.

'If I kiss you, it won't be on the cheek.'

She dropped her finger and faced him, her eyes narrowing in a look that was both new to him and very old. 'Oh, good.'

'Blast you, Olivia.'

She took his hand from where it rested on the desk, raising it to cup her cheek. 'Just a kiss, Lucas.'

Lucas closed his eyes, trying to gather the resolution to pull away, but that was worse. It was absurd that such a tame caress should make the act of pulling his hand away feel a Promethean task.

It was like watching a glass drop from across the room, fascinated by its descent towards destruction, knowing there was nothing one could do to stop the inevitable. Some sane corner knew there was something he could still do. Something as simple as take back ownership of his hand. *His* hand.

'Olivia.' He tried again, but her name was a torture in itself. It ran through him like water, warm and supple, like her body would be under his when he had her on her back, naked.

She shifted her head, sliding her mouth along his palm, her breath warm and moist on his skin.

'I told you last time, we cannot do this. Listen to me!'

'I'm listening,' she murmured, her breath heating the tips of his fingers.

'We cannot do this, not here, not now.'

She looked up from her demolishment of his defences, her eyes a fierce gold-shot green.

'I dressed to seduce you. I told Elspeth we had important matters to discuss and I shall be a while. Must I leave?'

'God help me, yes. Now.'

'Will you come to Brook Street later so I can tell you what I found?'

'Yes.'

'Then just one kiss and I will leave.'

She didn't even give him time to consider, her hands wound themselves about his neck and into his hair and with a whimper of need and pleasure she opened her mouth under his.

'One kiss… One simple, tiny kiss… Please, Lucas…'

His papers whispered on to the floor as he raised her on to the desk. She gave a small gasp as he moved between her legs, pulling her against him, but she merely adjusted herself, slid her fingers deeper into his hair, warm and supple against his scalp as she pulled herself towards him and he felt a wave of something sharp and hard and unfamiliar rip through him as he took possession of her mouth, answering her seeking lips, delivering his soul.

Olivia had come with the intent to appease, but she was more than happy to find herself being kissed into oblivion while seated on the edge of a desk. He wasn't gentle this time, and she didn't want him to be. She felt everything she saw in his eyes—the tension, the fear, the frustration, the unspoken yearning for something that might forever be beyond what she could give him. It burned and flared in every sweep of his mouth on hers, the heated caress of his tongue and lips and the way his hands and body moved against hers. She was alive and alight with need, her nerves crackling and sparking wherever they touched, making her squirm and whimper, trying to get closer, to merge their bodies as well as their mouths. But just when her hands tried to push their way under his shirt he caught them in a hard clasp, his mouth softening until he was only resting his lips against hers.

When he raised his head she remained with her eyes closed for a moment, listening to the music of her body vibrating from the tips of her toes to her scalp. This was no fading of a waltz or siren's call of an opera, this was the rising of wind before the storm and not just for her. She could almost hear the same thrum of determined need in Lucas as he remained frozen. So when he spoke she hardly regarded his words.

'You've had your kiss. Now go home.'

He was right, she should go, but she couldn't imagine moving from precisely where she was or breaking any point of contact with him. This was home.

The realisation struck her as powerfully as the desire he so easily loosed in her. This was home. She had lost her home because of Bertram, but that had merely opened her to find another home, one of her own choosing, with Lucas.

She didn't say the words aloud because it was far, far too early. But inside her she said them— *You are my home, Lucas Sinclair, and I am yours.*

She was not quite ready to leave it.

'As a rake you are a sad disappointment, Lord Sinclair. It is quite unfair that it always falls to me to seduce you when you have all the experience,' she admonished, running her hand over the soft lawn of his shirt. She liked the topography of his chest, it felt as powerful as he looked, and her fingers tingled at the rasp of hair beneath the white cotton. She wanted to see him, feel him, burrow into him…

'Olivia…'

She rushed on. 'I told Elspeth this was very important and that it was the last time I would ask of her to leave me alone with a man while I was under her protection. I left her downstairs with Miss Austen's novel and Jem promised to keep her plied with tea. Please don't make all my machinations go to waste.'

He laughed, leaning his forehead against hers, his hand curving over her cheek and his thumb pressing against her lips. 'Relentless.'

She parted her lips against the rough pad of his

thumb, instinctively touching it with the tip of her tongue. The groan that shook through him at that simple gesture thrilled through every muscle in her body, her legs clamping tight against his, her fingers burrowing deeper into his hair.

'Please don't send me away, Lucas, not yet. Just a while longer...' She spoke the words against his hand, tasting and testing its texture.

'Livvy...'

'I like that. No one calls me Livvy.'

'That's because you're mine. But you cannot stay, Livvy. After what happened today I'm not feeling strong enough to be noble. I don't want to be. I want to take you right here on my desk and devil take the consequences. So have pity on my conscience and leave. I will come see you this evening in Brook Street, I promise...oh, hell!'

She wasn't quite sure how her hands separated his shirt from his pantaloons, but the sensation of her hands skimming up his ribs was clearly as cataclysmic for him as for her, or perhaps his recoil was merely because her hands were cool on the warm silk of his skin. She tried to draw them away, hampered by the shirt.

'Are my hands cold?' she asked contritely and he groaned again and caught them, pressing them against his skin.

'No, they are deadly. Don't stop. I surrender.'

Every question she had he answered, in words or gestures. He took off his shirt at her demand and helped her with her dress, and every time he baulked and tried to convince her to stop, she used everything he was teaching her to overcome his qualms. She didn't want to stop any more than he did. She didn't want to wait on conventions. She wanted to show her trust in the most elemental way, and if she did not yet dare tell him she loved him, she could show him.

'I want you as naked as Mr Discus Thrower. I was thinking of you when I touched him...'

'I felt you were touching me. If we had been alone...' Lucas groaned, his hands fisting in her chemise, bunching it around her hips. She slid forward, pressing against the surging bulge in his pantaloons, her breath stopping as the pulsing heat between her legs rose to a high pitch and spread out in waves, making her skin tingle and her breasts ache. Every inch of her wanted to feel him, to brush against him. She wanted nothing next to her skin but him. The cotton fabric of her chemise felt rough and foreign on her skin. She wanted it off.

'We are alone now,' she whispered. 'What did you want to do to me?'

'Not to you, *with* you. This…this is what I wanted to do.'

She had no idea how she found herself spread out on the sofa by the fireplace, Lucas leaning over her, his mouth exploring her body, the stubble on his jaw a tantalising contrast to the silk sweep of his mouth and the damp caress of his tongue, finding and searing places she had never imagined could be so crucial to her.

Her own hands were exploring, touching where they could reach, mapping him as he mapped her. At some point she dragged his mouth to hers and he kissed her deeply, his body half-covering hers with heat and textures she wanted to explore and learn one by one. She felt her legs part, trying to making room for his and for the pressing heat between them, and his breathing quickened. But the kiss gentled suddenly and he raised his head. She wrapped her arms around him, afraid he might stop.

'Lucas, please don't stop.'

He shifted between her legs, his weight on his forearm, his eyes coal black and burning.

'I won't. Not before I show you what you are capable of, Livvy. I won't go any further, but whatever the law says, from today you are mine. If you have any doubts you want to be saddled with me for the rest of your life, tell me now.'

'Not one, Lucas.'

He touched his lips gently to hers, then to her cheek, his free hand continuing its teasing exploration downwards. She tried not to tense as it feathered over the curls at the juncture of her thighs. It was a single soft stroke that mapped a part of her that was as mysterious to her as the world she had entered when she met Lucas. She did not know why this was different from everything that preceded it. Even though she knew the heavy pulse just below where he was touching had to be reached somehow, it scared her.

'I won't hurt you, sweetheart. This is what the music is about. Do you trust me?'

His mouth brushed hers, the words like the touch of sunlight—caressing, warm, soothing. But though his fingers stroked just as lightly over the downy curls between her thighs, they were an agony, making her thighs shiver with tension. Surely nothing should feel so intense, so necessary and so foreign, and not threaten to destroy her.

'Do you trust me?' he repeated.

'Yes.'

He kissed one corner of her mouth and then the other. 'Then let yourself feel.'

His fingers slid against skin that felt like the surface of the water, shimmering and warm. Then he was at the core of her heat and she shuddered and her hips rose without thought, seeking, begging.

'I can't help it… Lucas!'

His mouth caught hers with a growl and he kissed her deeply. A hungry, plundering kiss that turned the fire below into a blaze and suddenly she was shaking with anticipation, trying to meet the rhythm of his fingers and body as they tossed her higher and higher.

His mouth moved downwards as well, over her exposed breast, brushing and coaxing and finally closing hot and moist over its crest just as the tension below reached a peak. She wanted to throw him from her, pull him on top of her, something, anything but remain in that unbearable, beautiful storm. She heard her own voice, but not hers, begging, urging and finally melting into a moan that caught in her throat. She clung to him, her fingers pressed hard into his back and nape as bolt after bolt of lightning slashed through her, harsh, brilliant, shattering her again and again into nothing but light and heat.

When her body gathered again, it was into

liquid warmth, as if she had moved one by one through all the elements, from the insubstantiality of air to the crude needs of earth to the all-consuming blaze of fire and finally to warm, embracing water. She rocked there for a while, warm and safe, cocooned against him. Slowly waking.

He had shifted and now she lay half on him, his arms holding her, and they stayed there, her cheek pressed against his chest, her body warm and heavy but utterly alert, as if the whole of creation was flowing outwards from her centre.

She could feel the empty house that would be filled, the cold, snow-covered streets that would thaw and fill with life, the winter that would bud and flower—all spreading out from the love inside her. She smiled at the foolish vanity of the sensation, but held it to her as well. This was love and this was her lover. Hers to care for and cherish and do everything she could to make him happy and free. She turned her head lightly to touch her lips to the hollow of his shoulder, sealing her vow. She never, ever wanted to move. Or only so they could do this again.

'That was…wonderful,' she whispered against his bare shoulder, revelling in the wonderful scent and feel of him. 'I thought it would hurt.'

His chest rose and fell with a shuddering breath. He shifted and she felt his mouth brush over her curls, the words whispering warmth over her scalp.

'Sweetheart, I'm afraid it might yet, but not today, though the way I feel now I don't know if I will survive the night. I just wanted you to know a little of what awaits you.'

She finally opened her eyes, pushing away a little to look up at him, realising that though she was utterly naked he was still in his pantaloons. It took her a while to even notice the tension in the arms that held her. He shifted finally, raising her so that she was on his lap, his arms around her. She tried to move so she could see him, but he hugged her to him in a convulsive movement. Then he laughed a little and brushed his lips over her temple.

'Relentless Livvy. Please don't squirm, sweetheart. My control has its limits.'

'What do you mean? Didn't you…?'

He shook his head and shifted her to the sofa as he retrieved her chemise from the carpet, followed by her dress and stays. She meekly allowed him to dress her as if he were Nora and not a very large, half-naked man, far more beautiful than the discobolus, perspiration glistening on the slopes and rises of his muscled torso and back.

'Didn't you want to?' she asked at last, the question forcing its way out. His hands jerked in the act of easing her tangled hair out from the back of her dress and the involuntary tug stung her scalp before he released her.

His hands settled on her shoulders, turning her. There was still the same midnight-black fire in his eyes as he took her hand and pressed it to the bulge she had felt at the juncture of his legs and she felt the hard, pulsing heat through the fabric. At the contact of her hand his eyes half-closed, a muscle leaping by the tense groove in his cheek.

'I would give my soul right now to be inside you, Livvy. Which is precisely why I won't.'

'That makes no sense. If you want—'

He smiled and pressed a swift kiss to her mouth before moving away to slip on his shirt.

'This is not the time to practise your relentlessness on me, Livvy. In my present state I do not have to make sense, I only have to cling to the cliff face of my good intentions and try not to slip. Now put on your bonnet and go to Lady Phelps. I can't imagine why she has not barged in on us yet, but I don't want to tempt the fates any more than we have. Up with you.'

'But I must speak with you about what Mrs Eldritch told me. I should have insisted on doing that first. Shall I tell her...?'

'No. What happened here was...beautiful. I don't want to mar it by discussing history and scandals, no matter what you have discovered. You will go home and rest and I will come this evening and we will discuss whatever you must tell me calmly and in the proper setting.'

The knock on the door was timid and the voice that spoke through the door even more so.

'My lord, Lady Phelps begs to inform you that the carriage has arrived and she and Miss Silverdale must be on their way.'

Lucas strode towards the door and Olivia lowered her hand before she could try to stop him. In any case, he was right. She wanted to stay enveloped in the magic of the moment and discussing the letter, no matter how important, would always overshadow the memory of the pleasure he had shown her and the care he had taken of her.

'She is ready, Tubbs. You may see her downstairs.' He turned to Olivia, drawing her towards the door. 'I will come by this evening, I promise. Try to stay out of trouble until then.'

He gave her a little shove out into the corridor and closed the door behind her.

Chapter Twenty-One

'Good evening. Miss Silverdale.'

'Good evening, Lord Sinclair. It is good of you to call,' Olivia replied as Pottle closed the door, leaving them alone in the drawing room. He moved so that the table was between them. He had come to Brook Street determined to treat what had occurred in his study just hours earlier with the lightest of touches and to keep as much physical distance between them as possible so his already fragile self-control would not have to take another beating. He was not at all certain he would succeed—the memory of her pleasure was seared into his mind and he felt greedy with the need to take her there again, even at the cost of deepening his suffering.

'Are you well?' His voice was stiff, which was fitting.

'Yes.' Her own voice was husky and he finally noticed she looked as uncomfortable as he felt.

'Are you nervous?' A sudden thought occurred to him. 'I did not hurt you, did I?'

'What? No, of course not! If I appear nervous it

is because I am, but not because…well, because of what happened. Are you not curious to learn what Mrs Eldritch told me?'

'I am postponing the inevitable. In any case, before you begin, please sit down for my sake if not yours. I would rather take this sitting down myself and I cannot if you insist on remaining standing. My mother did instil a few codes of polite behaviour in us after all, though I know they have been glaringly absent today.'

She sat and Lucas smiled a little wryly.

'That was the first time you did as I asked without argument. Should I be suspicious?'

She shook her head.

'Well, I am. Out with it. I may as well hear the worst.'

'But it isn't… Never mind. Remember that Mrs Eldritch mentioned Henry was helping her sort through her husband's papers prior to removing from her house? Well, after we left she remembered that Henry had become quite excited about a packet of letters between her husband and a mutual friend who worked at Buxted Mallory Shipping the same time your father did. She looked through those letters and finally she found this. That was why she sent for me.'

She unfolded the letter from Jasper Archer and held it out. Lucas remained seated.

'What does it say?'

'It is rather long. Perhaps you…'

'Just tell me what it says, Olivia.'

'Very well. I shall read only the pertinent parts.'

Time and time again I wonder what would have happened had old Lord Buxted not taken a hand in our affairs that day. If we had spoken the truth—that it was empty jealousy on George Buxted's part and childish foolishness on Ada Mallory's part that the duel ever took place, and that poor Howard Sinclair had no more amorous interest in her than in any of the women who sighed about him.

The poor fellow didn't even notice them, let alone encourage them, and so all the vicious slander Lord Buxted set about after the duel was as empty as my soul has felt since…

She looked up, trying to gauge his reaction but he said nothing and she continued.

Sometimes I marvelled at Sinclair's naiveté…a strange quality for any member of that family. Some matters flowed past him and others inflamed him without reason. I will never understand why George Buxted's accusation of cowardice blinded him to all our exhortations to reason.

Still, that makes it all the more heinous that Lord Buxted set it about it was Howard that discharged before the drop of the handkerchief when it was George Buxted who did so, though to be fair it was an act of clumsiness and fear, not malice.

I should have brought a constable, not Lord Buxted. But my sins truly began when I said nothing to counter him spreading those lies, painting that ludicrous picture of Howard Sinclair as a lecherous Lothario who set out to seduce Miss Mallory.

Only now that I have heard of the death of Lady Sinclair have I thought of the impact of those tales on his family...

'He goes on to ask Mr Eldritch to advise him about sending you and your siblings a letter. I presume he died before he acted on his conscience.'

Lucas watched as she placed the letter on the table with all the care of a mother laying a sleeping child in a crib.

'What will you do, Lucas?' she asked and her question forced him to the surface.

'What *can* I do? It is too late to do anything. Lord Buxted himself died two years ago and the current Lord Buxted is a boy of sixteen. Do you expect me to ruin his life as well?'

'No, but you will at least tell your brother and sister, won't you? They have a right to know.'

He stood and moved to the window. The snow was gathering, thick enough to render even the grey and brown of London beautiful. He tried to understand what he was feeling about her discovery and failed. All he knew was that he wanted her to come to him, do something unconnected with her quest and his past, unconnected even with the passion they shared that afternoon. But she remained seated, hands folded in her lap, and he thought again of Chase's assessment of her inscrutability. She was tied to him irrevocably, but he still had no clear idea whether she needed him. He tried to push the fear away. She was right about one thing—Chase and Sam had a right to know.

'Yes. I will tell them. I need to speak with Sam myself which means I must go to Oxfordshire.'

'Of course.'

'I will be as quick as possible and when I return we will begin the formalities. You can have your man of business draw up whatever legal documents you feel are necessary to protect your interests. I won't interfere with your business concerns in any case. We shall also have to discuss my own…activities at some point.'

'With your uncle?'

'Yes. I don't intend to continue as before, but I can still assist. You might even prove to be useful.' His smile was a little forced, but she smiled back, her eyes sparkling with interest. He would introduce her to Oswald and see what his uncle said. Probably nothing repeatable in polite company, at least initially. He changed the subject.

'Can you keep out of trouble while I am absent?'

She finally came to him and pinched the fabric of his sleeve between her fingers, giving it a little tug. 'Can *you*? Will you be careful? This weather is not suitable for travelling.'

He took her hand and pressed it between his, waiting for his lungs to make room for breathing again. The thought that this was how it could be, this concern, the right to touch her, small moments that he had no idea could mean anything let alone make life worthwhile…

'I am used to travelling in worse,' he answered, feeling foolish. 'I am more concerned about leaving you for a few days here in London. Perhaps I should stay until the gossip settles...'

Her hand turned to clasp his and her other curved about his nape as she rose to press her lips against his. It was a fleeting, almost shy kiss, in sharp contrast to the passion she had exhibited that afternoon, but it melted him. He pressed his hand into the warmth of her hair, holding her there, keeping the kiss hovering on the edge of the chasm he felt yawning below him. He wanted to say the words so badly. He wanted to go down on his knees and beg her to say them back.

When he finally left he was aching with holding everything inside, but he was glad he had. While he was at Sinclair Hall he would begin to make it ready for her. She would need her own study, with plenty of room for her lists and her Walls of Conjecture. And when he returned he would take his time wooing her. He had rushed her into this engagement and she had rushed him into physical intimacy, but from this point forward he resolved he would not allow these new emotions to set the pace. He did not want to ruin this. It was too precious.

Chapter Twenty-Two

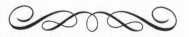

The smell of baking hit Lucas full force as he opened the area door in Spinner Street and the tension that had been plaguing him since he left London three days earlier dropped a notch, but remained somewhere around chest level.

'Good morning, Nora. Pottle informed me Miss Silverdale and Lady Phelps were here.'

Nora watched him wipe his boots with a judicious eye. 'Miss Olivia and Lady Elspeth are at the dressmaker's, but they'll be here any moment now so you can wait in the study. We're almost done with packing. You'd be amazed how much nonsense can accumulate in just a few weeks. Once the bannocks cool I will send Jem with a plate. Off with you, now.'

Lucas went upstairs obediently, but inside he felt anything but tame. He had wanted her to be here. He had *needed* her to be here. He hadn't known it was possible to miss anyone so much after a mere few days. Despite his need to tell Sam the revelations about their father, he had wanted to turn around the moment he drove his curricle out of London with Chase. Or at least take Olivia with him. It was her gift after all. She had wanted to give the Paytons back the man they thought they knew and instead she had given him and Chase and Sam back the man he had been so certain they knew but lost twenty years ago. He could see his father more clearly for it—still flawed and weak and naïve, but loving, caring, conscientious. His father.

Even Sinclair Hall appeared different this time. Good memories peeked out from the corners like timid but hopeful children waiting to be coaxed out to play. He would be making new memories there now. New life even. The thought of Olivia with him there…their children…

He finally allowed it to take possession of him. Not just the love and need that had been creeping up on him for the past few weeks since she summoned him, but hope.

In the doorway to her study he stopped abruptly. The bareness of her Wall of Conjecture was almost like an open wound. She had removed everything and the whole room rang with its absence. He pressed his hand to the bare felt. The only remnants of her plotting were the tiny pinpricks in the fabric and a stray colourful shawl from her Madame Bulgari days still draped over her chair.

He wandered over to her desk and picked up the shawl, running it through his hands. A new trunk stood in the corner and on the desk were neat piles of papers, lists, and arranged on top of the wooden box she had bought him was a piece of brown paper on top of which lay the remaining pencils and bundles of coloured strings removed from her spider's web. He inspected the collection on the desk, his memory bringing back an image of the wall—intricate, demanding, begging for answers. Rather as if someone had tried to sketch Olivia's mind itself. He smiled. She would not appreciate the comparison. Or perhaps she would.

He sighed and glanced at the clock. He wanted the quiet of those first days in Spinner Street back. He should have appreciated it while he had it. As soon as it was decently possible he would marry her and take her somewhere where they could be alone, somewhere warm where she could raise her face to the sun. Somewhere…

The thought died as his gaze settled on a stack of lists at the corner of the desk.

Lord Sinclair. Characteristics.

He did not immediately look away and by the time he did the entries were seared into his mind.

Arrogant
Overbearing
Opinionated
Selfish
Handsome and well aware of it
Cares only for himself
Needs to be coaxed and led
Bait—curiosity?

He turned the small collection of lists over before that very bait of curiosity made him read further. The packet of lists was practically branding itself into the palm of his hand as he pressed down on it. There must be at least five long strips of paper there. What other expletives, complaints and machinations had she jotted down at his expense?

Not that it was any of his business. She could, and would, think whatever she liked of him.

He picked up his hand and the bottom list clung to it. He shook it free and it fluttered face up on to the desk. There were only five words on it: *he is lost and sad.*

He stared at it, his heart thumping as if he had just gone a bout with Gentleman Jackson.

It was true. As in everything she had dissected him with brutal accuracy, extracted the core and put it to use for her aims.

It hardly mattered. It shouldn't matter.

It certainly shouldn't hurt.

What had he expected? Eulogies? Admiration? Some girlish expression of attraction?

Idiot.

She had never made a secret of what she wanted from him. She was attracted to him, that was obvious—for someone as passionate as she the physical fascination was a powerful allure. And he had proven useful, hadn't he? Clearly useful enough to compensate for being *'lost and sad'*. She had taken everything she learned about him and used it to achieve her ends, to manage him like a tethered bull.

Certainly he should introduce her to his uncle Oswald, master manipulator. They were clearly two of a kind. Of all his faults, which she so accurately penned on her list, he had never considered himself naïve, but clearly he was as much a fool as ever his father had been, blundering after her, trusting her with his weaknesses just as he wanted her to trust him with hers.

He had called her relentless, but he had not known the half of it...

A knock at the door roused him.

'Mrs Jones's bannocks, my lord,' Jem said, placing the plate on the table. The warm smell spread through the room and, irrationally, Lucas's resentment burned even brighter.

'Take them back, Jem. I won't be staying.'

Jem's response was cut off by a knock at the door and Lucas strode towards the back stairway, but not quickly enough. Jem had already opened the front door and Olivia and Lady Phelps hurried inside. Olivia's eyes widened as she saw him and she stepped forward, but then her smile doused like a candle dropped into a puddle.

'Lucas? What is wrong?' she asked.

He forced himself to answer. 'Nothing. I cannot stay.'

'Lucas...'

'We will speak later.'

Lady Phelps and Jem melted past them as he headed towards the front door, but Olivia caught his arm.

'Lucas. I can see something is wrong. Has something happened? Tell me.'

'It has nothing to do with your investigations, if that is what concerns you.'

'No, that is not what concerns me. *Has* something happened? To your brother or sister?'

'No. I will speak with you later.'

She slipped between him and the door. 'You are angry with me.'

'I am not angry.'

She grasped the lapels of his coat, crushing them in a manner that was certain to give Tubbs palpitations. She stared up at him, her eyes searching his. 'I don't understand. What have I done?'

He tried prying her hands from his coat. He was so tempted to press her back against the door, capture her face, kiss her until she was panting with need, until she was begging for the only thing she valued in him. And then he would tell her to go to hell...

'Nothing. You have done nothing but be honest, as always. Now there is an overvalued quality. Still, it is better than any quality you managed to ascribe to me in your charming little list, so I should keep my peace.'

He tried to move her out of his way, but she flattened back against the door, her hand closing on the knob, her eyes flashing in the direction of the study and widening in realisation. The blush was so sudden and violent he could almost feel the rush of blood upwards through her body.

'My lists...' It wasn't a question. 'You read my lists?'

'I didn't read them. They were on your desk. If you must denigrate me, I would prefer you at least do it to my face rather than leave lists around for all to see.'

'I didn't… It isn't… You weren't meant to see that…'

'Evidently. I really don't wish to speak with you just at the moment, Olivia. Surely you should know better than to try to placate someone as overbearing and selfish as myself.'

She shook her head, looked a little bemused. 'You couldn't possibly have read them through.'

'Acquit me of that fault at least. I turned them over once I realised you were dissecting me. I am all too aware of my failings; I don't need anyone else listing them for me. My vanity is becoming accustomed to being crushed into the mud since I met you, Olivia, but there are limits.'

She pressed her hands against her cheeks. She looked shocked and scared, like a child caught *in flagrante delicto*. He turned and headed towards the servants' door, but she grabbed his hand.

'Lucas, please. I began writing them the first day you came here, before I knew you. But you didn't read all of them…' She looked flushed and miserable, but that only made him feel worse and he pulled his hand from hers. That must have been quite a list of abuse for her to be so guilty. Did she really think so poorly of him? 'They aren't all failings.' Her voice was muffled, hushed.

'Thank goodness for small mercies. I imagine there must be something in there about my utility and how easily I am dispatched on errands.'

'Lucas...'

'I feel I should be apologising for imposing my arrogant, opinionated and uncompromising self on you, but if you find me so objectionable, you have only to say the word and I will be on my way. Unless you are concerned I might become lost without your superior guidance?'

'Lucas, listen to me.'

'I don't think so. I've done enough of that.'

'Lucas, I love you...'

She moved forward, her eyes beseeching, her hand outstretched, and he felt such a welling of anger and pain at the blatant manipulation he reacted before he could think. He took her hand, his other hand closing round her nape, pulling her towards him.

It hurt, the first brush of his lips on hers, struck through him like an icicle being shoved into his flesh. Like the time he had been pushed overboard in the Baltic Sea. Everything contracted, focused on a pain so sharp it felt it would shred him, turn him first to glass and then shatter him.

Her body pressing against him, as if she already sensed his descent into the cold and was trying to revive him as they did frozen soldiers with body heat. He clung to that warmth, the lie of it. To her passion. Whatever she thought of him, this she couldn't deny.

He felt something break, spread. It was like watching cracks form on the ice cover of the Baltic, the faint white line snapping off at wild angles, rushing towards collapse as black water seeped upwards. The words were almost out of him before he stopped them.

I trusted you. You made me hope.

'Go to the devil, Olivia.'

He turned and left.

Chapter Twenty-Three

'The Honourable Charles Sinclair,' Pottle announced and stood back as Chase entered. As at the opera, Olivia felt the momentary surprise at the similarity to Lucas; they looked more like twins than brothers, even with the slight difference in colouring. There was something harder about Chase's face or perhaps that was simply that she was already familiar with Lucas's expressions and could see beyond the stony façade to the complex clockworks beneath.

'Thank you for coming, Mr Sinclair.'

'I couldn't resist the summons. I am impressed you succeeded in having Jem hunt me down; the Tubbs clan does not usually lend themselves to infringing on Sinclair privacy.'

'I can be persuasive when I must. Where is Lucas? Jem tells me he has left London.'

'My brother is his own master, Miss Silverdale. Why do you believe I know where he is?'

'I would be exceedingly surprised if you didn't, Mr Sinclair.'

'Even if I did, why do you believe I will tell you?'

'Because however much Lucas may hate me at the moment, he must still consider himself betrothed to me and he would not appreciate if I were to do something foolish behind his back. If he knew you were aware that I was contemplating such a course of action and did nothing to prevent it, he might be angry with you as well.'

'Do you know, it is usually advisable to spend a little longer making a polite appeal before you go on the offensive. What precisely *are* you contemplating?'

'I don't know yet, but I assure you it will rank as foolish. Take your pick.'

'Ah, I see. We are negotiating.'

'Precisely.'

'And your terms?'

'You tell me where Lucas is.'

'You clearly do not have a clear concept of the notion of negotiations. They are based on give and take. I am already aware of your objective, but you must offer me something for that information aside from your vague threat.'

'If you tell me where Lucas is, you may ask me for anything you wish.'

He sighed and bent to stroke Inky in a gesture that was all too familiar for Olivia's bruised heart.

'You are taking all the pleasure out of the process, Miss Silverdale. Very well. Give and take. Tell me why you wish to find my brother and I shall consider my response.'

'Because I love him and I hurt him and I must speak to him.' The words came out of her a little too loudly and in the silence that followed she could hear the blood thumping in her ears. She felt cold and hot and when he took her hand and led her towards the sofa she realised she was shaking.

'Lucas told me you keep a decent brandy. It is freezing out there.'

'I do at Spinner Street, but Pottle keeps some for guests in that cupboard there. Kindly pour me a measure as well.'

'Here.' He returned, handing her a glass with a finger's width of brandy, and she took it in both hands. 'Drink. It will either clear your head or muddle it. Either option is an improvement on making decisions while driven by emotion.'

'Lucas does that, too.' She sniffed and sipped the brandy.

'What, talk sense?'

'No, try to calm me with brandy. I am thinking *very* clearly!'

'He is in the region of Dover right now.'

She met his eyes. 'Dover! Is he leaving England? Where is he travelling to? To Russia? You *must* tell me!'

'Why? You could hardly go after him...' He trailed off, his mouth curving in a surprisingly warm smile. 'I'm curious. How *would* you go after him?'

'I would take poor Lady Phelps and commandeer my brother Ralph. He has travelled extensively and he would know how to make the arrangements.'

'I see. And he would lend himself to such an exploit?'

'If I told him it was important to me. The Silverdales never ask anything of each other unless it is important. We pride ourselves on our self-sufficiency.'

'Well, not being a Silverdale, I am afraid you shall have to elaborate. What precisely did you do to send my brother off in such a fury? It is very out of character. He rarely allows his temper to rule his actions. He's certainly had enough practice keeping it under his thumb.'

She flushed in memory of that evening. 'He saw something I wrote about him. I write lists, you see.'

'Lists.'

'It is a foolish habit, but it helps me keep my

world in order. I was packing away the papers relating to our enquiries and the lists I had written about Lucas were on the desk. I don't know how much he saw, but I think he saw the worst of it. He certainly cannot have seen all of it, because... Well, it hardly matters. He was furious, as you said.'

'What was the worst of it?'

She rolled her shoulders. Lord Chase Sinclair was demanding his pound of flesh.

'I wrote that I thought him arrogant, opinionated, uncompromising and vain. And a few other things. We had just met and I was rather annoyed with him at the time.'

'Understandable. Well, at the very least this is quite promising.'

'Promising?'

'I believe it is best you have a fair understanding of my brother's faults before you wed. That way you will more likely be able to identify his finer points. He does have a few, you know.'

'I do. The other pages were mostly an itemisation of those. It is rather embarrassing, but I wish he had read them through before his conscience intervened. Though then he might have run away for very different reasons. He told me once the last thing he cares for is a clinging, overly emotional female.'

'Are you a clinging, overly emotional female?'

'I never thought I was in the past. I certainly don't think I *cling*. Perhaps sometimes I would like to, though. Sometimes I definitely am overly emotional; sometimes not at all. I do not know any more. Just tell me what I must do so that you will disclose his direction.'

'I already did. Dover.'

'Yes, but where is he continuing from there?'

'I am almost tempted to send you after him to Dover, but since he will be engaged on some rather sensitive business and since he will soon be returning, that would be rather redundant and possibly damaging. To the best of my knowledge he is due back in London in a few days, so I suggest you allow him to conclude his business and wait patiently for his return.'

She was already seated, which was lucky, because her stomach rose and fell, her nape turning cold and clammy. She wouldn't cry, but she wanted to. She wanted Lucas there, with her. She shook off the queasiness and straightened.

'I could always travel to Dover and make enquiries.'

His smile flashed wide and warm. 'I would

wish you good luck, my dear, if I wanted to see you run into some serious trouble. First, I did not say he is *in* Dover, but in the region of Dover, and second, should you by some miracle uncover his direction, he is meeting with some rather unsavoury individuals who would not in the least appreciate being interrupted by a proper young woman and might vent their frustrations on my brother. Since I cannot allow that to happen, that would require me…ah, putting my foot down. I would rather not have to take such steps with my future sister-in-law.'

She tried to unfist her hands and failed. 'I need to see him.'

'And so you shall. Whatever my brother's failings, he takes his responsibilities very seriously. He might be angry, but he will not run so you need not be concerned he will try to weasel out of the betrothal. I prescribe patience. I will inform you the moment he is back in London, I promise. Then you can and should descend on him in all your fury.'

She breathed in. It would be all right. What mattered was that Lucas had not fled to the Russian Steppes. He was returning to London. He might not know it, but he needed her. She certainly needed him. He thought her relentless—

well, she would prove just how relentless she could be. She put down her brandy.

'Thank you, Mr Sinclair.'

'Chase.'

'I beg your pardon?'

'My family and friends call me Chase.'

She smiled. 'Thank you, Chase.'

'You are welcome, Miss Silverdale. Now I will exact my recompense.'

'Anything.'

'You really shouldn't say that to an accredited rake, my dear.'

Olivia smiled. 'Please don't trot out that Sinful Sinclair nonsense. Just tell me what it is you want from me.'

'I want you to do your utmost to make a friend of our sister Samantha. She has had a difficult time and might not be open to overtures, but you strike me as a determined young woman. Well, you would have to be to have so thoroughly routed Lucas, so I am asking you to apply some of that determination to winning her over. Will you make that effort?'

'I will do whatever is necessary to make Lucas happy.'

He nodded and headed to the door. 'That will do, then. He is very protective of her. Well, I shall be on my way for now, but I shall certainly be seeing you again before the bridals.'

'If there are any,' she murmured.

He stopped at the door and glanced back over his shoulder. 'I, for one, shall be very disappointed if they fall through, Olivia Silverdale.'

Chapter Twenty-Four

Lucas reached across the bed, his fingers hovering above the lush curve of her thigh. He could feel the heat from here, and his hand was preparing to gather her towards him, his gaze feasting on the sight of her rose-tipped breasts and then rising to meet the slumberous green and gold eyes.

'Do you want me?' His voice hung between them and her lashes rose and she smiled.

'Don't you know?'

A bolt of triumph sheared through him and he finally allowed his hand to pull her to him—and grunted with pain as it connected with the wooden wall.

Damn it. Damn *her*.

He dragged himself into a sitting position on the uncomfortable bed of the inconspicuous house leased for the meetings, leaning his elbows on his knees as he rubbed his face. His head felt as if a door-knocker was being plied with vigour inside it. He was getting too old for the lethal combination of three days and nights of tense negotiations and too much vodka.

No, that wasn't the problem. Peach-scented and far too lifelike erotic dreams were the problem. Being dragged through a wringer by the most intense and confused emotions since his childhood was the problem.

For three days he had focused on the negotiations with Nesselrode's men with the tenacity of a bull terrier, but underneath this façade he was a roiling mess—swinging between wounded anger at her manipulative insensitivity, fury at himself for being so gullible and bouts of corrosive self-pity that he would have derided in anyone else.

And every night he dreamed of her entering his study, coming to him and...

He groaned, pushing his hands deeper into his disordered hair.

The fire had gone out and the floor was freezing beneath his bare feet. He could use a foot-warmer himself. No, he didn't need a foot-warmer. He needed an infuriating, demanding, wary young woman who was half fear and half fierce. Sometimes much more fear than fierce...

The memory returned—of her leaning against his study door—but this time instead of setting his body ablaze it showed him only her shy, uncertain smile as she leaned against the door, determined to go forward but prepared to be rebuffed.

What the devil had he expected of her?

Had he really expected that the same miracle that had stripped away his protective layers and laid him open to this mawkish thing called love would occur to her just because he so desperately wanted it to?

The girl was as mistrustful as he, and just as scared of feeling. She would not love easily, but when she did...

Instead of thanking the powers-that-be that she desired him and wanted to be with him, and recognising that this was an excellent foundation upon which to coax that resistant but resilient plant to the surface, he had thrown a tantrum and run off like a callow youth at the peak of his first infatuation.

Right here, right now, he could not explain it.

It was just that he had not been prepared for that brand of pain. It had wrapped itself around the whole of his world and echoed back into a bellow that had followed him for the last three days like the ringing in his ears after a burst of cannon fire.

You should love me, just as I love you.

A bellow followed by a whimper.

Why don't you?

Perhaps she never will. Not the way you need. And you will have to live with that because she is still enough. More than enough. Being with her is being alive in a wholly different way. So go back to London, apologise and then make her as happy as you can.

He stood and went to tug on the bell-pull.

With any luck his relentless little field marshal was as confused as he about the whole thing—which was why he should be with her and not hiding in his work, feeling sorry for himself and missing her like the greenest of green youths.

It was time to go home.

The noise struck him the moment he entered the Mausoleum and he groaned at the sight of the stacks of timber and carpeting in the hallway. He had forgotten about his instructions to Tubbs to begin the refurbishment of the Mausoleum.

There might not be a point if there was to be no wedding.

Stop it.

There would definitely be a wedding. He would change and go immediately to Brook Street and make very certain of that.

'Good afternoon, my lord.' Tubbs came up from the nether regions and helped Lucas with his coat. 'Mr Chase heard from Sir Oswald you were due back in Town and said to expect you presently. There are fires in your room and the study and water almost ready for a bath. Mrs Tubbs has a light repast ready when you wish. There is some correspondence for you in the study. I believe Mr Chase said it was important. He said you are to wait for him here as he has something important to discuss with you.'

Lucas rubbed his face. He had no patience for business now. He had no patience for anything but Olivia.

'Very well, Tubbs. Have the food and bath ready and then I am going out. If Chase arrives before I leave, fine. If not, tell him I have gone to Brook Street.'

His study was blessedly warm and he went to his desk as he tugged off his cravat, expecting a stack of documents from Oswald. But there was only one item on the desk. His heart and lungs tried to rearrange themselves in his chest and he pressed his palm over his sternum as he approached the thick cream rectangle. There was no direction, only his name: Lucas.

He felt a little ill, but he picked it up. His mind

rushed forward, telling him that whatever was written there it would make no difference, he would not let her go, she was his and he would keep her and make her happy and nothing she could say, or write, could stop that from happening. It was a babbling, high-pitched chatter as his mind marshalled its defences, but underneath was an aching sludge of fear, like the great ice floes of the North Sea as they shoved towards the shores—heavy, grey, inexorably destructive.

His fingers were shaking as he unsealed it. Even her handwriting hurt. Perhaps he should not read it—reading what she wrote when she was not there had landed him in hell once already. He could not bear it a second time. He should put the letter down and find her. Once they were in the same room he would be able to see her, touch her, make her remember why she liked him after all.

Oh, God, please.

He almost succeeded in putting it down, but the soft, creamy paper clung to his fingers. He had bought her this paper. Had spent some time choosing it just as he had the pencils. He had wanted to buy the whole stationer's store, but pride and embarrassment had held him back each time. And fear, again.

He breathed deeply and forced himself to read.

Dear Lucas,

This whole affair began because of notes and letters and this one might mark the end of it unless you can find it in you to forgive me and also accept that I love you.

You have called me relentless and believe me when I say that is precisely what I intend to be. I am writing this letter in the event that you somehow succeed in evading me upon your return to London and to give you fair warning that I will not be fobbed off and I will not stand by as you disappear. So you had best resign yourself.

I told Chase that I would follow you to Russia if need be and that is precisely what I shall do. I will employ every tactic and strategy at my disposal, because I love you and, though I do not know if you reciprocate that particular, peculiar emotion, I know I am good for you. Sometimes.

You refused to listen to what I wrote on those lists and I shan't bore you with everything, but you should at least know what I wrote at the end of my lists about you. This is what I wrote after our visit to Mrs Eldritch, verbatim:

Lucas is so much more generous than I—

for a man who claims to be so selfish he is forever aware of others—their needs and wishes—from foot-warmers and compassion for me to a helping hand for Nora and apparently for all the Tubbs clan if what Jem lets slip is true.

I can see he sometimes wants to walk away and cannot. I could bind him merely by needing him, but I would never wish to.

I want to do the same for him as he has done for me. Be his champion in everything that seems small and mundane, but in the end that is the fabric of loving. I want to be the one who holds his hand when he is lost and sad.

That was my last entry. There is more before that, some of it even more embarrassing, but I will spare you.

This is a rather poor attempt at what is my first love letter, but it is hard to shout into an abyss without knowing what one might hear in return.

Sometimes I see something in your eyes that gives me hope that you truly want me in your life. At least part of you. I hope that part can convince the rest of you, but I admit I will not be surprised if it doesn't.

I will always be grateful for everything you have done for me these past weeks. I cannot imagine not having known you, however painful losing you might be.

I do love you.

Olivia

PS I almost forgot. I asked Jem to take the box with your father's letters to Sinclair House. I wish I could have met him and your mother. I think I would have liked them.

'Livvy...' he whispered as the words blurred. 'They would have loved you. Adored you. Blast you, Livvy—'

'Is that an exasperated *Livvy* or a pitying *Livvy* or an affectionate *Livvy*? I cannot tell.'

His heart, already sorely abused, tried to catapult out of the room altogether. He had not even heard her enter. She stood again with her back to the door, her brown-and-gold pelisse like a continuation of the warm wood colour behind her, only her face, pale, and her eyes, huge pools of forest and amber, stood out. Her hands were splayed back against the door, as if trying to hold back furies beating on the other side. Or trying to steady herself.

Olivia. Livvy.

His.

She did not move as he approached, just watched him as she had once in the carriage—without expression, prepared to stand strong and show nothing of what was inside her. Relentless and so very scared.

He took her hands from the door and somehow he was on his knee before her, breathing them in, her.

'Forgive me, Livvy. I am so sorry...'

She crumpled on to the floor next to him with a little cry, her hands tightening on his.

'Ah, no, Lucas, please, please not yet. Please just a few moments. I cannot bear it. I told myself whatever you said, whatever you decided, I would be strong, but I'm not, I'm not. I don't want to hear it, not yet. Not ever.'

His mind was clearly suffering from the same upheaval of his other inner organs because for a moment he had no idea what she was talking about. Then the world settled and he could think again. He pulled her shaking form against him, sliding back so that he could lean against the wall as he drew her on to his lap, stroking her hair, wiping the damp from her cheeks as she cried. He spoke, soothingly, lightly, easing her out of her pain because he knew now just how it had clung to her from the day he left, just as it had clung to him. A chain and ball of ice dragging with his every step.

'I never thought my first declaration of love would elicit such a response, my darling Livvy. I understand it takes some strength of will to contemplate a lifetime in my company, but there are compensations, surely? Do you really not want to hear me tell you how much I love you? Not ever? I shall have to be creative then. Would other languages count under that interdiction?' She had stopped crying and he took advantage to extract his handkerchief and dry her face as she stared at him as at a Bedlamite hanging upside down from the rafters of St Paul's.

'I prefer to make love to you in English, but I can do it in Italian—*amore mio*—or Spanish, or even Russian and Arabic—*habibti*. German might be a little stilted, but my Greek is tolerable—*agapi mou*. And if you consider that cheating, I could write it. I am not as gifted a writer of love letters as you, Livvy mine. In fact, I have never written a love letter, poem or epistle in my life, but I can try. I will start with notes, perhaps, and pin them to our bedroom wall so you cannot ignore them.'

'Lucas…'

'Yes, my…sorry. I forgot you did not wish to

hear you are at the very core of my world and that I cannot imagine my life without you any longer. What is it you wished to say?'

'Lucas. Are you saying this…because of my letter? Because I am in love with you?'

'I know I made a mistake that day. I should not have acted the coward and run simply because I was hurt. But you once told me you trust me, Livvy. Do you?'

'With my life.'

'Then trust me with your heart. Look at me. You know I am not lying. You are only scared and that is fine, for now. God knows I am just as terrified, but that is no longer an excuse for either of us.'

She touched his jaw, lightly, just a grazing of two fingers, and he heard the faint rasp of her skin on his stubble and felt it through to the palms of his hands and the soles of his feet. Then she smiled, her beautiful smile—promising both a blaze of heat and aching tenderness. Again the burning blurred his eyes and he pulled her to him, burying his face in her hair, in her scent, in his love for her, in her love for him.

'God, Livvy. I love you. You shouldn't trust me, not an inch. I don't think I can live without you and that terrifies me. I want to be strong for you and keep you safe and make you happy, but how the hell can I if everything I want revolves around you? I don't know how to find my centre any more.'

'Oh, Lucas. It's right here. What fools we both are. I love you so. Three days I was in purgatory, waiting and worrying and wanting. Do help me take off this pelisse.' She squirmed on his lap as she tried to unbutton the row of tiny buttons and his body woke from its stupor with all the abruptness of a sleeping wolf being hit over the head with a club—snarling and ready for the attack. He groaned and grabbed her hands.

'We can't. Chase will be here soon and...'

She sighed and sank against him, tucking her head under his chin and her hand under his coat, pressed to the rapid tattoo of his heart.

'He already is here. He brought me. I suppose you are right, and I have already broken my word to Elspeth not to come here unchaperoned.'

'Chase brought you?'

'I made him promise he would inform me the moment you returned.'

'You made him.'

'We negotiated.'

'I see. And what did my brother receive in this negotiation?'

'Nothing but the truth. He loves you, too.'

He leaned his head back against the wall and breathed in and out. Really, he was going to have to find a more manly way of dealing with these waves of mawkish joy that struck every time she told him she loved him. She touched her lips to the base of his throat and he could feel the curve of her smile, could feel the words forming against his skin as she spoke.

'I love you, Lucas. I shall have to remind you of that every day until you believe it. You will probably beg me to stop.'

He bundled her closer, tipping her head back so he could do something with her damaging, delectable mouth.

'I won't. I will hold you to that promise, my impossible, relentless, adored love. Every day.'

Epilogue

Venice

Lucas worked his way upwards through the Palazzo Montillio. On the floors below, his cousins were preparing for the night's entertainment at the casino they managed and which hosted the elite of Venetian and European society, but on the upper floors everything was still and empty.

He reached the large bedroom at the end of the corridor and sighed. *Too* empty. He continued his climb through the next floor which was part-storeroom and part-attic and then even further to the wooden staircase that led to the roof. The moment he stepped out he saw her leaning against the stone balustrade, looking out over the mouth of the Grand Canal towards San Marco and the Campanile. Beyond, the sky faded to grey and violet with a hint of the darkening lands beyond. He smiled in appreciation at the tumble of curls that picked up the remnants of the setting sun in the west, a gilded goddess overlooking the city of carnal pleasures. She was wrapped in a dressing gown of brocade silk in the colours of sea and sand, the shimmering material pressed against her by the Adriatic breeze, outlining her body as clearly as any of the marble statues in the Uffizi. It was a beautiful sight, but he would much rather see that gown spread out beneath them on the bed below. As much as he would like to strip her here and make love to her with the view of the city spread out around them, February was not the month for such fanciful gestures.

She turned as he stepped on to the roof, her smile as warm as the setting sun in her hair. He smiled back, a reflexive reaction he had no control over. He had no control over the surge of joy, either. *Mine,* his body said. *Thank God*, chorused his mind.

She walked into his arms and he gathered her against him, mapping her with his hands and mouth, a little scared by the force of his need. He had only been absent for a couple of days; that could hardly be considered deprivation.

'I missed you,' he said into her curls. Then, a little more dignified, 'I trust Giovanni and Maria took good care of you in my absence?'

'Excellent care. Maria thinks I'm too thin and has been working to rectify matters. Soon I shall have to buy a new wardrobe. Or spend my days wearing nothing but dressing gowns like now.'

'Bless Maria, then. I thoroughly approve of that outcome.'

She laughed, leaning back to look at him. 'I know we are planning to leave for Egypt, but if you'd rather stay here and help your uncle, do just tell me. I am perfectly content to stay here or go wherever you wish.'

'Excellent. Downstairs to make use of our bed and then to see what Maria's cooks have concocted.'

'Lucas, you know what I mean. The last thing I wish is for you to become bored with your life with me. When you wish to return to your duties with your uncle you have only to say. I admit I am looking forward to being of use…'

'You do realise my plans before I met you were to spend another dismal winter in Russia? The last time I was in St Petersburg the sun only showed its face for one day out of thirty and that was for less than an hour. I know all about boredom, love. I can safely say that I cannot remember the last time I have lived through a period less boring than this that did not involve something best forgotten. I am happy with you.'

The simple truth of those words still astonished

him. She hugged her arms around him, rubbing her cheek against his chest.

'I am glad, but keep in mind my need to be useful. I have something else I wished to say to you, though. While you were gone Maria took me to the attics.'

'To the attics? My cousin certainly knows how to entertain…' His laughter faded at her expression. 'What is it?'

'She found a small case with some of your mother's belongings. Some books and two very lovely fans and a pendant I think Samantha would like, but in one of the books she found a letter. From your father. I recognised the handwriting.'

'What does it say?'

'I did not read it, but I did see the date. It is dated the day before the duel.'

She held out her hand and he took it and let her lead him downstairs to their room.

It was a short letter, the handwriting looked a little larger and rounder than he remembered, as if his father had written slowly, etching each word against his will.

My darling Tessa,
I wish you were here. You and Lucas and Chase and Samantha. I need all of you around me—I am not myself without you. I

thought it would be easier away from Father and John, but as they have so often said the fault is in me, not them. Clumsy, awkward, I stumble into trouble whether intending to or not.

I certainly never dreamed I would find myself in such straits. I still pray I will wake and discover it was all a dreadful mistake, but I cannot in honour withdraw. You know only too well how that word strikes—coward. I cannot stand down.

Whatever the outcome tomorrow, please forgive me and do not judge me too harshly. With luck I will be with you very soon and perhaps now Father and John are dead we can begin anew, but not at the Hall. Somewhere that is purely ours.

You are and have always been the bright shining star in my life and I am grateful for every moment you have given me.
Your loving, devoted husband,
Howard

He folded the letter and tucked it back into the book. Olivia wrapped her arms around him again and leaned her cheek against his shoulder.

'Whatever she thought happened there, she could not doubt he loved her.'

'I don't think she did,' he answered, pulling her on to his lap. 'Thank you, Olivia.'

'For what? I keep bringing back painful memories. Just when you were happy.'

'You know better. You do realise that if none of this had happened I never would have met you?'

She leaned back in the circle of his arms, her smile bright with love.

'I adore how you transform my misdeeds into virtues, Lucas.'

'I learned that skill from a master, or rather a mistress. Now, I am very glad you found my father's last letter, but we have more important matters to attend to.'

'Yes, Giovanni did say the Archduke will be a guest at the casino today and...'

'I am not the least bit interested in archdukes. I have realised your soul is in peril. I distinctly remember you promised to tell me you love me every day and it has been three whole days since your last profession of adoration. You are in breach of our covenant and so as your knight it falls to me to rescue you.'

'Not that I wish to question your championing skills, but it is hardly fair to say this is my fault when it was you who was absent.'

'Don't split hairs. Wearing nothing but a shift

and dressing gown is a good beginning, so I will let you go with only two protestations of your undying love.' He untied the belt of the robe, sliding his hands up over the gossamer-thin shift underneath. Need, love, lust barrelled through him.

'Oh, God, I missed you, Livvy. You don't know how much. I kept telling myself, it is just three days. But it ached like hell. No, not there, here.' He pressed her hand to his heart. 'I feel like a damned fool, but I need you to tell me you missed me, that you want me with you.'

She kissed his chest, the harsh striking of his heartbeat magnified by the warmth of her lips, her breath feathering over his skin as she spoke.

'You are wrong that I am in breach, Lucas. I wrote you two terribly soppy love letters where I was very clear about how much I miss you and need you. Amongst other things.'

'You did? Where are…?'

'Later. Actions first, words later… Lucas, my love.'

* * * * *